Praise for the Arc

'This is a cracking tale o
The 7

'Prepare to wonder at the Museum
of Magical Miscellany.'
Sunday Express

'This book sent tingles of excitement and
wonder down my spine . . . I couldn't stop reading!'
Evie, age 10

'A fast-paced tale full of mystery and excitement.'
Publishers Weekly

'A series of thrilling adventures.'
Booklist

'An exciting adventure.'
Julia Eccleshare, *LoveReading*

'This is page-turning fantasy of the highest quality.
A fast-paced plot and enjoyable characters . . .'
Kids' Book Review

'I couldn't put it down. One of the best books
I have read recently. Fantastic!'
Tomasz, age 9

'Young 'Harry Potter' fans would
love this book.'
Mathilda, age 8

Archie Greene

and the
Raven's
Spell

D. D. Everest

ff

FABER & FABER

First published in 2017
by Faber & Faber Limited
Bloomsbury House,
74–77 Great Russell Street,
London WC1B 3DA

Printed and bound by CPI Group (UK) Ltd, Croydon, CR0 4YY
Typeset by Faber & Faber Limited

A CIP record for this book
is available from the British Library

ISBN 978–0–571–30964–1

FSC
www.fsc.org
MIX
Paper from
responsible sources
FSC® C020471

2 4 6 8 10 9 7 5 3 1

For Sara, Dan and Erin

Contents

The Three Types of Magic

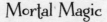

Natural Magic

The purest kind of magic comes from
magical creatures and plants and the
elemental forces of nature, such as
the sun, the stars and the seas.

Mortal Magic

Is man-made magic. It includes the magical
instruments and other devices created by
magicians to channel magical power.

Supernatural Magic

The third and darkest type of magic uses
the power of spirits and other
supernatural beings.

The Three Apprentice Skills

Finding

Binding

Minding

The Five Lores of Magical Restraint

In 1666, a magical accident caused the Great Fire of London. The Lores of Magical Restraint were agreed to prevent another magical disaster. (Lores is the magical spelling of laws.)

First Lore All magical books and artefacts must be returned to the Museum of Magical Miscellany for inspection and classification. (They are classified as level one, two or three in magical power.)

Second Lore Magical books and artefacts may not be used or bought and sold until properly identified and classified.

Third Lore The unauthorised use of magic outside of magical premises is prohibited.

Fourth Lore The hoarding of magical books and artefacts to accumulate personal power is outlored under the prohibition of dangerous practices.

Fifth Lore The mistreatment of magical creatures is expressly forbidden.

Inside the Scriptorium in the Museum of Magical Miscellany, a black flame flickered across an open page. The letters of the spell twisted and distorted in the dark fire until there was nothing left but cinders. A single breath of foul air carried the ashes away, leaving only a scorch mark to show where the dark flame had been.

1

Worms for Supper

Archie Greene stared into the gloomy room. The only light came from a solitary sunbeam that entered through a slit window. There was no furniture, just a pile of rags in one corner and a heavy iron chain.

A raven appeared at the window. For a moment it blocked out the light. Then it folded its wings and slipped through the narrow opening. The heap of rags moved and two eyes gleamed in the dark. A man was chained to the wall.

'Hello, my old friend,' he croaked. 'What have you brought me today?'

The raven opened its beak and a juicy fat worm fell onto the floor. The man seized it and hungrily gobbled it down.

'A banquet fit for a king,' he laughed, bitterly.

'Now I will tell you my story once more so that you may pass it on to your children and they to theirs. For one day, the ravens will carry the warning.'

The raven put its head on one side to listen. The man wheezed, and Archie could see that although a streak of white ran through his black hair, he was still a young man.

'There was once a foolish alchemist called Fabian Grey . . .' he began.

'Archie, wake up!' said Bramble Foxe. 'I only went to get another book and you're out for the count!'

For a moment Archie was disorientated. The aroma of old parchment filled his nostrils and he realised his cheek was resting on the open page of the book he'd been working on. He must have fallen asleep. He opened his eyes and found himself in the Scriptorium, the room at the Museum of Magical Miscellany set aside for writing magic.

Archie and Bramble were apprentices at the museum, where the world's most magical books were kept. The museum was hidden beneath the Bodleian Library in Oxford.

Bramble was holding a stack of books in her arms, but something wasn't quite right. Her face looked green. In fact, everything had a greeny tinge to it. Archie frowned. Then it dawned on him that the Emerald Eye, the magical pendant given to him by the ghost of the magician John Dee, was lying on the open book in front of him so that he was looking at Bramble through it.

Relieved, he sat up and tucked the pendant back inside his shirt. The golden quill he used to write magic was lying on the desk. It must have slipped from his hand when he'd nodded off. He picked it up and felt a pulse of magical energy surge through it. It had once belonged to the seventeenth-century alchemist Fabian Grey, one of Archie's ancestors.

Archie was nearly thirteen, with mousey brown hair that stood up in a spike. At first glance he looked much like any other boy his age. The only real clue that there was anything magical about him was the colour of his eyes. One was green and the other was grey, a condition known as 'magician's eye'. He also had two tattoo-like marks on the palm of his right hand called firemarks, which denoted which magical apprenticeships he had begun. The first was in the shape of a needle and thread, the firemark he'd received when he started his apprenticeship as a magical bookbinder. The second firemark looked like a dragon swallowing its own tail and was even more rare because it meant that Archie was a magic writer.

Archie rubbed his eyes.

'Careful of that ink!' exclaimed Bramble,

3

indicating a crystal inkwell dangerously close to Archie's elbow. 'We haven't got much left.'

The ink contained a precious magical substance called azoth, which was used for writing spells, and was notoriously hard to make. Archie and his friends had managed to make some when they discovered a formula in Fabian Grey's notebook.

Bramble set down the books she was carrying. 'That's the second time you've fallen asleep this week. And we've got all of these to get through,' she added, indicating the pile of books.

Bramble was Archie's cousin and two years older than him. She flicked her long, dark hair over one shoulder and pointed at the clock on the wall. 'It's nearly eight o'clock, and I don't want to be late again tonight.'

Working at the museum was exciting but recently there'd been a lot of late nights. Archie yawned and stretched. These days he seemed to be tired all the time. It must be the long hours they'd been putting in at the Scriptorium.

Besides the two of them, there were three other apprentices who could write magic – Archie's younger cousin Thistle and their two friends Rupert Trevallen and Arabella Ripley. They called themselves the Alchemists' Club after Fabian Grey's original club. Lately, though, there had only been Archie, Bramble and Thistle.

'Arabella's back tomorrow, so that should help,' said Bramble. 'I hope she's had a nice time visiting Prague with her parents.'

'I really miss Rupert,' Archie sighed. 'At least we got a break when he was here.'

Until a month ago, Rupert had been working in the mythical menagerie in the Natural Magic Department of the museum. But as he was a bit older than the rest of the apprentices, he had now finished his training and was working at the Royal Society of Magic, in London. The Royal Society controlled all the magic in Britain, and it reported to the Magical League, the international magical authority. Archie himself didn't know much about the Royal Society except that it had a centuries-old reserve of precious azoth.

'How's Rupert getting on anyway?' asked Archie. He knew that Bramble kept in touch with him.

'He's working with Orpheus Gloom,' she said. Gloom was a magical assessor who had worked at the museum for a while. 'The Royal Society is experimenting with new ways to make more azoth using ingredients from magical creatures. Gloom chose Rupert because of his experience in the menagerie.'

'Who's taken over from him in the menagerie?' asked Archie.

'They haven't decided yet. Thistle applied for the job, but he's not sure he'll get it,' said Bramble. 'That reminds me,' she added. 'Edith Drew told me that there's some sort of problem with the magical creatures. Apparently a couple of snufflings have gone missing.'

Snufflings were small creatures that resembled guinea pigs and produced a magical enzyme that meant they could vanish if they sensed danger.

'How do they know they're missing?' asked Archie. 'They might just be hiding.'

'Snufflings disappear for a few seconds, not for entire weeks like these have,' said Bramble. 'And its not just the snufflings – some of the other creatures are getting sick. Simon the red-bellied salamander hasn't changed colour in weeks!'

Salamanders were distantly related to dragons and changed colour depending on their mood. Simon was temperamental and usually changed several times a day.

'Perhaps he's just feeling a bit washed out,' suggested Archie, hopefully.

Bramble shook her head. 'No, there's something wrong. He's got no appetite, and you know how dragons like their food. I think he might be pining for Rupert.'

Archie smiled to himself. Sometimes he still couldn't quite believe he was having these sorts of conversations – talking about dragons and magical ink. His life hadn't always been so exciting.

He'd spent his first twelve years living quietly with his gran in a small seaside town after his parents and sister had disappeared while he was still a baby. But everything had changed for Archie the previous summer when he'd met his cousins and found out he was descended from the Flame Keepers of Alexandria, a secret community that guarded the Flame of Pharos, an ancient magical flame, and who were devoted to finding and preserving magical books.

When Archie had started his apprenticeship at the museum he'd discovered a rare ability that allowed him to talk to magical books. He had used his magical talents to thwart a plot to free an evil warlock called Barzak from *The Book of Souls,* one of the Terrible Tomes, the seven most dangerous magical books ever written.

Since then Archie had also had another exciting adventure involving another of the Terrible Tomes, *The Grim Grimoire*, which had cursed Fabian Grey and the original members of the Alchemists' Club. The lives of Archie and his newly formed Alchemists' Club companions were also in great danger until Archie had managed to defeat the *Grimoire* and lift the curse on his friends.

That was three months ago, and since then

the five of them had been practising their magic-writing skills. Now, under the supervision of Gideon Hawke, the head of Lost Books, but unbeknownst to the magical authorities, they had begun the task of rewriting the fading spells in the books in the museum.

Archie realised Bramble was looking at him quizzically. 'Anyway – when I came in you were mumbling something in your sleep. Bad dreams?'

Archie remembered his strange dream. 'I dreamed about Fabian Grey in the Tower of London,' he said, gazing at the golden quill in his hand.

Bramble raised her eyebrows. 'Him again!'

Grey had featured in Archie's dreams a lot lately. The alchemist had been imprisoned in the Tower after he'd accidently started the Great Fire of London with his magic.

Bramble looked thoughtful. 'I'm sure Grey's got something to do with whatever Dad is working on at the moment, too,' she said. 'I heard Mum mention him the other day when they were talking.'

Archie's uncle, Woodbine Foxe, worked as a finder, locating unidentified magical books. Woodbine spent most of his time scouring second-hand bookshops and following up leads. Occasionally the museum would send him to collect a missing book. He had been very distracted lately and the children suspected he was on a secret mission.

Even though there was no one else in the room, Bramble dropped her voice to a low whisper. 'I'm pretty sure it's got something to do with the Greaders, too. Dad says they are getting bolder.'

Greaders were the sworn enemies of the Flame Keepers and had been behind the plot with *The Book of Souls* and *The Grim Grimoire*. In public, most Greaders appeared to be upstanding members of the magical community, but in secret, they practised dark magic and were greedy for the magic contained in the books. Archie had noticed that the museum elders seemed on edge. An increase in Greader activity would explain it. Bramble interrupted his thoughts.

'So what happened in your dream?'

'Grey was chained up in the Tower,' said Archie. 'He was talking to a raven.'

Bramble gave him a sharp look. 'Did the raven say anything?' she asked.

In their previous adventures with the Alchemist's Curse, a talking raven had delivered Fabian Grey's gold ring to Archie. The ring's secret was that it was really Grey's magic quill in disguise. Archie wore it on his finger whenever he wasn't using the quill to write magic.

'No, it just brought him a worm to eat,' Archie said, pulling a face in disgust at the thought. 'But Grey said something about the ravens carrying a warning.'

'Warning about what?'

Archie shrugged. 'You woke me up before I could find out.'

'Well, you can finish the dream tonight. We've got work to do now.' She glanced at the open book on the desk. 'What's taking you so long anyway? You're normally so fast and you've been working on that spell for hours.'

'It's finished,' said Archie indignantly. 'It's right there.' He glanced down at the spell he'd written. 'Well, it was . . .'

A black flame had appeared on the page. As they watched, the carefully formed letters Archie had written ignited, twisting and distorting until there was nothing left but cinders. A single breath of foul air carried the ashes away, leaving only a dark scorch mark where the spell had been.

'What on earth was that?' said Bramble.

2

The Stolen Book

That night Archie lay awake in bed thinking about the black flame and the disappearing spell. It had been too late to find anyone at the museum to ask about it. He'd made up his mind that he should tell Old Zeb the bookbinder in the morning, but it was still bothering him when he eventually fell into an uneasy sleep. In his dreams a raven was tapping on the window. It had a message in its beak, but Archie couldn't open the window to let it in.

He awoke with a start. He could hear a murmur of voices. For a moment he wondered if he was still dreaming, but when he opened his eyes he was in the bedroom he shared with his younger cousin Thistle. The voices were coming from downstairs.

His aunt Loretta was talking to Woodbine. His

uncle had been away for a couple of days but must have returned some time during the night. Archie glanced at the clock on his bedside table. It was six in the morning. Normally, if Woodbine got back late he would sleep in. So why was he up so early?

Archie slipped out of bed and crossed the room to the door. Leaning out into the landing he strained his ears to catch what they were saying. The house always felt more secure with Woodbine there, but Archie could tell these weren't his uncle and aunt's usual cheerful voices. They were speaking in serious, low tones.

Archie stood on the landing, listening. He couldn't make out all the words, but he was sure he heard Loretta say, 'Keep still or you'll make it worse.' Her voice sounded strained.

It was followed by a grunt of pain from Woodbine.

'Careful, woman, that stings!'

Something was wrong. Archie felt a hand on his shoulder and nearly jumped out of his skin.

He turned to see Thistle behind him. His cousin was a few months younger than him, with freckles and a mop of dark hair that was standing up where he'd slept on it.

'What's up?' Thistle asked, stifling a yawn.

'Shhhhh!' Archie whispered. 'Listen.'

The low voices had started speaking again.

Thistle leaned past him over the bannister, a look of concentration on his face.

'Dad's back from his trip,' he said over his shoulder. 'He was doing a job for Gideon Hawke.'

Archie nodded. 'Yes, I know, but something's wrong. Come on.'

They tiptoed along the landing and down the stairs, avoiding the creaky steps so that they wouldn't be heard. The kitchen door was closed and the voices were coming from inside.

The two boys were creeping along the corridor towards the small dining room when they heard Bramble whisper:

'What are you doing?'

She was standing at the top of the stairs with her dressing gown pulled tightly around her.

Archie put his finger to his lips and pointed towards the closed kitchen door. Bramble nodded that she understood and slipped quietly down the stairs. With Archie leading, the three of them stole into the dining room. The serving hatch that connected it with the kitchen was slightly ajar. Archie had overheard conversations this way before. He felt a bit guilty about eavesdropping, but adults were annoyingly cagey about the truth and sometimes it was the only way to find out what was really going on. They crowded around the hatch peering through the open crack.

What they saw made them gasp. Woodbine was slumped at the kitchen table, but he was barely recognisable. His face was covered with cuts and one eye was so swollen that it was almost closed.

Loretta was sitting across the table from him with her back to them, dabbing at his injuries with a piece of cotton wool. Woodbine flinched whenever she touched an open wound.

'We didn't stand a chance,' he muttered between grimaces. 'We got there at eight because we thought it would be quiet. We picked up the book but they were lying in wait outside. They hit us with an immobilising spell, and then when we couldn't protect ourselves they threw a drubbing spell at us for good measure. Wolfus was the first one out of the door so they clobbered him the worst. You should see his face.'

'You were lucky to get away with just a drubbing,' said Loretta. 'You could've been killed!'

Woodbine shrugged. 'We should have put up more of a fight,' he said, shaking his head ruefully. 'But it all happened so quickly. Gideon will be furious. He was already angry that the Royal Society had the book all those years without telling anyone. Everyone thought it was lost but it was there all the time.'

Loretta dabbed at his puffed-up eye. 'The book,' she said. 'What happened to it?'

'Gone,' growled Woodbine. 'They took it. They knew we were coming. Someone must have tipped them off.'

'But the Royal Society of Magic,' gasped Loretta. 'I can't believe they would dare to take it from there!'

'They dared all right,' muttered Woodbine, darkly. 'The Greaders sense that the wind has changed in their favour. This is just the start; you mark my words. They're gathering their forces – and they have people in high places.

'Why do you say that?' asked Loretta, a note of fear in her voice.

Woodbine touched his swollen eye and winced. 'Arthur Ripley,' he said. 'It's been four months without any sightings of him. Someone must be sheltering him – covering his tracks.'

Arthur Ripley was Arabella's grandfather and a notorious Greader. He had been behind the plot to free the warlock Barzak, and had instigated the second plot with the Alchemist's Curse and *The Grim Grimoire*. Archie also knew that Ripley had had a hand in his father's disappearance, as *The Grim Grimoire* had let slip that Ripley had trapped Archie's father, Alex Greene, inside a magical book. Archie suspected Ripley was also responsible for the disappearance of his mother and sister, as they had all gone missing at the same time.

Archie had spent every spare moment since trying to discover what had happened to them, so his ears pricked up at the mention of Ripley's name. Gideon Hawke had promised Archie that when Ripley was caught they would find out what he knew about his family.

'But why would anyone want to protect Ripley after what he's done?' asked Loretta.

Woodbine's brow darkened. 'There are people in the magical realm who agree with what he's trying to do. They would have no qualms about using dark magic, and they would follow Ripley if he rose to power.'

On the other side of the serving hatch the three cousins exchanged anxious glances.

'And now they've got the book,' said Woodbine.

Archie felt a prickling sensation in the palm of his right hand. He glanced at the small tattoo-like firemarks there.

Woodbine continued. 'The authorities will have to do something, and quickly.' He paused. 'If the Greaders get a chance to open that book . . .'

His voice trailed off and he seemed to slump a little lower in his chair.

'That's enough of that sort of talk, Woodbine,' snapped Loretta. She was trying to put on a brave face but her voice shook. 'The children will be down soon.'

The three cousins took this as their cue to leave. They crept quietly back up the stairs. They hurriedly threw on some clothes and came back down, making plenty of noise this time to announce their arrival.

When they entered the kitchen, Woodbine was wearing sunglasses to cover his black eye.

'You're up early,' said Loretta, with an unconvincing smile.

The children sat down at the table.

'What ho, young 'uns,' said Woodbine, trying to sound his usual upbeat self.

'How did you get on?' asked Bramble, studying him for a reaction. 'With the mission, I mean.'

Woodbine looked away. 'I'm not allowed to talk about it,' he said.

He absentmindedly touched his bruised cheek.

Loretta shot him a sharp look. 'Yes, well, never mind all that. How about some cake and eggs for breakfast?'

Loretta was famous in the Foxe household for her unusual combinations of food. She had a shelf full of cookery books – gifts from well-meaning friends and family – but she never opened them. Loretta preferred to make up her own eccentric dishes. Archie had found it disconcerting at first but he'd almost got used to it now.

'How is Rupert getting on, by the way?' Loretta

asked a short while later, plopping a greasy fried egg onto a large slice of sponge cake and passing the plate to Bramble. 'I hear the Royal Society asked for him specially. His parents must be very proud. Does he like it there?'

'I think so,' said Bramble. 'But he misses the animals from the menagerie.'

'Bound to,' agreed Woodbine, his mouth half full of cake and eggs. He scraped up the last of his eggy cake crumbs with his fork and shovelled them into his mouth. He'd forgotten that his lips were swollen and winced.

Archie pushed a knife into his own egg and watched the yellow yolk soak into the porous sponge. He added some tomato ketchup for good measure and hesitantly took a bite. In fact, the combination of sweet and savoury was surprisingly good.

A short while later, their stomachs full, the three cousins set off for the museum. There was a start-of-term meeting and they didn't want to be late.

It was a bright spring morning and the sun was warm on their backs as they walked from the Foxe family home in Houndstooth Road to the centre of Oxford.

As well as his magic-writing duties, Archie was still apprenticed to Old Zeb, the bookbinder, at the magical bookshop called the Aisle of White. The bookshop was on one side of a small courtyard just off a square near the Bodleian Library. The bookshop served as a place to sort the magic books from other books that people came to sell. It was the only part of the museum open to the Unready – people who didn't know about magic.

The main museum was on the other side of the courtyard and strictly off limits to the non-magical world. To enter it, apprentices went through Quill's Coffee & Chocolate House, which was where they were headed now.

When they arrived at Quill's, Pink, the waitress, was standing behind the bar. A tall, slim woman with pierced eyebrows and lots of tattoos, she controlled the door ray, the secret entrance which connected the front of Quill's, the part that was open to the public, and the back of house where the apprentices met before going to the museum.

Separating the two sides was a magical barrier called a permission wall, which was enchanted so that the back of house was invisible to the Unready.

'Hurry up,' said Pink, waving them through the door ray. 'The meeting starts in five minutes.'

The back of house was full of excited chatter. Archie, Bramble and Thistle had spent the Easter break in Oxford, but some of the apprentices had been away on holiday and hadn't seen their friends for a while so there was a lot to catch up on.

The three cousins found Arabella. She told them about her visit to Prague.

'There's a place called Alchemists' Alley inside the castle,' she said. 'My parents insisted we go there. They wanted to see the bookshop where that Greader attack happened last year.'

Archie shuddered at the memory. A Greader named Amos Roach had killed an elderly couple called the Krones on the instructions of Katerina Krone, their adopted daughter. Katerina was descended from the Nightshade family whose ancestors included Hecate the witch, the author of *The Grim Grimoire*. Arthur Ripley had written to Katerina to tell her that the book was hidden in the Darchive inside the museum and was her inheritance. When Katerina had tried to make Archie complete the unfinished spell so she could take Hecate's powers for herself, the *Grimoire* had put a curse on her, which had left her spellbound.

Archie and the Alchemists' Club had foiled the plot, and Katerina had been sent to an asylum for the magically ill. Amos Roach, like Arthur Ripley, was still on the run.

Bramble told Arabella about the black flame and the vanishing spell.

'That's weird,' said Arabella. 'I've never heard of spells disappearing like that. I wonder what it means. Have you told the elders?'

Archie shook his head. 'Not yet,' he said. 'I'll tell Old Zeb straight after the meeting. He'll know what it means.'

Feodora Graves, the head of Supernatural Magic, clapped her hands and cut their conversation short.

'Welcome back to another term at the Museum of Magical Miscellany,' said Graves in her clipped voice. 'If you would please take your seats we have some very important notices to give you.'

Arabella and the three cousins joined the crowd of apprentices making their way to the function room in the back of house at Quill's, where the meetings were held.

The four of them sat down together, leaving an empty seat. Then they remembered that Rupert wouldn't be joining them because he was in London. Archie felt a pang of nostalgia for the days when the five of them were always together. He knew that Rupert was excited about working at the Royal Society, but that didn't stop him missing his friend.

As usual, the museum elders had taken their places on the raised platform at the front of the room. Dr Motley Brown, the head of the Natural Magic Department, a short man in a tweed jacket, was talking to Gideon Hawke, the head of Lost Books.

It was the job of the Lost Books Department to track down dangerous magical books. Brown and Hawke were having an animated conversation. Archie guessed they were talking about Woodbine's failed mission. Brown was shaking his head. Archie caught a few words.

'It's too bad, Gideon, but you really should have collected it yourself. I mean, of all the books to have stolen from under your nose, it had to be *that book* ...'

'Someone tipped them off,' said Hawke.

Archie switched his attention to Hawke. The head of Lost Books was of medium height with dark hair, and wore a brown moleskin jacket. It was well known among the apprentices that he was the most magically talented of all the museum elders. Archie had seen him perform spells on several occasions. But to look at him there was little to indicate his magical abilities, except that, like Archie, he had different-coloured eyes: one was blue and the other grey. Archie had often wondered how old he was, but it was impossible to tell.

Just then, he noticed a tall man, with long, grey hair and a beard that was frosted with white, sitting next to Hawke. He was dressed in a midnight blue velvet jacket, with pointed shoes that had silver buckles. The man was listening to the other two in rapt concentration. He had a faintly amused expression as if he knew something that no one else did. By the deep creases in his face he looked old, but the twinkle in his eye was youthful.

Graves took her place among the elders. She wore a worried frown. Standing, she raised her voice above the hubbub of chattering apprentices. 'Please take your seats so we may begin.' She cast a sharp-eyed look around the assembled faces.

'First, I'd like to introduce Faustus Gaunt,' she said, indicating the tall man with the beard. 'Faustus is an expert on magical prophecies. He is helping with some research in Lost Books, and we are delighted that he will be filling the vacancy as head of Mortal Magic.'

At the mention of his name, Gaunt gave the slightest of nods.

Graves paused, and took a breath. 'I have some other important news,' she continued. Her frown deepened. 'A very dangerous book has been stolen from the Royal Society of Magic. If you or anyone you know has any information concerning the missing book, you must report it to one of the elders.'

As she spoke, her gaze fell on the four members of the Alchemists' Club and seemed to linger on

Arabella. 'It is very important that we recover the book. Do I make myself clear?'

The apprentices left the function room chattering about the stolen book.

'It must be the same book that Dad was talking about,' said Thistle, as soon as the four of them were alone. 'The elders seem really worried about it. I've never seen them so jumpy.'

'Woodbine said that the authorities would have to act quickly,' said Archie, 'before the Greaders got a chance to open it. I wonder what book it is?'

'It's got to be the last of the Terrible Tomes,' said Arabella. 'It's the only thing that would alarm them like that.'

There were seven Terrible Tomes in all. When Archie had first arrived at the museum, four had already been found and locked away in a room called the crypt inside the museum. Thanks to Archie and the Alchemists' Club, two more of the Tomes – *The Book of Souls* and *The Grim Grimoire* – were also now under lock and key. That left one unaccounted for.

'The seventh Tome . . .' said Bramble.

'Yes, but what is it?' mused Archie.

None of them had an answer, but Archie had just had another thought. 'Woodbine said the book was stolen at just after eight o'clock. That's when you woke me up in the Scriptorium, and the spell disappeared shortly after. Do you think it could all be connected?'

Bramble shot him an anxious glance. 'It's possible,' she said. 'That's even more reason to ask Old Zeb about the black flame when you see him.'

3

The Diviner's Mark

The bell clanged noisily as Archie opened the door to the Aisle of White and stepped inside. He made his way between the dark wooden bookcases towards the counter at the back of the bookshop. The shelves were full of old books, but the magical ones were kept behind a velvet curtain, waiting to be mended or sent to the museum for classification.

Geoffrey Screech, the bookshop's owner, was standing behind the counter as usual. A narrow-shouldered man with a goatee beard, Screech wore a green waistcoat and a yellow bow tie. It was his job to check if any books that came into the shop were magical.

'Hello, Archie,' he said, looking up, his face creasing into a friendly smile.

'Is Old Zeb in yet?' Archie asked.

'He's downstairs,' Screech said. 'Is something wrong?'

But Archie had already disappeared through the curtain. He glanced at a bookcase there as he passed. It was full of repaired magical books waiting to go to the museum.

'Hello, Archie,' said a papery voice.

A chorus of other rustling voices joined in. Archie was only just beginning to understand the importance of being a book whisperer – especially as he was the only one – but it still gave him a thrill of excitement every time a book spoke to him. Today, though, he had to get on.

'Sorry, I can't stop to chat,' he said. 'I'm in a hurry.'

'Shame,' said another papery voice. 'It's so nice to talk to someone who isn't a book.'

'Yes,' said a deeper voice coming from a large book with a red leather cover. 'We don't get out much.'

Archie smiled to himself. 'All right then,' he said. 'But just for a moment.'

He glanced at the book's spine. Its title was *Magical Mysteries*. He remembered repairing it a few days earlier.

'Broken binding,' he said, 'with a small rip in the cover?'

'That's right,' said the book. 'But you fixed me up like new.'

Archie glanced at the other books.

'You were in for a broken clasp,' he said to the first one. 'And you had a crooked spine,' he said to the next. 'And you ...' he added, touching the cover of the fourth book, 'now let me see. Hmmmm. No, don't tell me ... you needed a new jacket because your old one was worn out!'

'Yes!' said the book. 'You gave me this smart new blue one.'

'You repaired all of us,' said the big red book, 'and we'd like to repay you in some way.' It lowered its already whispering voice. 'We heard your father was trapped in a book – maybe we can help you find out which one?'

'Really?' said Archie, suddenly very interested.

'We like solving mysteries,' said the deep voice. 'When we get to the museum we'll ask around. One of the books will know something.'

'That'd be brilliant, thank you! Now I must dash. There's something I need to ask Old Zeb about.'

He heard a chorus of voices wishing him good luck and promising to keep in touch.

At the bottom of the stairs he stepped into a long, dark corridor, lit by flaming torches.

Three arched doors led off the corridor. The

first was green; it was a magical portal called the Enchanted Entrance. Old Zeb had once shown Archie how to use it to get to other magical buildings. The second was blue, and led to the frozen lair of the bookend beasts, the stone griffins that had guarded the Great Library of Alexandria. Archie walked past these. The mending workshop was behind the third door, the red one. Beyond it, the passageway disappeared into shadows, and there was a fourth, black door, that led to Fabian Grey's secret laboratory. This was where the Alchemists' Club met, but they hadn't had a meeting in weeks due to Arabella and Rupert being away.

Archie pushed the red door open and stepped into the workshop.

The Word Smithy, the furnace containing the Flame of Pharos, was open and Old Zeb, the bookbinder, was standing by it. He looked like a mad professor with his straggly, white hair standing up in clumps. A stack of damaged books was on the workbench waiting for the old man to repair them.

'Mornin', Archie,' wheezed Old Zeb. 'Didn't expect to see you so early. Aren't you meant to be at the meeting in Quill's?'

'I've already been,' replied Archie.

'That was quick!' said the old bookbinder.

'I thought you might want to catch up with your friends.'

'Yes, I did, thanks. But there's something I wanted to ask you about.'

'Ah, curiosity!' said Old Zeb, his eyes sparkling. 'That's what I like to see. Good lad. Stick the kettle on.'

Old Zeb never did anything without a cup of tea first. Since becoming his apprentice, Archie had grown very fond of the old man and his eccentric ways.

Archie filled up the copper kettle and put it on top of the Word Smithy. As he did, he felt the prickling sensation in his palm again. He felt uneasy and wondered briefly if he was about to get another firemark. Apprentices received a new firemark when the Flame of Pharos determined it was time for them to learn a new magical skill. But the last time he'd received a firemark it had spelled danger for the museum.

Old Zeb noticed him scratching his hand. 'Is that what you wanted to ask me about?' he said.

'No, it's something else,' Archie said, trying to ignore the itching in his palm. He finished making the tea and the two of them sat on stools at the workbench sipping from chipped teacups.

'So then ...' said the old man after a while, 'what's bothering you?'

Archie sighed. 'Why would a spell suddenly disappear from a magical book?' he asked.

'You mean an old spell starting to fade?' asked Old Zeb.

Archie shook his head. 'No, a new spell that's just been written with azoth.'

'Impossible!' said Old Zeb. 'If the spell has been written properly then it can't just vanish!'

Archie shrugged. 'That's what I thought. But it did!'

Old Zeb's expression turned grave. He pursed his lips in thought. 'To make a freshly written spell vanish like that would require very powerful magic indeed.'

There was a crackling sound from the Word Smithy, and the Flame of Pharos seemed to gutter. Old Zeb peered into the furnace.

'What's the matter, old girl?' he said, eyeing the Flame with concern.

'Is it all right?' asked Archie, anxiously. 'It looks like it might go out.'

'Just hungry I expect,' said the old man. 'Magical flames aren't easily extinguished. There are only two things that can snuff them out: griffin's breath and dragon's blood, and there aren't many griffins or dragons in Oxford these days,' he added with a twinkle in his eye.

Archie knew the breath of a griffin was so cold it

could be fatal. He'd seen the frozen lair of the two stone griffins called the bookend beasts behind the blue door. He also knew that dragons had unusual magical properties because ... well, they were dragons. But he also had proof as he had a dragon-skin bag that prevented magical spells escaping.

The old bookbinder picked up a log from a stack and put it in the furnace. The Flame immediately burned brighter. He went to close the door but as he did an ember shot into the air and exploded, showering the room in sparks. Archie and Old Zeb gasped.

Archie felt a familiar tingling sensation in his hand. He slowly opened it and stared at his palm.

A new firemark had appeared. It was shaped like an open eye, with three red tears falling from it.

'Let me see,' said the old bookbinder, kindly. Grasping Archie's hand, he peered at the mark. 'How extraordinary,' he muttered. 'Three firemarks in such close succession. I've never heard of such a—'

'Oh,' he breathed, his eyes wide, 'it's the diviner's firemark. The last person to get that was Wolfus Bone thirty-five years ago. Strange that it should appear now when Wolfus is injured! Mind you, Gideon had a hunch that one of the apprentices would get it soon. It's been so long, you see.'

'What does it mean?' asked Archie, still staring at his hand. 'What do I have to do?'

The old man smiled. 'It's nothing to worry about,' he said. He looked into Archie's eyes. 'But it means you'll be starting a new apprenticeship. You must report to the Lost Books Department this afternoon.'

'But I've still got so much to learn about bookbinding!' said Archie. He loved working with the old man and didn't want to leave.

Old Zeb smiled again. 'No,' he said firmly. 'It's time. I was going to tell you myself anyway. It's all here,' he added, handing Archie a scroll tied with a red ribbon. 'Go on, read it!'

Archie slipped the scroll from its ribbon and unwound it. To his great surprise it was a diploma.

This is to certify that Archie Greene
has completed his training as a magical
bookbinder and has passed with
flying colours!

It was signed:

Zebediah Alluitious Perret,
Master Bookbinder at the Museum of
Magical Miscellany.

'There,' said the old bookbinder, beaming. 'I told you you were a natural.'

Archie was speechless. As he gazed at the diploma he felt a strange mix of emotions – great pride that he had measured up to Old Zeb's exacting standards, but at the same time sadness that their time together was coming to an end.

The old man seemed to read his thoughts. He patted Archie on the shoulder.

'I remember the day I gave your father his diploma,' he said with a wistful smile. 'I can see him now, standing just where you are. I wish he could be here to see you today,' he added. 'He'd be very proud. Very proud indeed.'

Archie wished his father was there now, too, and his mother and sister. If only the mended books could find out where they were.

Archie shook the old man's outstretched hand. 'It's been a pleasure teaching you,' said Old Zeb. 'Now it's time for you to start your new training in Lost Books.'

'The Flame has a plan for you, Archie,' he added. 'It always did!'

When Archie caught up with his cousins in Quill's at lunchtime he was bursting to tell them his news. He showed them his bookbinding diploma and his new firemark.

'Wow!' gasped Thistle. 'I've never seen that firemark before.'

'Wolfus Bone was the last person to get it,' said Archie. 'I'm to report to Lost Books this afternoon.'

'That's quick!' exclaimed Bramble. 'How exciting!'

'Its also a bit daunting,' said Archie. 'I mean, Gideon Hawke is nice enough, but he's a bit intimidating. What if I'm not up to the job?'

'You'll be fine,' said Bramble. 'You're a fast learner. And Lost Books is a brilliant place to work; it's the most important department because it's where all the newly discovered books go to be classified.'

'Lost Books?' said a voice. 'How come you get all the cushy jobs? It's not fair!'

They looked up to see Peter Quiggley's round face. Quiggley had started his apprenticeship at the same time as Archie and Arabella. He'd had a rather unfortunate start to his career at the museum. On his first day Greaders had mistaken him for Archie and kidnapped him, believing he was the book whisperer.

Quiggley's captors had released him after a few hours when they realised their mistake, but Quiggley was very angry about it. It wasn't clear whether he was crosser about being abducted or being released because he wasn't considered magical enough to keep.

He'd had a chip on his shoulder about it ever since. He seemed to resent Archie in particular, and never missed an opportunity to put him or his cousins down. Quiggley also had a reputation for being lazy and was always looking to score points against the members of the Alchemists' Club and get them into trouble.

'Mind your own business, Quiggley,' said Bramble. 'We didn't ask for your opinion.'

'Perhaps not,' said Quiggley, 'but you lot won't always get the best jobs.'

He gave them a smug smile and moved away.

'I wonder what he's looking so pleased with himself about,' said Thistle.

'He's not worth bothering with,' said Bramble. 'Come on, Archie, it's time you made an appearance in Lost Books. Let's get some motion potions.'

Motion potions were the antigravity potions needed to ride on the seats of learning – the flying chairs that the apprentices used to transport themselves to the museum underground.

'All right, Arch? All right, Bram? All right, Thistle? What'll it be today?' asked Pink as they approached the bar. It was her job to make the motion potions.

'I'll have my usual,' said Bramble.

Pink smiled. 'Right you are – one shot in the dark,' she said. 'In a choc-tail?'

'Yes, please!' said Bramble smacking her lips.

Motion potions came in lots of different flavours, and the apprentices could choose to drink them with hot chocolate as a choc-tail, or with fruit juices. A shot in the dark tasted of wild berries and citrus.

'What about you, Arch?' inquired Pink.

'He's starting in Lost Books today!' Thistle jumped in excitedly.

'Lost Books!' said Pink. 'Better make it something special then. How about a missing link?'

Archie scanned the menu of motion potions pinned up behind the bar. A missing link was a blend of strawberries, bananas and blueberries with 'added zip'.

'What's "added zip"?' he asked.

Pink winked. 'That's the missing link. It just makes the ride a bit quicker,' she said. 'Perfectly safe – I use it all the time myself.'

'All right, then,' said Archie, 'I'll have a missing link.'

'And I'll have the same,' said Thistle, rubbing his hands together with excitement.

'One shot in the dark and two missing links coming right up,' said Pink. 'And which seats of learning will you be using?'

'The box seats,' said Bramble.

Each of the seats of learning had its own history.

Some, like the box seats, allowed more than one apprentice to travel together.

'They're all yours,' said Pink, lining up three glasses. She took down a bottle from a shelf and poured two drops of a thick crimson liquid into the first glass, adding a few drips from a blue bottle and a drop from a black bottle. Then she picked up three bottles at the same time and poured them into the other two glasses. Finally she added a slug of a bright blue liquid to the two glasses.

'That's the added zip,' she said, smiling at Archie. She tipped the glasses into three tall mugs and topped them up with steaming hot chocolate.

'Here you go,' she said.

They collected their motion potions and crossed the room to the snugs where the seats of learning were located.

The box seats were a row of ancient wooden theatre seats behind a red and gold curtain. The three cousins buckled themselves into their chairs and closed the curtain.

'Bottoms up!' said Archie, clinking his glass first with Bramble and then with Thistle.

'Down the hatch!' said Thistle.

They downed their motion potions. Archie's fingers and toes had just begun to tingle pleasantly when the floor opened and the box seats plunged through the gap.

4

The Lost Books Department

The next thing they knew they were hurtling through the underground passages and caverns that led to the Museum of Magical Miscellany. It didn't matter how many times he rode on them, Archie never tired of the seats of learning. They were like the best-ever roller-coaster ride and flying all rolled into one. Sharing it with his cousins made it even more fun.

Every time they went around a bend, all three of them whooped with delight. Archie and Thistle's seats seemed to be moving even faster than normal today.

'Keep up, Bram!' Thistle called over his shoulder as the two of them pulled ahead. It must be the added zip in the motion potion, Archie thought.

The tunnel ended abruptly and they flew into

the Bookery, a cavernous space, where magical books flew about like flocks of birds. The flying books swooped and soared all around them, dodging out of their way at the last moment.

Ahead of them in the gloom a light shone. The box seats flew towards it, descending in a series of circles and coming to a halt in a long corridor called the Happy Landing.

'We're here,' said Archie, unclipping his belt and hopping out of his seat.

As usual, the museum was full of apprentices. Most of those working in the Great Gallery were doing their minding apprenticeships. Minders made sure all the magical books were in good order and filed in the right place.

The finders were assigned to one of the three magical departments: natural, mortal or supernatural magic. They learned to identify which sort of magic a book contained. There was usually only one apprentice bookbinder at a time who, until a few days ago, had been Archie but the position was now vacant.

The air above their heads was filled with flying books, flapping their covers like wings. There was an enchantment on the building that allowed the books with a special stamp to move. It saved the apprentices work because the books filed themselves on the shelves.

Archie made his way to the West Gallery and up the first set of stairs leading to the Scriptorium. Lost Books was on the next floor, up a second staircase.

'Good luck, Arch,' said Bramble. 'Not that you need it, you'll be fine.'

'Tell us all about it after work,' added Thistle.

Archie reached the top step and waved. One of the double doors was open.

Gideon Hawke was sitting behind his desk staring at a green glass bottle that looked like the sort that contains medicine. When he saw Archie, he quickly slid it into a drawer.

'Ah, Archie!' he called. 'Come on in.'

Archie was slightly in awe of Hawke. Recently the head of Lost Books had taken a keen interest in Archie's book-whispering talents and the magic-writing skills of the Alchemists' Club.

It had been Hawke's idea that Archie and the others should start rewriting the magical books in the museum in secret. Some of the other elders knew what they were doing but Hawke had said it was better if the Magical League and the Royal Society of Magic didn't know. It would only cause trouble, he said.

'Come in and sit down,' Hawke said, indicating the battered leather sofa in the middle of the room. There was a fire burning in the hearth.

On the desk, Archie noticed some magical tools. The black-handled imagining glass Hawke used to examine magical books was there, and the Shadow Blade, the enchanted blade made from the reflection of a shooting star.

Archie took a seat on the sofa. The room was as cluttered as ever but a table had been cleared next to the desk and a crystal ball the size of a very large goldfish bowl placed upon it. Archie was sure it hadn't been there before.

'It's an oculus,' said Hawke, answering Archie's unspoken question. 'It allows me to communicate directly with the magical authorities. Unfortunately, it also enables them to communicate directly with me!' he added with a wry smile.

Archie peered at his own reflection in the oculus, noticing how his nose and lips were magnified in the glass.

When he looked up, Hawke was studying him. 'But you aren't here to learn about magical instruments,' he said. 'Zeb tells me that you have the magic diviner's mark. Show me.'

Archie held out his open hand. Hawke picked up the imagining glass and inspected the new firemark there. When he was satisfied, he stood up and began pacing the room, a sure sign that he had something on his mind. After a while, he crossed to the fire and stared into the flames. 'I suppose you heard about what happened to Wolfus?' he asked.

Archie knew that Bone had received a nasty drubbing because he'd overheard Woodbine telling Loretta. There was no point lying to Hawke – he always seemed to see straight through him.

He nodded. 'Is he badly hurt?'

Hawke stoked the fire with a poker. 'He'll recover,' he said, 'but it was a vicious attack. He'll be out of action for some time.' He paused. 'It leaves us without a diviner at the museum at a time when we need one most.'

'A diviner can sense magical activity,' Hawke added, 'and provide an early warning of danger.'

Archie had seen Wolfus Bone use a dowsing rod to tell where magical energy was coming from and how strong it was. Bone could also tell what sort of magic it was – natural, mortal or supernatural.

Hawke began pacing again. He stopped abruptly and turned on his heel, as if he'd made up his mind about something.

'I want you to take Wolfus's place until he is ready to come back,' he said.

'But I don't know anything about magic divining!' Archie exclaimed.

'You have the firemark,' said Hawke. 'That's the most important thing. I can show you the basics and Wolfus can teach you the rest when he's back on his feet.'

'Erm, well, if you think I'm up to it,' said Archie, 'I'll give it a try.'

'Good,' said Hawke. 'Come back tomorrow and we'll get you started.'

At that same moment fifty miles away in London at the offices of Folly & Catchpole, the oldest lore firm in England, Horace Catchpole shifted uncomfortably in his chair. He studied the open ledger on his desk. He'd heard that a dangerous book had been stolen from the Royal Society of Magic, and it had unsettled him. Horace knew enough about magic to know that there was something going on and it might be connected to one of the firm's clients.

Folly & Catchpole specialised in the storage of magical items and other secrets in its underground cellar known as the dungeon. Instructions were kept in ledgers like the one in Horace's hands. An entry dated 6th September 1666 was troubling him. He had been looking at it all afternoon.

Folly & Catchpole's reputation was built on two simple principles: minding its own business and not making mistakes. It was the first of these that was bothering Horace. The firm's clients expected their instructions to be followed to the letter. No one knew that better than him. And yet, as he read and reread the entry in the ledger, he couldn't help wondering whether he should report it to the magical authorities. It said:

Property of Fabian Grey.
Do NOT remove.
Owner will collect.

5

The Oculus

It was the day after Archie's new firemark had appeared and he was sitting on Gideon Hawke's leather sofa. He still couldn't quite believe he was working in the Lost Books Department, the most exciting and secretive part of the museum. It only seemed five minutes ago that he had started his bookbinding apprenticeship, and now here he was learning about magic divining. Bramble had told him it was one of the most advanced magical apprenticeships of all.

He tried to focus on what Hawke was saying.

'Today, I'm going to tell you about one of the most important divining skills – delving. Delving is usually something only finders learn at the end of their apprenticeship, but it's fundamental to divining. It's when you deliberately seek out a magical source. It can happen when the diviner is awake, or sometimes in their unconscious mind.'

Archie thought about the strange dreams he'd been having lately. He wondered whether he should say something, but Hawke interrupted his thoughts.

'Have you ever sensed magic around you?'

Now that Hawke mentioned it, Archie realised that he had felt something like that, most recently in the Scriptorium, but also sometimes when he was working in the mending workshop.

'Sometimes I can feel it in the air like static electricity,' he said, surprising himself. 'Like a background tingle or hum.'

Hawke looked pleased. 'Good,' he said. 'I thought you might have.'

'And there's something else,' added Archie. 'When I write magic I can feel it flowing through my body. It's almost as if it's part of me.'

Hawke beamed at him. 'Excellent!' he said. 'That means you are channelling magic. This is even better than I hoped for. It proves you have the natural ability to be a diviner, and now all we need to do is hone it.'

'Let's start with some simple delving spells,' he said. 'The first one is used to find magical books that are mixed up with non-magical books. See the shelves over there?' he asked, pointing at a tall bookcase against the wall crammed with the spines of books. 'Some of the books are magical, but which ones? Now watch.'

Hawke concentrated his full attention on the bookcase and spoke the words of a spell.

'Books of magic
On the shelves
Secret volumes
Reveal yourselves!'

As he said the last word, three books on the top shelf slid forward so that their spines stuck out proud from the others.

Hawke regarded the books sternly. 'Hmmm,' he said after a brief pause, 'and the rest of you?'

Three more books on the second shelf eased out. 'Come along,' said Hawke, raising his eyebrows. 'We haven't got all day!'

Two more books on the next row stuck out their spines.

'I'm still waiting,' he said. He began to drum his fingers on the desk. 'Do I have to say the spell again?'

There was a rustling sound from one of the lower shelves and four more books shuffled forward. Hawke pursed his lips and looked at the ceiling. 'And finally?'

A large, dusty tome on the very bottom of the bookcase slowly edged out of its row.

'Thank you,' said Hawke.

Archie couldn't help grinning. The books reminded him of reluctant children in a classroom dragging their feet when the teacher asks the naughty ones to come to the front. He heard a bossy voice from the top shelf.

'You heard the spell, wot kept you?'

A sleepy voice replied from the large book on the bottom shelf, the one that had been the last to come forward. 'All right, all right, keep your cover on. I was nappin',' it said, defensively.

'Nappin'?' said the first voice. 'This is no time for nappin'! You gotta look lively with a delvin' spell.'

The books were bickering among themselves. Archie smiled to himself. When he looked up he was aware of Hawke's eyes on him. For a brief moment he wondered whether the head of Lost Books could hear the voices, too. But Hawke wasn't a book whisperer so it would be impossible.

'Your turn,' said Hawke, giving Archie an encouraging look.

He took out a white quill and a crystal inkwell and placed them on the desk. Then, dipping the quill into the ink, he scribbled something on a piece of parchment and handed it to Archie.

'It's another delving spell,' he explained. 'This one's for finding magical books that are hidden from sight. Go ahead and read it.'

Archie took the parchment and read out the spell.

'Secret volume
Placed in stealth
Book of magic
Reveal yourself.'

For a moment nothing happened. Archie felt disappointed. Then just as he was beginning to think the spell hadn't worked, he heard an angry exclamation and a thud as a book fell from where it had been concealed on top of the bookcase and landed on the floor.

Hawke stepped from behind his desk and picked it up. He raised his eyebrows. 'I wondered where that had got to,' he said. 'It's been missing for a while.'

Later that day, Archie was having lunch with Bramble and Arabella in Quill's when Peter Quiggley walked past with a smirk on his face.

'What's he looking so pleased with himself about?' asked Archie.

Arabella rolled her eyes. 'Haven't you heard?' she

said. 'He's the new apprentice at the menagerie. He's taking over Rupert's job, working with Motley Brown.'

'That's why he made the comment about getting the best jobs – he must have known!' exclaimed Archie. 'But why did they give it to him?'

'Brown likes him. Thinks he has great potential. And Quiggley's been sucking up to him for months.'

'What will Thistle say when he hears?' asked Archie. 'He'll be devastated.'

'He already knows,' said Bramble, gloomily.

'Poor Thistle,' said Archie. 'I bet he's really upset.'

'He'll get over it,' said Arabella. 'Besides, we've got our work cut out just trying to keep up with rewriting the magical books.'

When Archie arrived at the Scriptorium that evening, he found a fresh pile of books on his desk waiting to be rewritten.

Most of the books in the museum had originally come from the Great Library of Alexandria. When his attempt to open the Terrible Tomes had failed, Barzak had set fire to the library burning it to the ground. The books had been rescued and brought to Oxford by the Flame Keepers, but many had been scorched in the flames and their spells damaged, so now they were fading and had to be rewritten with azoth or their magic would be lost forever.

Archie regarded the stack of books. There were eight thick volumes. It was going to be another long night. Arabella was meant to be joining him, but there was no sign of her yet. He decided to make a start without her. He slipped Fabian Grey's gold ring from his finger, transforming it into a quill. Dipping the nib into the inkpot, he opened the first book, a book of gardening spells to help plants grow more quickly.

The words were still visible in places, but where the spells had faded completely the magic writers had to write new magic to fill the gaps and complete the spell.

Archie tried to let the magic flow through him. First he had to relax his body and let the magic in. He had found that when he was tense he couldn't write magic at all. He took three deep breaths.

Then he closed his eyes and opened his mind. For a moment he sat perfectly still, with the quill held lightly between his finger and thumb. He felt the familiar tingle of raw magical power and began tracing the lines of the spells. Slowly at first, but getting faster as he got into his rhythm, he felt the magic flowing through his body and into the golden quill. As he rewrote each spell, he turned the page and moved on to the next one.

He heard the door to the Scriptorium open. Archie opened his eyes, and saw that Arabella had brought some more books. She put them down on the desk.

'Hawke put these out for us to work on, too,' she said. 'There's a lot to get through so we'd better get cracking.'

They set to work, both rewriting spells with the magical ink. It was a demanding job because they had to concentrate on what was still legible while also using their own magical ability to fill in the empty spaces where the spell had completely disappeared. Archie enjoyed filling in the missing lines the most. The other members of the Alchemists' Club all agreed that he was the best at it, and they gave him the most badly faded books to work on.

The collection of gardening spells took Archie half an hour because there were lots of spells to trace, but the second one, a book of popper spells, only took him twenty minutes because there were more gaps he could fill in. He was careful to turn the page as he finished each one so that the spell did not pop out of the book. The third, a book of love potions, was quicker still. By the time he reached the fourth book, a series of enchantments for musical instruments, his quill swooped and curved across the parchment making a scratching sound as it went. He finished the fifth and sixth books – some spells for preparing a banquet and a book of lucky charms – in short order. By now, Archie was lost in the act of creation, his mind full of magic and his quill hand a blur of activity.

'You're on fire tonight, Archie,' said Arabella, noting how many books he had already finished. 'That must be a record.'

Archie gave her a thin smile. He was starting to feel lightheaded. The magic flowing through him could do that. Sometimes it gave him a headache.

'How many more are there?' he asked.

Arabella glanced at the stack of books she'd brought in. 'Another two,' she said. 'Do you think we can manage them all tonight?'

Archie nodded. 'Yeah, I'm on a roll,' he said, although in truth he felt his energy was utterly spent and he just wanted to get home and go to sleep. He felt his bed calling to him.

He picked up the book on the top of the heap and opened it. He was about to start writing, when he heard Arabella cry out.

'What is *that*?'

Archie glanced up and saw that she'd dropped one of the books and it had landed on the ground with its cover open. Arabella was pointing at it with a startled look on her face.

A black flame was burning inside the open book

of popper spells. It turned the letters of the spell to ash. Archie felt the air rush past him. It smelled foul, like rotting fish. The cinders blew away. Where the spell had been a moment earlier there was just a blank page.

The breeze turned the pages and one by one the spells that Archie had written burned to ash.

'What does it mean?' asked Arabella, frightened.

'I don't know,' said Archie. 'It's the same thing that happened last night! Old Zeb said it would have to be a very powerful magic. We have to tell Hawke.'

A frightening thought crossed Archie's mind. The black flame was only attacking the spells he'd been working on! The ones that Arabella had rewritten didn't seem to be affected. Could it be something that he'd done? Perhaps the spells he'd written were corrupted in some way?

The two of them hurried up the stairs to Lost Books. When they reached Hawke's office, the door was ajar and they could see into the room. They were about to knock when they heard a voice coming from the oculus.

'Gideon? Is that you?'

Hawke was sitting at his desk in front of the large crystal ball. The oculus was glowing and a face had appeared in it. Archie and Arabella recognised the bald head of Orpheus Gloom, the magic assessor from the Royal Society of Magic.

'Good evening, Orpheus,' said Hawke.

'Ah, there you are, Gideon,' said Gloom. 'Terrible business the other night. How is Wolfus?'

'He'll live,' said Hawke, 'but no thanks to you.'

'Yes, well, it was all a bit of a mess,' blustered Gloom. 'If your chaps had arrived a bit sooner, the whole situation might have been resolved.'

Hawke stiffened in his chair. 'Surely, you're not blaming us for your mistake?' he said sharply. 'If you had told us where the book was sooner – and that you had been harbouring it inside the Royal Society for the last three hundred years – then we might have stood a chance!'

'Yes, yes, but the Royal Society thought it was safe here,' said Gloom, looking shifty.

'And you were wrong!' declared Hawke crossly. 'What is the point of having a lore about hoarding books when the people who are meant to enforce the lores ignore them?'

'All right,' said Gloom, holding up his hand. 'We should have told you we'd got the book before, but it didn't seem important. Locked away in the library here it was out of reach of the Greaders.'

'*Library?*' exclaimed Hawke. 'How many magical books have you got?'

Gloom looked sheepish. 'Well, it's not really a *library*,' he said. 'The Royal Society has a small collection of rare books, that's all. They date back to before my time. I only found out recently myself. It's a bit irregular, I know, but they didn't seem to be doing any harm here.'

'So what changed your mind about *The Book of Night*?' asked Hawke. 'Why did you ask us to collect it?'

Archie and Arabella exchanged excited looks. So the stolen book was called *The Book of Night*! What sort of magic did it contain?

Gloom looked even shiftier. He glanced over his shoulder as if he thought someone might be listening. 'We received some threats,' he said.

'Threats?'

'Yes. Letters. They said they knew we had the book and that if we didn't hand it over there would be serious consequences.'

Hawke leaned forward. 'What sort of consequences?'

Gloom swallowed hard. 'The Royal Society would be closed down,' he said.

'And you believed them?'

'We couldn't take any chances. I thought it was time to move the book somewhere safer. That's why I contacted you.'

'Hmmm,' mused Hawke, 'but someone knew that the book was being moved and took it for themselves.'

Gloom nodded. 'Yes. And if *The Book of Night* is opened, Gideon . . . Think of it . . .'

'I am thinking of it,' snapped Hawke. 'It's all I think of these days! But the seventh Tome should never have been at risk.'

Outside the door, Archie and Arabella made eye contact again. So they had been right – it was the seventh Terrible Tome.

'Who else knew it was being moved?' demanded Hawke. 'Who did you tell?'

Gloom shook his head. 'Apart from the museum elders, no one.'

Hawke's brow creased into a frown. 'And the only people I told were Wolfus and Woodbine Foxe. They're men I would trust with my life. But someone knew and told the enemy.'

'A traitor!' breathed Gloom.

Just then, there was a crackling sound and another face appeared in the oculus next to Gloom's. It was a man's face, framed with long, black hair, threaded with grey, and combed back to reveal a pronounced widow's peak.

'Did you say traitor?' the man asked, and his voice was cold like a knife in winter.

'Uther,' said Hawke. 'Good of you to join us, but I didn't know the Magical League had started listening in on private conversations.'

Archie felt Arabella tug at his sleeve. 'That's

Uther Morgred, the chief magic enforcer at the Magical League,' she whispered. 'He's very bad news.'

Archie peered around the door to get a better look. The man held his head high. His sallow face was finely boned with deep lines etched into his cheeks and the corners of his eyes. He was clearly not in the first flush of youth but it was impossible to know just how old he was. Archie noticed that one of his eyes was a moss green and the other was so dark that it appeared to be black.

'We monitor all magical activity,' Morgred said. 'A very dangerous book is missing, and I just heard you say there is a traitor operating inside the Royal Society or the Museum of Magical Miscellany. That is a serious allegation, very serious indeed. I will have to investigate. If there is a spy amongst us I will find him or her.'

'And what will the Magical League do about the stolen book?' asked Hawke.

Morgred's brow furrowed. 'We will issue a proclamation. Something carefully worded,' he said. 'People already suspect that it's one of the Terrible Tomes; if they knew which of the seven there would be panic. But spreading a little fear might loosen some tongues.'

Morgred's eyes roamed around the room, making Archie uncomfortable. He had the feeling that the magic enforcer could sense them standing there in the shadows.

'Good evening, gentlemen.' Morgred's face disappeared from the crystal orb leaving only Gloom's face illuminated.

'I'd better be going as well,' said Gloom. He held up his hand in farewell. 'Goodnight, Gideon. If anyone can recover *The Book of Night*, then it's you. Good luck.'

The oculus went dark. Hawke put his head in his hands and gave a long sigh.

'Let's get out of here,' whispered Archie.

'What about the disappearing spells?' asked Arabella.

'Not now,' said Archie. 'I think he's got enough on his plate. I'll tell him first thing tomorrow.'

6

The Light and the Shade

The next day, when Archie told Hawke about the vanishing spells, he looked concerned. 'And you're sure it was a black flame?' he asked.

'Positive,' Archie confirmed.

Hawke paced up and down a couple of times in silence, his brow creased in thought.

'Could it be connected with *The Book of Night*?' Archie blurted out.

Hawke swung round to look at him. 'How do you know about that?' he snapped angrily.

'I overheard you talking to Gloom in the oculus,' Archie said, his face colouring.

'I see,' said Hawke, glowering at him. 'So you listen at keyholes now! Spying on people is becoming a bit of a habit of yours, Archie!'

Archie stared at his shoes.

Hawke resumed pacing. His brow darkened. 'Old Zeb tells me you have dreams about Fabian Grey?' he said.

Archie was too embarassed to feel annoyed that the bookbinder had gone behind his back. He told Hawke about his most recent dream of the raven and the Tower of London.

Hawke listened attentively. 'You must tell me if you have any more dreams like that,' he said when Archie had finished. He gave a grim smile. 'Fabian Grey seems to haunt us all!'

Hawke started pacing again, and he looked like he was carrying a great weight on his shoulders. He stopped by the fire with his back to Archie. For a long moment he stared into the flames, as if he was weighing something in his mind, unsure which direction to go in. Then he turned to face Archie.

'I want you to come and work with me in Lost Books,' he said. 'And I don't just mean as a magic diviner – I mean as my personal apprentice. I need some help. The Greaders are planning something very big, I'm sure of it. The theft of *The Book of Night* confirms it. It's my job to stop them. We have to find that book before the Greaders open it. But I won't lie to you, Archie, it is dangerous. So what do you say?'

Archie was flattered. Coming from Hawke this was praise indeed.

'What about rewriting the books?' he asked.

Hawke was studying him again. 'After what you've just told me about the black flame and the disappearing spells, I think it's best that you don't write any more magic for the time being.'

Archie felt a sudden panic. Did Hawke think that he was to blame for the spells disappearing? 'Why?' he asked.

'Something is consuming the newly written spells and I don't want to feed it. Tell the others, too – it's not safe for any of you to be writing magic.'

Archie was relieved to hear that Hawke wasn't singling him out. Still, it was a blow. They'd been making good progress rewriting the books. Archie felt disappointed. But at least it would take some of the pressure off the remaining members of the Alchemists' Club.

'The black flame – what do you think it is?' he asked.

Hawke blew out his cheeks. 'I think it's related to the stolen book, and if I'm right then we must proceed very carefully indeed.'

'We can continue your delving training while you're helping me,' he added. 'I'll ask Wolfus to give you some lessons as soon as he's well enough. Kill two birds with one stone.'

The mention of birds made Archie think about the raven in his dream. He wondered again what it meant and why Hawke was so interested. Interested enough to want Archie to be his apprentice.

Normally, Hawke was cautious about teaching apprentices magic. This was out of character. Archie knew whatever had caused the change in him must be serious. He swallowed hard.

'I'll do whatever I can to protect the museum,' he said. 'But why me?'

Hawke's lips creased into a half smile and the shadow that had fallen over him seemed to lift a little. 'You're a book whisperer,' he said, 'which is a very useful talent for finding books, and therefore should be helpful in tracking down *The Book of Night*.'

He saw Archie's puzzled expression and continued.

'A book whisperer has an advantage when it comes to delving. You instinctively know when magic is present. The first time you entered the Aisle of White, you could hear the magical books talking to each other even though you didn't know what it was.

'And there are other magical talents that come naturally to you, too. You were able to release Barzak from *The Book of Souls*. To do that you must have used a very powerful unbinding spell. And to send him back into the book you must have used an even more powerful binding spell.'

Archie's jaw fell open. 'But I had no idea,' he gasped.

'No,' said Hawke, 'I don't suppose you did.' He looked thoughtful.

'I wondered how you were able to defeat Barzak. It shouldn't have been possible for someone untrained in magic to resist such a powerful darchemist, even though he was weakened by years of imprisonment in the book.'

Hawke's eyes wandered to the flickering fire and he stared into the flames.

'I have to admit, Archie, it troubled me greatly at the time. Then you saved Orpheus's life by breaking the dark quill's spell.'

He was referring to the time that Orpheus Gloom had picked up a hexed quill that would have killed him if Archie hadn't managed to write a spell to stop it.

'Again, you did that without any proper training. You were practising very advanced magic – yet you had no knowledge of how or what you were doing. Even the most able magister would take years to learn what you did instinctively. And then I was sure.'

Archie felt a knot in his stomach.

Hawke gave him a thin smile. 'It seems, Archie, that you are practising your own kind of original, instinctual magic – and that's very, very rare. You used original magic to defeat Barzak and save Orpheus. Those spells are your own. They are inside you.'

Archie felt the knot in his stomach tighten. Somehow he was able to perform amazing feats of magic without knowing what he was doing. It had worried him, too. He'd pushed it from his mind, or tried to dismiss it as a fluke, but deep down he had always known there had to be some other explanation. He remembered how he'd been able to understand the magical language called Enochian Script when it had taken Horace Catchpole hours to decipher the meaning.

For the first time, Archie felt frightened by his own abilities.

'But I have no control over it,' he said. 'I didn't mean to perform any of that magic – it just happened. What if I accidentally hurt someone?'

'You can learn to control it,' said Hawke. 'That's what I'm going to help you with.'

Archie felt a wave of relief. It would be all right. Hawke would help him channel his magical ability.

The head of Lost Books turned away and began pacing again. 'But first you need to understand what we're up against. I'm going to tell you some things that may alarm you,' he said. 'I only tell you now because the stakes are high and you need to know.'

Archie wondered what he was going to say. Hawke picked up a log and placed it on the fire. For a moment he watched it burn and then he began to speak.

'*The Book of Night* is the last of the seven Terrible Tomes. It's the darkest book of all. Until very recently its whereabouts was known only to a handful of people at the Royal Society of Magic. Even I did not know it was there,' he added, with a trace of bitterness.

He was speaking in a low voice now. Archie felt a change in the atmosphere of the room. Despite the fire in the grate, it felt cold. He had goosebumps on his skin.

He waited for Hawke to explain, but the head of Lost Books seemed reluctant to say more. He gingerly placed another log on the grate, watching as it nestled into the orange glow at the heart of the fire. The flames licked its surface and soon the dry wood caught. Hawke gazed into the writhing tongues of fire.

'See how the log burns?' he said, flicking his eyes towards Archie and then back to the fire. 'The flames are hungry, they devour the wood and it makes them stronger.'

He replaced the fireguard in front of the hearth. 'The spells you are rewriting in the books are like the logs,' he said. 'They feed the magical flames.'

'Flames?' said Archie, surprised. 'There's more than one?'

Hawke nodded. 'The Flame of Pharos isn't the only magical flame. There's another – the Flame of Pandemonium – the Dark Flame. It is the dark twin of Pharos. Both flames seek to control the path of magic. Each tries to consume the spells of the other. But only one can prevail. It's the light and the shade, you see, Archie.'

As he watched the flames in the hearth devouring the log, Archie felt a shiver run up his spine.

Hawke continued. 'The Dark Flame would turn the magical realm to dark magic. It has its own firemark, the Black Dragon, and it has its own deadly servants. There are three of them and they are called the Pale Writers. They are the corrupted spirits of long-dead darchemists. They have only one aim: to find *The Opus Magus*.'

Archie remembered hearing about *The Opus Magus*. It was the great work of magic, but no one had seen it in centuries.

'I thought *The Opus Magus* was just a legend?' he said.

Hawke shook his head. 'No, it's real. It is the

primary spell that created magic and made all the others possible. If the Dark Flame were to control *The Opus Magus* then there would only be dark magic in the world.'

Hawke stared at the twisting fire in the hearth as its yellow tongues consumed the last of the burning log.

'*The Book of Night* contains the Dark Flame,' he said. 'Whoever opens it will release the Pale Writers. Think of it, Archie – a dark master to rule the magical realm.'

'How do you know this?' asked Archie, shocked.

'Because the new spells are burning black,' said Hawke. 'Stealing the book must have woken the Dark Flame. Now it is devouring the fresh spells. It is still weak but it seeks their power to regain its strength. The book has not been opened yet so the Dark Flame remains contained. It will take a strong spell to release it and probably at a time of dark power, during a lunar eclipse. We must hope we can recover it before that happens.'

'But if *The Book of Night* is opened?' Archie gasped. 'How can we stop the Dark Flame?'

Hawke's brow darkened. 'If the book is opened then the magical realm will be in great danger – probably the greatest danger it has ever faced. Magic itself will be in peril. But there may be a way to stop it even then.'

His brow furrowed. 'We found something in the archive. When Morag was looking through the old texts, she discovered an old notebook that belonged to John Dee.'

Morag Pandrama was the museum's archivist. It was her job to look after the old magical records. Archie's ears pricked up at the mention of Dee's name.

'It contains a prophecy,' added Hawke. 'It's written in obscure language but it suggests that there is a way to defeat the Dark Flame. That's why Faustus Gaunt is here. He's an expert on magical prophecies. I've asked him to examine it and give us his opinion.'

Hawke paused. 'Faustus and Morag are searching through the archive now to see if they can find anything else that might throw some light on the matter.'

'And as my apprentice, you will have access to the archive. I'll ask Morag to put out some reading materials for you.'

'You'll need this,' he said, producing a silver key and sliding it across the desk. Archie put it in his pocket.

That afternoon, the museum elders called an urgent meeting at Quill's. Work came to a standstill and the apprentices filed into the function room.

Archie barely had time to tell Bramble, Thistle and Arabella what he'd learned from Hawke about the Dark Flame and the prophecy before Motley Brown rounded up the stragglers and closed the doors.

The apprentices were restless.

'What's all this about?' demanded Peter Quiggley, sitting down in the place where Rupert would have sat.

'Dunno,' said Arabella, giving him a disdainful look that said he wasn't welcome.

'It must be something to do with the stolen book,' continued Quiggley, ignoring her hint. He turned to Bramble and Thistle. 'I heard it was your dad's fault that it was taken in the first place.'

'It wasn't his fault,' growled Thistle, 'he was just doing his job!'

'Or rather *not doing* his job!' snickered Quiggley, with a smirk. 'Wasn't he expelled from the museum, too?'

It was true that Woodbine had been asked to leave the museum a few years earlier after he'd opened a popper, releasing the spell for a rhinoceros in a collection of priceless antique china. Thistle, like all the Foxe family, was sensitive about the subject.

'That was an accident,' he said, squaring up to Quiggley.

'A bit accident-prone, your dad!' sneered Quiggley.

'Stop it, both of you,' said Arabella. 'The meeting is about to start.'

'He's asking for it!' said Thistle, hotly.

'It's not worth fighting over,' said Bramble. 'It's done now.'

The two boys glared at each other. But before the hostilities could escalate, Graves took her place among the elders. In her hand she held a parchment scroll with a blue wax seal. Something about the scroll looked ominous.

'Please take your seats so we may begin.'

The apprentices shuffled their feet. There was a nervous energy in the room. All eyes were on Graves now. She paused and took a breath. 'I have an important announcement to make,' she continued, holding up the scroll so they could all see it. 'Along with every other magical institution, we have received a message from the Magical League. I have been instructed to read it to you.'

She broke the wax seal and unwound the scroll. Her eyes scanned its contents, her lips moving soundlessly as she absorbed its meaning. Her face, always solemn, had turned even more dour than usual. She glanced at the other elders then coughed once to clear her throat.

'By order of the Magical League, I hereby proclaim a state of heightened alert in the magical realm. A book has been stolen from the Royal Society of Magic. It is one of the Terrible Tomes and is highly dangerous. This is in direct violation of the Lores of Magical Restraint, and appears to be part of a Greader plot. Anyone with information about this crime or the whereabouts of the missing book must inform the magical authorities immediately. Under no circumstances should anyone open this book. I repeat, do not attempt to open this book!'

The room had fallen silent. Graves looked up from the scroll. 'It is signed by Uther Morgred himself,' she said, looking at the other elders.

One of the younger apprentices gave a strangled sob and burst into tears. There was a cry of distress from the back of the room, and all heads turned just in time to see Meredith Merrydance collapse in a faint.

Archie, Bramble and Thistle walked home from the museum together. Now that Hawke had suspended their magic writing they had the evening off. Archie was still thinking about the proclamation and what Hawke had told him about *The Book of Night*. He felt the silver key in his pocket.

'What's actually in the archive?' he asked Bramble.

'All the old records and texts about magical books,' she replied. 'It's the first place the elders look when they find an unidentified magical book or artefact. Why?'

'That's where they found Dee's prophecy,' mused Archie. 'I wonder if there's anything else in there connected to the Dark Flame.'

'Apprentices aren't allowed inside,' said Bramble.

Archie smiled. 'I am,' he said. He opened his hand to show them the key.

Thistle stared at it. 'Why has he given you a key?' he asked.

Archie shrugged. 'I suppose it goes with being his apprentice,' he said. 'If I'm going to work in Lost Books I need to know my way around.'

'Just be careful,' said Bramble. 'There's some strange stuff in the archive. You might get more than you bargained for.'

Archie smiled. 'Come on, Bram, we're talking about the archive here, not the Darchive!'

'Don't mention that place to me,' said Thistle with a shudder. 'I don't want to go anywhere near it ever again.'

Archie agreed with Thistle. The Darchive

was definitely not on his list of places to revisit. But he was sure the archive couldn't be nearly as bad. And if Morag Pandrama had found Dee's prophecy there, there might be other valuable information. He decided to check it out the following day.

7

Inside the Archive

Security in the Lost Books Department had been increased after the incident with *The Grim Grimoire* and the Alchemists' Club a few months earlier. The door to the archive, which also led to the Darchive, was locked and reinforced.

But when Archie had been to the Darchive he'd travelled there by the seats of learning, so he had never seen the archive before.

He fitted his key in the lock and was surprised to feel it turn of its own accord, making a loud click. Twisting the door handle, he stepped inside. He found himself in a long, low-ceilinged chamber, like an underground vault. Ahead of him he could see other smaller rooms opening off the main one and a series of alcoves where fat white candles flickered. The way the wax had melted and run down, they looked like stalagmites in a cave.

Bookcases lined the walls and there were racks containing scrolls and other parchment documents. In the centre of the main room were several reading tables with crystal lanterns suspended overhead casting a golden light. A pile of books and scrolls had been placed on one of the tables. Archie guessed that these were the documents Hawke had asked Morag Pandrama to leave out for him.

He casually flicked through the titles. Mostly they were historical texts relating to individual magical books and artefacts. He opened one and read a description of the dagger Hawke kept on his desk.

Shadow Blade: An enchanted blade made from the reflection of a shooting star captured in the black glass of obsidian. A shadow blade is a potent weapon against dark magical creatures because it can penetrate any darkness – and the darkest of hearts.

But it was a thick black book with the title *Most Wanted* that caught Archie's attention. It was a catalogue of the most sought-after lost books and artefacts. He looked up the one that was on his mind.

The Book of Night: (proper title *The Book of Nightmares*): was written by three darchemists to summon the Flame of Pandemonium from the underworld. Opening *The Book of Night* will release the Dark Flame and the Pale Writers, the spirits of the darchemists who wrote it. The Pale Writers seek *The Opus Magus* to control the primary spell and bring a dark age of magic.

Archie flicked on through the book until he found *The Opus Magus*. He had once looked it up in his father's reference book *Magical Greats: The Good, the Bad and the Ugly*, but this was more detailed.

The Opus Magus: 'The Great Work' is the founding spell of magic. The original *Opus Magus* was housed in the Great Library of Alexandria, and disappeared when the library was destroyed. Only when *The Opus Magus* is rewritten will magic be restored to its former glory.

The wording reminded Archie of the pledge the Alchemists' Club, always recited at the start of their meetings: 'We swear allegiance to the Alchemists' Club. We promise to do all we can to restore magic to its former glory.' They had taken it from Fabian Grey's original Alchemists' Club oath.

Once again, Archie felt Grey's shadow. He glanced at the gold ring on his finger. It felt suddenly tighter. Archie didn't seem to be able to get away from the alchemist.

Archie walked up and down between the bookcases and racks of scrolls. He wasn't sure what he was looking for but he was enjoying exploring. It was a chance to practise his delving skills, even though the archive didn't contain magical books; it just contained historical documents and reference books.

He closed his eyes and practised looking with his mind. Hawke had said it was possible to detect magical energy that way.

He was wandering with his eyes shut when he felt something. He had a tingling sensation. It seemed to be coming from Fabian Grey's gold ring on his finger. As he walked down the aisles he could feel it getting stronger. It was accompanied by a strange sense of déjà vu, as if he'd been there before. Something felt familiar – like a forgotten secret.

He opened his eyes and came face to face with a creature with bat ears and fangs. It gave him a start until he realised it was a stone gargoyle. Another one crouched on the other side of a large door with iron studs and a heavy lock. They looked as though they were guarding it. Archie had seen the door and the gargoyles before – they marked the entrance to the Darchive.

That explained why he could detect magic. The Darchive contained all sorts of dark magical objects, which was why it was strictly off limits.

'Don't worry, I'm not going in!' he said aloud, patting the first gargoyle on the shoulder. It stared back at him stony-faced.

Archie moved away, heading back the way he'd come. He was just about to enter the first vaulted chamber when he noticed an alcove off to one side. A small door led into another room. He was beginning to realise what a maze the archive was. He felt the tingling sensation again and an urge to see what was behind the small door, but he was interrupted.

'Archie?' It was Hawke's voice. The head of Lost Books must have come looking for him.

'In here,' Archie called.

Hawke appeared in the doorway connecting the two rooms. 'Ah, there you are,' he said. 'I want to show you something.'

Archie glanced at the alcove, made a mental note to come back and investigate it later, then hurried after Hawke. The head of Lost Books led him into a small antechamber that opened into another room with a very low ceiling. It was so low that he had to duck to enter. This room had a domed ceiling carved out of rock, in the Gothic style.

In the middle was a glass case containing two strange objects. They were the size and shape of duck eggs and made of an opaque golden waxy material that looked like amber. Around the outside were two protective bands of silver, one running lengthways and the other widthways so that they crossed each other. When Archie reached out his hand he felt a pulse of magical energy.

'What are they?' he gasped.

'Torchstones,' said Hawke. 'The magisters used them to transport the Flame of Pharos to Oxford.'

Hawke opened the case and picked up one of the objects, holding it between his thumb and forefinger so Archie could see it more clearly.

The silver band had a verse engraved on it.

'I carry the flame
To light the dark.
Let shadows flee
My sacred spark.'

It was hinged in the middle. Hawke squeezed it gently and the Torchstone sprang open, the two halves separating to reveal a hollow chamber inside.

'Embers from the Flame of Pharos can be placed in here,' said Hawke, indicating the hidden compartment. 'The Torchstone protects them from harm.'

'Why are there two?' asked Archie.

'That's the spare. It's a precaution,' said Hawke. 'Two flame carriers are selected from among the Flame Keepers. If the Flame of Pharos is threatened, then they carry the Torchstones. It's a great honour to be chosen.'

He flicked his wrist and the Torchstone clicked shut, returning to its egg shape once more. Hawke placed it back inside the glass case.

He gave Archie a meaningful look. 'I am a flame carrier. But if something were to happen to me, I hope that as my apprentice you would take my place,' he said.

Archie made his way to the Aisle of White. Hawke had told him to go on practising his delving skills and he'd decided to try his luck in Fabian Grey's secret laboratory. Only the members of the Alchemists' Club knew where it was so he'd have the place to himself.

It also gave him an excuse to drop in on Old Zeb. He hadn't seen the bookbinder since he'd started working in Lost Books over a week ago and he missed him.

As he crossed the courtyard to the bookshop, Archie was still thinking about the Torchstones.

He'd never really considered how the Flame of Pharos had been transported from Alexandria to Oxford. He tried to imagine the long journey. He could see why carrying a torch on such a long voyage wouldn't be advisable, or even very safe. The Torchstones were an ingenious solution.

When Archie opened the door to the bookshop, the bell clanged loudly. Marjorie Gudge was standing behind the shop counter. She filled in for Geoffrey Screech when he had to go out.

'Hello, Archie,' she said, her eyes magnified by her thick glasses. 'If you've come to see Old Zeb, he's not here. He's taken some books back to the museum.'

Archie was disappointed to have missed him. He knew the old bookbinder hadn't found a new apprentice yet so he would have to run his own errands.

'Actually, I've come to pick up my tool bag,' he said, saying the first thing he could think of so that Marjorie wouldn't wonder what he was really up to. 'I'll let myself in,' he added, smiling.

The mended books in the bookcase behind the black curtain, the ones that had volunteered to help Archie find his family, were gone. They would be the ones the old bookbinder had taken to the museum. Archie felt his hopes rise that they might discover which book his father was trapped in.

In their place was a box of new arrivals to be repaired. Archie picked up the box, out of habit, and carried it down the spiral staircase and along the corridor to the mending workshop.

Putting the box on the workbench, he took the black key to the lab, which was kept on a hook with lots of other keys, and hurried along the corridor.

It smelled earthy down here and the only light came from burning torches set in brackets in the wall. Even these ended just past the door to the workshop so that the part of the passageway where Archie was now was poorly lit.

The laboratory was behind a black door that was concealed in the shadows.

Three members of the original Alchemists' Club, Braxton Foxe, Roderick Trevallen and Angelica Ripley, had taken refuge in the laboratory after they had accidently started the Great Fire of London. But after a scorpion sting had killed Roderick as part of the Alchemist's Curse, the lab was sealed up and forgotten about. For three hundred and fifty years its location had remained unknown, until Archie and Thistle had discovered it.

Archie fitted the key into the black door and unlocked it. The door groaned open. When he stepped inside, the room smelled stale, with traces of amora, the smell of magic, and burnt chemicals. It had been weeks since he was last in here. There hadn't been an official club meeting since Rupert had joined the Royal Society.

Archie lit the torches on the wall and surveyed the room. It always gave him a thrill to think that this was where the original Alchemists' Club had met.

It was where Grey had carried out his magical experiments while he was still an apprentice at the museum and had first produced the magical substance azoth.

A wooden plaque above the bench said: 'We pledge to restore magic to its former glory.'

The *Most Wanted* book had said that rewriting *The Opus Magus* would restore all the fading magical books.

Archie inspected the glass jars on the shelves. They were filled with murky solutions. One contained a perfectly preserved scorpion – the same scorpion whose sting had killed Rupert's ancestor Roderick Trevallan.

Down the middle of the room ran a long wooden bench with glass flasks connected by a tangle of rubber tubing, like a mad chemistry experiment. Grey's old magical reference books were in a neat stack at one end where Archie and Thistle had put them for safekeeping. Black scorch marks all along the bench were evidence of magical experiments that had gone wrong.

Archie closed his eyes and tried to concentrate. He reached out with his mind, delving for hidden sources of magic. He spoke the spell that Hawke had taught him.

'*Secret volumes*
Placed in stealth
Books of magic
Reveal yourselves.'

Silence. He tried again but nothing happened. So there weren't any magical books concealed in the laboratory. But that didn't mean there weren't other secrets hidden there.

Archie was still thinking about this when he spotted an envelope on the bench. It was sitting in full view and he wondered how he could have missed it before. He had been so preoccupied with his thoughts that he hadn't noticed it. It was addressed to the Alchemists' Club in a firm hand. Whoever had put it there wanted it to be found. He glanced around the room.

As far as he was aware the only people who knew about the laboratory were the five members of the Alchemists' Club and Katerina Krone.

But she was now in an asylum for the magically

ill, so she couldn't have left the message. So where had it come from?

He opened the envelope. There was a note inside.

I fear the Greaders are preparing to open *The Book of Night*. When they do, you must be ready to fight for the future of magic.

I will contact you again when I can.

FG

Archie's heart leaped into his throat. The letter was signed FG, and next to the initials was a picture of a raven. His mind raced. Could it be from Fabian Grey? But no, that was silly. The real Fabian Grey had been dead for over three hundred and fifty years. It must be someone who wanted them to think he was alive. But were they friend or foe?

When Archie showed the mysterious note to Bramble, Thistle and Arabella that evening, they all shook their heads. None of them had any idea how it could have got there. Someone else

obviously knew about the lab and had used that knowledge as a way to get a message to them.

The Alchemists' Club had already arranged to meet on Saturday, as Rupert would be back in Oxford for the weekend, so they could all be together. But finding the note made the meeting even more urgent. The secret informer had indicated they would make contact again, but how, and when?

8

Faustus Gaunt

When Archie arrived at Lost Books the next day, Hawke was sitting in his office staring into space. On the desk in front of him was the green glass bottle Archie had seen before. It definitely looked like a medicine bottle. When he heard Archie come in, Hawke slipped it into the side pocket of his moleskin jacket.

'Ah, it's you, Archie,' he said, turning to face the door. 'I thought it might be Faustus. I'm expecting him any moment.'

Archie began tidying the room. It was his routine now every morning. He stacked up the books that were strewn all over the floor, being careful not to close any open ones so that he didn't lose Hawke's place in them. He gathered up the scrolls that were all over the armchair by the fire and put them back on the shelves. After a few minutes of picking up he could see the Persian carpet again.

Yet no matter how often he cleared up, the room was just as cluttered by the next morning. Hawke must spend every night poring over books. Archie guessed that he was searching for clues about how to defeat the Dark Flame.

'I wondered where that had got to,' said Hawke, as Archie picked up the imagining glass with the silvery lens from the mantelpiece and replaced it on the desk. 'I must have put it there last night and forgotten.'

He shook his head absent-mindedly. Archie noticed he was looking a little dishevelled, as if he'd slept in his clothes. It occurred to him that he didn't know very much about Hawke. Did he live at the museum or did he go home at night like the other elders? Perhaps he slept on the leather sofa. It certainly looked comfortable enough for a bed and Hawke was very attached to it. He was still pondering this when there was a knock at the door and Faustus Gaunt appeared in the doorway. In his hand he held a battered old notebook.

'Ah, good morning, Faustus,' said Hawke, rising to greet his visitor.

'Is this a good time?' enquired Gaunt.

'Yes,' said Hawke. 'In fact your timing couldn't be better. Archie is here now and I want him to hear what you have to say.'

Gaunt cast a look at Archie. 'Very well, Gideon, if that is your wish.'

'Archie is my apprentice,' explained Hawke. 'He must know everything that we know.'

Archie felt flattered by Hawke's confidence in him. He hoped he could live up to it.

Gaunt took a seat at one end of the old sofa with the notebook on his lap, and Hawke indicated for Archie to sit at the other end. The head of Lost Books sat facing them in the wing-backed chair next to the fire, his fingers steepled in thought. When they were all sitting comfortably, Hawke's keen eyes bored into Gaunt's.

'Well, what have you discovered, Faustus?'

Gaunt took a deep breath. 'I have examined the text that Morag found in the archive, and I can confirm that it is genuine. It is one of John Dee's final prophecies, written towards the end of his life.

'As you know, Dee was the greatest scryer in England. He used his magical ability to see into the future. Like most of Dee's prophecies, it is written as a riddle.'

Gaunt took some spectacles from his jacket pocket, unfolded them and perched them on the end of his nose. Then he opened the old book to a marked page and read out what was written there.

'When white burns black
And shadows prey
Then hope must lie
With all that's grey.

The raven knows
What was forgot
The secret key
To magic's lock.'

When he finished, there was a silence. Archie tried to absorb what he'd just heard.

'The meaning is deliberately veiled,' said Gaunt. 'That is Dee's way. But I believe it foreshadows what Fabian Grey saw in *The Book of Prophecy.'*

Archie gave a start. Grey again! Wherever he turned, the alchemist's name seemed to crop up. He turned Grey's gold ring on his finger, trying to loosen it. Gaunt was still speaking.

'We know that when Grey was an apprentice at the museum he consulted *The Book of Prophecy* and it changed him. Grey believed that he had a special destiny. He'd seen a vision that showed that the future of magic rested on his shoulders. He told Braxton Foxe as much.'

Archie had heard this before from Braxton Foxe's book ghast, the spirit of his unfulfilled dream.

'I think what Grey saw in his vision was how to defeat the Dark Flame. Dee's riddle hints at it. "When white burns black" could be a reference to the Dark Flame burning on white spell parchment. "When shadows prey" could refer to the Pale Writers being released. And the last line of that verse is surely a direct reference to Grey himself.'

'And the second verse?' asked Hawke.

'The second verse refers to the key to magic's lock,' said Gaunt. 'That can only mean one thing.'

'*The Opus Magus*,' breathed Hawke.

Gaunt nodded. 'Exactly.'

Archie's mouth fell open. 'But ... That's not possible,' he gasped. 'Is it?'

Gaunt leaned forward. His face took on a new intensity. '*The Opus Magus* disappeared two thousand years ago when the Great Library of Alexandria burned down,' he said. 'Its physical form was destroyed but the spell itself must have survived somehow or magic would have disappeared long ago. I think *The Opus Magus* is the secret that *The Book of Prophecy* revealed to Grey.'

Archie's mind was racing as he tried to fit it all together.

Hawke was sitting motionless. He hadn't moved so much as a muscle since Gaunt had started speaking. 'And what is your conclusion from this?' he asked.

Gaunt folded his spectacles and slipped them back into his pocket. 'If Dee's prophecy is right, then Grey saw two things: *The Opus Magus*, and a vision of how to use it to defeat the Dark Flame.' He paused. 'The *only way*.'

Archie left Lost Books with his head spinning. He had so many thoughts buzzing round his brain that he felt quite dizzy. He was still turning over what it all meant in his mind when he heard a rustling sound. It was coming from the bookshelf next to him.

'Psssssst,' said a papery voice. 'Over here. We've got some information for you.'

'What?' said Archie, still trying to gather his wits.

'We've been asking around about your father,' said the voice. 'I told you we like solving mysteries.'

Archie's heart leaped and he recognised the voice now – it was the mystery book from behind the curtain at the bookshop! He scanned the bookcases until he spotted its red spine on one of the shelves. It must have been put there after it was delivered to the museum.

'What did you find out?' he asked, desperate for news.

The book rustled again. 'I've talked to the reference books – the ones that can speak – and they all agree that if he was trapped inside a book then it must be a drawing book.'

Drawing books had the power to draw people into their pages so they became part of the story and could get trapped if the book was closed while they were still inside.

The only drawing books Archie knew of were *The Book of Yore* and *The Book of Prophecy*, but he supposed there could be others.

'How can I find out which drawing book it is?' he asked, his heart beating faster.

'That's harder,' said the mystery book.

'I need to know!' said Archie. 'I have to find out what happened to him and my mum and sister.'

'How old is your sister?'

Archie stopped to think. 'Rosie was nearly three year's older than me, so she'd be almost sixteen now.'

'Right,' said the book. 'Leave it with me. I'll get back to you when I know more.'

Archie was suddenly aware of Thistle's freckled face staring at him. 'So you've started talking to yourself now!' he said.

Archie smiled. 'I was talking to one of the books,' he said. 'Anyway, what are you doing in this part of the museum?'

'I've just come from the menagerie,' said Thistle. 'I told Rupert I'd keep an eye on the place for him so I was just checking up, and there's something wrong. Simon the salamander has not been well at all – and now he's disappeared!'

'What?' cried Archie. 'A six-foot lizard can't just disappear!'

'That's what I thought,' said Thistle, 'but this one has. I've asked Quiggley and he has no idea where Simon's gone. In fact, I'm not even sure Quiggley knew that he had a red-bellied salamander in his care. He doesn't seem to know the first thing about magical creatures, and he certainly doesn't know about how to look after members of the dragon family.'

'But this is terrible. Where can Simon have gone?' asked Archie, shocked.

'Quite,' said Thistle shaking his head. 'I've got my curiosity compass and I thought it might help us find him.'

Bramble and Archie had given Thistle the curiosity compass for his twelfth birthday. It was a magical device that looked like a pocket watch and could detect the direction of magic. Thistle and Archie had used it to locate Grey's secret laboratory.

Thistle flicked its cover open. Inside was a compass with the design of the sun on its face and a black needle that would change colour and spin if the curiosity compass detected magic nearby.

Archie and Thistle both regarded the needle. It was glowing with a bright golden colour and turning slowly.

'Hmm,' mused Thistle. 'There's a lot of magic in this part of the museum. That'll be the books. I've worked out how to use the compass properly now,' he added. 'You can set it for different types of magic. I'll set it to detect natural magic because Simon is a magical creature.'

He turned a dial on one side of the compass to a picture of a lightning bolt striking a tree.

'There,' he said, holding up the instrument so that they could both see.

The needle was still. 'Oh,' sighed Thistle. 'Well I guess that means Simon is nowhere around here.'

'I guess not,' mused Archie. 'But if he's not here, where is he?'

At that moment the needle suddenly turned red and began spinning madly. 'Hang on,' cried Thistle. 'There's something naturally magical and it's on the move. 'Come on!'

Thistle held up the compass and began to walk in the direction the magical energy was coming from, glancing at the needle every few moments to make sure he was going in the right direction.

Archie followed him. He felt a tingling sensation, too, indicating a strong magical presence.

'It's over here!' Thistle said, striding through the Great Gallery like some intrepid explorer in a jungle.

'This way,' he added, ducking into an aisle of bookcases. They weaved in and out of the bookshelves. 'Getting stronger. It's very strong here.'

They both stopped and looked around.

'I don't understand it,' said Thistle. 'According to the compass we should be right on top of the source of the magic.'

They stared around but there was no sign of anything that might be producing natural magic.

Thistle scratched his head and shook the compass. 'Its never been wrong before,' he said. 'Perhaps Simon's behind this bookcase . . .'

He took a step forward and tripped over something that left him sprawling on the ground. 'What the . . .'

There was a low growling sound like an engine throbbing.

'Uh oh!' cried Thistle scrambling to his feet. 'I recognise that sound. Duck!'

The two boys ducked behind a bookcase just as a flame appeared in the air.

'It's Simon,' cried Thistle. 'But why can't we see him?'

At that moment there was a fizzing sound and a smell of wet straw, and Simon the red-bellied salamander appeared in front of them, looking as startled as they were. For a moment the lizard stared at them with big sad eyes and then with a sound like a whimper, it collapsed on the ground.

Thistle leaped forward. 'He's sick,' he cried. 'He looks horribly pale.'

'Look!' said Archie pointing to a cut on the salamander's leg. 'He's bleeding. We need to get him back to the menagerie right now.'

'That might be easier said than done!' said Thistle. 'Simon's lost weight but he still weighs a tonne.'

Thistle stayed with Simon while Archie went for help. The first person he found was Feodora Graves. When she heard what had happened she came at once.

'How is he?' she asked when she saw the salamander lying on the ground with Thistle stroking its head.

'He's alive at least,' said Thistle, 'but he's very weak. He's lost a lot of blood.'

'I'll use a heavy-lifting spell to get him back to the menagerie,' said Graves. 'When did he last flame?'

'Just now,' said Archie, 'but it was pretty pathetic.'

'Should be safe to get close then,' said Graves.

She stroked Simon's head, and then she put her head close to his and sniffed. 'Hmmm,' she said. 'He's been given some sort of concealment potion to make him invisible. I can smell it on his breath. It must have worn off just as you found him. Just as well because we don't want an invisible salamander on the loose.'

'But why would anyone want to make Simon invisible and let him out of the menagerie? And hurt him?' asked Thistle.

Graves looked thoughtful. 'Those,' she said, 'are very good questions.'

9

The Secret Informer

Saturday morning couldn't come soon enough for Archie. The five members of the Alchemists' Club had agreed to meet at Quill's and then go to Grey's laboratory. They had a lot to talk about.

Archie, Bramble and Thistle got there first and were just ordering hot chocolate and buns when Rupert arrived with Arabella.

'Rupert!' cried Bramble, giving him a big hug.

Rupert blushed. He looked pleased and embarrassed at the same time. He glanced around Quill's. 'How I've missed this place!' he said, beaming a smile at Archie and Thistle.

'How long are you in Oxford for?' asked Thistle.

'Just the weekend. I was planning to drop in at the menagerie, to see how the animals are doing. I wanted to see the Pegasus and I heard about the trouble with Simon the salamander. Dragons can be very tricky unless you know what you're doing.'

'Peter Quiggley has taken over from you and I'm not sure he knows much about dragons, or any magical creatures for that matter!' said Archie.

Rupert looked bemused. 'Quiggley? Really?' he said. 'How did he get the job?'

'That's what we thought,' said Bramble. 'Did you put in a good word for him?'

Rupert shook his head. 'You must be joking!' he said. 'Quiggley is about the last person I'd have suggested. I don't think he likes ordinary animals – let alone magical ones. When Brown asked me who I thought should take over from me I recommended Thistle.'

Thistle looked pleased. 'Thanks, Rupert,' he said.

'It's a shame the Flame of Pharos doesn't decide,' said Bramble. 'I'm sure it would have chosen you, Thistle.'

'Why *doesn't* the Flame decide?' asked Archie.

'Some jobs are at the discretion of the elders,' said Rupert. 'They choose their own personal apprentices. That reminds me, I hear you are Hawke's apprentice. That's brilliant. Congratulations!'

'Thanks,' said Archie, swelling with pride.

'So tell me what else has been going on at the museum,' said Rupert. 'And don't leave anything out.'

'Let's go to the lab and talk there,' said Archie, casting a glance around the other tables. 'We don't want to be overheard.'

Archie let them into the Aisle of White using his key. They hurried down to Old Zeb's workshop and collected the key to the black door.

When the door opened four pairs of eyes went straight to the bench. But there wasn't another note.

'What's the matter with you lot,' asked Rupert, noticing their serious faces. 'Anyone would think you'd seen a ghost.'

'Funny you should say that,' said Archie. 'I wonder if ghosts can write.'

They told Rupert about the secret informer and showed him the first note, which Archie had brought with him.

'Someone's trying to warn us,' said Rupert.

'Yes,' mused Archie, 'but who?'

'Someone who wants us to think that Fabian Grey is still alive,' said Rupert.

'Or it could be Faustus Gaunt?' said Thistle. 'He's FG.'

'Good thinking,' said Bramble. 'But how would Gaunt know about the lab?'

'He's the magical prophecies expert, isn't he?' said Rupert, looking thoughtful. 'Tall with long, silver hair?'

'Yes, that's him,' said Archie. 'He's helping Hawke with John Dee's prophecy.'

Rupert nodded. 'Thought so. He's a fellow of the Royal Society. I've seen him around the place a couple of times. He must be looking at the records there, too.'

Arabella interrupted. 'Hold on, let's not forget the club rules. We can't start the meeting properly until we've all said the pledge.' She broke into a smile. 'The five of us here in the lab with a mystery to solve. It's just like old times!'

They all grinned at each other. It was good to be back together. They'd all missed the camaraderie and closeness of their secret meetings.

'All right, I'll go first,' said Bramble. 'I, Bramble Thornbush Foxe, pledge to restore magic to its former glory.'

Archie thought about *The Opus Magus*. One by one the others said their names and pledged themselves to the Alchemists' Club. Rupert was last and no sooner had he finished than Thistle turned to him.

'So what happened at the Royal Society when *The Book of Night* was stolen?'

Rupert's brow creased into a frown. 'How do

you know it's *The Book of Night*?' he said, his eyes sparkling with interest. 'All Gloom told me was that it was one of the seven.'

'We overheard Gloom talking to Hawke about it in the oculus,' said Arabella. 'And from what Archie has found out, it's the worst book they could possibly have got their hands on. So what happened?'

Rupert looked pensive. 'I'd only just started working at the Royal Society, but I could tell there was something going on. Gloom seemed nervous and now I know why. He asked me if I thought a dangerous magical book would be safe if no one knew where it was. I told him that as far as I was concerned there was only one safe place for dangerous magical books – and that was in the museum!'

'What did he say to that?' asked Thistle.

'He didn't say anything, but I could tell it wasn't the answer he wanted to hear. Shortly after that he must have contacted Hawke and asked him to send someone to collect it.'

'Yes,' said Thistle. 'Hawke sent Bone and Dad, but when they got there they were ambushed.'

'So now the Greaders have got it,' said Rupert. 'What will they do with it?'

Archie explained what he'd discovered about *The Book of Night*. Rupert looked shocked.

'So if *The Book of Night* is opened then the Dark Flame will release the Pale Writers to find *The Opus Magus*,' gasped Rupert. 'I thought *The Opus Magus* was just a legend?'

'No,' said Archie, shaking his head. 'Hawke says it's real. If the Pale Writers find it then the Dark Flame will use it to turn all magic into dark magic.'

'So all of our work rewriting the magical books will have been for nothing,' groaned Arabella.

'Yes,' said Archie. 'The Dark Flame has been consuming the new spells – that's why they burned with a black flame. And worse than that, all the spells we have already rewritten will turn dark as well. *The Opus Magus* is the key to everything. It's the primary spell. Whoever controls *The Opus Magus* controls magic.'

'But there must be something we can do,' said Rupert. 'There must be some way of stopping them.'

'The vision *The Book of Prophecy* revealed to Grey,' Archie said. 'That's the only way to stop the Dark Flame. Gaunt thinks Grey saw *The Opus Magus*, and we know he had a bibliographical memory so he'd remember every spell he ever saw.'

'I bet that's what he was going to use the azoth for,' said Arabella, 'to rewrite *The Opus Magus*!'

'But just seeing a spell wouldn't have turned

109

his hair white,' said Thistle. 'He must have seen something else as well.'

'Gaunt and Hawke also think Grey saw a vision of what he had to do with *The Opus Magus* to defeat the Dark Flame,' said Archie.

'Well, whatever it was drove him half mad,' said Arabella. 'Braxton Foxe said Grey couldn't remember what he'd seen, which is very odd for someone with such a good memory!'

'Couldn't remember or wouldn't remember?' asked Rupert.

'Perhaps whatever Grey saw was so frightening he didn't *want* to remember,' said Archie.

'But surely he would have left a clue,' said Bramble. 'We are talking about the greatest alchemist of all time – and he was desperate to restore magic! Perhaps Hawke and Gaunt are looking for it, too.'

'So what are we going to do?' asked Arabella.

'We have to help them discover what Grey saw in the vision,' said Archie, 'before the Greaders open *The Book of Night* – or worse, discover *The Opus Magus*.'

By the end of the meeting they were already formulating a plan. Now that they weren't writing magic every night, they could concentrate on trying to solve the mystery.

Bramble and Thistle would find out all they could about *The Book of Night* and the Dark Flame, including the Pale Writers. Arabella would keep her eyes and ears open around Ripley Mansion, her parents' house in Oxford where the Greaders met, for any information about what they were up to.

Archie was determined to help Hawke and Gaunt discover what Grey had seen in *The Book of Prophecy* using his book-whispering and delving skills.

Rupert, meanwhile, would keep them informed of developments at the Royal Society and try to find out what the magical authorities were doing to recover *The Book of Night*.

They agreed to meet again as soon as there were any significant developments.

After the meeting, Rupert said he was going to drop in at the menagerie. The others decided to go with him. Thistle was the only one of them who had visited that part of the museum since Peter Quiggley had taken over Rupert's old job.

The five of them made their way to the West Gallery of the museum and through the door to the Natural Magic Department. They climbed the wooden staircase to the second floor. The heavy oak door was locked, but luckily Rupert still had a key and was able to let them in.

When he opened the door, the smell of animal dung and urine was almost overpowering. The menagerie usually smelled pungent but clean. This was something else.

The animal pens were on either side of a long passageway. Lanterns cast a golden light, but even in the gloom they could see that the place had not been properly mucked out for days. The animals were strangely quiet in their pens.

'What on earth's going on?' demanded Rupert, striding down the corridor. 'This place is filthy!'

He gestured at some overturned wooden buckets. 'It should be feeding time now. Where's their food? When were the creatures last fed?' he said angrily.

Rupert was getting very worked up now. He picked up the overturned buckets and began filling them with different types of food. 'What's all this I hear, too, about snufflings going missing?' he demanded. 'I turn my back for a few weeks and the whole place goes to rack and ruin!'

'Don't look at me,' said Thistle. 'I used to come all the time and help out but Quiggley doesn't like me hanging around. He told me to stay away.'

'Charming,' said Bramble. 'Anyway, where is Quiggley?'

Just then, Rupert gave another indignant shout. 'Never mind Quiggley, where are all the snufflings?'

At the sound of his voice, several of the small guinea-pig-like creatures appeared inside the pen and began nuzzling around his ankles.

'They recognised your voice,' said Bramble. 'They must have been hiding before, so we couldn't see them.'

'But where are the rest of them?' asked Rupert, incredulously. 'There should be twice as many as this!'

He threw some food down for the snufflings and moved on to the next pen, which housed the dodo.

'Desmond!' cried Rupert. His call was answered by a plaintive honking sound as the large-billed short-legged bird waddled into sight.

'He's losing his feathers. At this rate, he'll be extinct by the end of the week!' said Rupert, shaking his head. He threw a couple of fish to the dodo, which caught them in its bill and swallowed them whole.

'And there's the dryads,' he added, moving on to the next pen, where the tree pixies lived. 'Oak! Ash! Elm! Are you all right?' He threw them some nuts and berries.

The little figures caught them and hungrily gobbled them down. The dryad called Oak waved his acorn hat in appreciation.

The next pen was covered with wire mesh and had a tall gate with blacked-out glass. It contained the flesh-eating birds called stympalians, which could kill a human with one look. The sound of metal wings could be heard on the other side. Rupert approached the pen, but then thought better of it, especially if they were hungry.

The children heard a bellowing, snorting noise coming from two pens down. They recognised the sound of the Minotaur. Rupert froze in his tracks. It was only a few months ago that the bull-headed beast had got loose from its pen. Driven mad by an enchanted musical locket, the monster would have killed Rupert and the winged horse called a Pegasus. It was only Archie's intervention that had saved them.

Rupert, though, was oblivious to the Minotaur now. He was staring at Simon the red-bellied salamander in the next pen. The great lizard looked a washed-out grey colour.

'Oh dear, Simon,' muttered Rupert, shaking his head. 'Whatever is the matter with you? Been eating too many cufflinks?' he asked, referring to the time that the salamander had swallowed his grandfather's lucky cufflinks.

'He hasn't changed colour since he escaped from his pen,' said Thistle, casting a worried look at Simon. 'What do you think's wrong with him?'

Rupert put down one of the buckets he was carrying and opened the door to the pen.

'Is that a good idea?' asked Bramble. 'He is a dragon after all!'

'If he hasn't changed colour in a while he won't be able to flame,' said Rupert. 'Besides, he knows me.'

He held out his hand and the salamander's long tongue licked it. 'All right, old boy,' Rupert said. He looked into the lizard's eyes, and put his nose down near its mouth to smell its breath.

'Graves said that someone gave him a cloaking potion to make him invisible,' said Thistle.

'Well, he's definitely anaemic,' said Rupert, after a moment's thought. 'His blood is too thin. He needs building up. I'll make him a tonic with some phosphor in it – that's what dragons need to keep their blood healthy.'

He patted the salamander on its head and stepped out of the pen, closing the gate behind him.

'I almost don't dare look at the Pegasus,' he said. He walked over to the biggest pen, which housed the winged horse. He whistled and there was a movement in one corner of the pen. The Pegasus had been kneeling on the ground with its wings strapped to its back. At the sound of his voice, it stood up and trotted unsteadily towards him. The once-beautiful creature looked thin and emaciated.

'I've never seen the creatures look so neglected,'

said Rupert, angrily. 'I'll be having a word about this.'

As soon as he'd fed and watered all the animals, he stomped off to Motley Brown's office in the Natural Magic Department with the others trailing after him. When they got there the door was closed, but Rupert barged into the office.

'Hello, Rupert. What a pleasant surprise,' said Brown, smiling. 'How nice to see you. How is Orpheus treating you at the Royal Society?'

'Have you seen the state of the menagerie?' demanded Rupert.

Brown blinked at him. 'Well, erm, not recently,' he said. 'I've been rather busy with one or two other aspects of Natural Magic. How is young Quiggley getting on?'

'He's a disaster!' said Rupert, hotly. 'The place is filthy and the creatures aren't being properly looked after. The snuffling population has been decimated, and Simon the red-bellied salamander is so anaemic he probably needs a blood transfusion!'

'Oh dear, that's not very good. Not very good at all,' muttered Brown. 'I will talk to Peter. He's obviously not coping very well. Yours are big shoes to fill, Rupert. But you have my assurance that I will put it right.' He paused. 'Thank you for drawing this to my attention.'

*

As the five friends made their way back to Quill's, Rupert's mood had not improved.

'I can't believe he gave Quiggley the job instead of you,' he said to Thistle. 'It's madness.'

Thistle shrugged. 'I wasn't best pleased either. But at least Brown knows what a lazy little weasel Quiggley is now, so he'll make sure the animals are properly cared for.'

'Maybe,' said Rupert, doubtfully. 'The trouble is that Brown has got his hands full with the rest of the Natural Magic Department. He hasn't got time to go running around after Quiggley in the menagerie. And by the look of the place, Quiggley doesn't give two hoots about the animals.'

Rupert shook his head, sadly. 'I'm down in London most of the time now so I can't keep an eye on things.'

'Well if you give me your old key, I'll come in from time to time just to make sure Quiggley is looking after them properly.'

'Would you?' said Rupert.

'It'd be my pleasure,' said Thistle, grinning.

Rupert dropped the key into Thistle's hand. 'Thanks,' he said. 'I'll feel a lot better knowing there's someone looking out for them. Oh, and give Quiggley a kick for me when you see him. And make it a big one!'

'That would be a pleasure, too,' said Thistle.

10

Dark Dreams

That night, Archie retrieved the shoebox he kept under his bed and placed it on his pillow. Seeing Rupert again had left him feeling wistful. Removing the lid he took out a bundle of letters and postcards from his gran, Gardenia Greene. The top one had a picture of a mountain and a postmark from Kathmandu. That had been the first place she had visited after leaving her cottage in West Wittering. Since then she had sent Archie and his cousins regular updates on her travels in India, and most recently China.

Beneath the letters and postcards was an assortment of his father's things. There was a pen, some faded photographs, a pair of gloves and some books. One of the photographs showed a boy and a girl standing outside Quill's. The girl was wearing purple shoes and was clearly recognisable as a young Loretta. She looked to be about ten. The boy, Archie's father Alex Greene, was a couple of years older, about twelve.

Another photograph was of Alex in his late teens, holding hands with a pretty girl of about the same age. They were both smiling broadly. Archie recognised his mother, Amelia Grey as she had been then. It was on his mother's side that Archie was related to Fabian Grey.

He picked through the books until he found an old scrapbook with some newspaper cuttings that Loretta had kept. He idly flicked through, reading the headlines.

There were several local news stories about Quill's. One article said there had been a substantial refurbishment and the café was reopening to the public. Archie smiled when he saw his father and Loretta at the front of the queue for hot chocolate.

Another headline caught his eye:

**CROCKERY VANDAL CHARGED
WITH SMASH AND GRAB**

It was the story about Woodbine being taken to court for breaking antique china at an exhibition in Oxford. It was the incident Peter Quiggley had referred to when Archie's uncle had opened a popper releasing a rhinoceros spell, which had led to Woodbine being asked to leave the museum.

Woodbine Foxe, a resident of Houndstooth Road, Oxford, was fined £500 and bound over to keep the peace. Foxe apologised for the breakages and promised to be more careful in future. He added that stories about a rhinoceros being loose in Oxford were wildly exaggerated. A neighbour told reporters that the Foxes were a strange family who mostly kept to themselves and that the more respectable residents of Houndstooth Road preferred it that way.

The story included a picture of a contrite-looking Woodbine leaving the courthouse wearing a tie and a badly fitting suit. A woman was covering her face in embarrassment. Archie recognised Loretta.

The final headline read:

FIRE AT OXFORD COFFEE HOUSE

It was a report of the fire started by Arthur Ripley in the museum thirteen years earlier when he'd tried to open the Terrible Tomes. Archie read the first couple of paragraphs.

The fire started in the early hours of Saturday morning. Aurelius Rusp, an Oxford resident who was passing at the time, raised the alarm. Local historian and book antiquarian Arthur Ripley is missing and believed to have died in the inferno.

But Archie knew that Ripley had not died in the fire. He had hidden at Ripley Hall, the Ripleys' family house in Cornwall, planning the Greader plot to release Barzak from *The Book of Souls*. After that Ripley had been locked up in the asylum for the magically ill but he had still managed to write to Katerina Krone to convince her that *The Grim Grimoire* was her inheritance. Ripley had disappeared when the Alchemist's Curse plot failed. Archie wondered where he was now, but the next paragraph drove the thought from his mind.

The whereabouts of Ripley's assistant Alexander Greene remains unknown. Greene and his wife disappeared two weeks ago and have not been seen since.

So his parents had gone missing about the same time as the fire. Archie hadn't made this connection before. The mystery book had said that if they were trapped inside a book it would have to be a drawing book, but which one? The mystery book had said it would try to find out for him. He wondered if it had made any progress.

He was putting the things back in the shoebox when he caught sight of his father's reference book, *Magical Greats: The Good, The Bad and the Ugly.* It seemed a very long time ago now that he had first looked at it. He was just discovering magic then. So much had happened since. Archie smiled to himself and opened the book.

A familiar title caught his eye.

The Book of Yore: An ancient codex that contains the history of magic, including many secrets about the past. *The Book of Yore* is sometimes included with the Books of Destiny, but strictly speaking it has no power to predict the future. Rather, the secrets it reveals about the past may alter the fate of those who discover them. *The Book of Yore* may be consulted by asking it a direct question, although what it reveals may not seem immediately relevant. The book never lies but it has a dark side, which makes it dangerous.

'You can say that again,' Archie muttered under his breath, remembering how it had trapped him in the burning Library of Alexandria. Hawke had rescued him with the book hook, a magical staff, but he'd had a very narrow escape. He didn't trust *The Book of Yore*. Could it have trapped his family, too?

Archie knew that his father had consulted another drawing book, *The Book of Prophecy*. That was how he had discovered that Archie had a forked fate. It meant that, like Fabian Grey before him, Archie's destiny and the future of magic depended on which path he chose to follow at critical moments in his life.

The Book of Prophecy had helped Archie before, but it, too, had a dangerous side. It had nearly driven Fabian Grey mad. Perhaps it had trapped his parents and his sister?

He looked up another entry.

The Pale Writers: servants of the Dark Flame of Pandemonium. The Pale Writers were once great magic writers who turned to writing dark magic. By writing *The Book of Night* they summoned the Dark Flame from the underworld of Pandemonium. They thought they could control it but its power was too great and they became its servants instead, each trapped within the book by his own weakness: the first by doubt, the second by dread and the third by despair.

Archie gave a start. A terrifying notion had just occurred to him. What if his family were trapped inside *The Book of Night*? He felt his blood run cold as he read the next paragraph.

Cursed for all eternity, the Pale Writers seek *The Opus Magus* – the primary spell of magic that will give the Dark Flame dominion over the Flame of Pharos. Legend has it that when *The Book of Night* is opened and the Pale Writers are released, the final battle between the two flames will begin.

'Cursed for all eternity!' That was a very unsettling thought to go to sleep on.

Archie lay awake for a long time. Through a gap in the curtains he could see there was a new moon in the sky that gave off very little light. When he finally fell asleep he dreamed about the raven again, but this time *he* was the raven.

In his dream, it was night-time and he was flying over the rooftops of Oxford. He could hear the wind and the beating of his wings as he soared over the ancient college buildings. There was barely any light from the moon, but his keen raven eyes could see the neatly tended lawns in the courtyards and the dark shape of the spires that punctuated the skyline. Arrow-straight he flew until he reached a dark, brooding house set back from the street. A single light flickered in a downstairs room with a large leaded-light window. He made straight for it, landing on the windowsill, where he could observe.

The windowpane was dirty but through the grime he could see a group of cloaked figures. Standing in the centre of the circle was another figure in black, holding a thick book with a dark cover, who began to chant.

> *'Darkest of the two*
> *We pledge ourselves to you*
> *By the power of the Flame*
> *We blacken magic's name!'*

Uttering the final words of the spell, the hooded figure opened the book.

A flame smouldered inside the pages. But this was no ordinary flame: it burned with a black fire. Three white phantoms rose like smoke from the book's pages. Their bodies were semi-transparent, their features distorted, and their eyes blazed with a hungry dark fire. They turned towards the window and Archie felt a sudden terror grip him like an icy hand on his heart.

The cloaked figures watching sank to their knees and held out the palms of their left hands. The one holding the book passed among them. The first of the figures thrust his hand into the book's dark flame and Archie heard him cry out in pain. As he did, a symbol appeared on his palm. With his keen raven eyes, even from outside, Archie could see that it was not like any firemark he had ever seen before. It looked like a black dragon.

He felt goosebumps at the sight of it. The ritual was repeated as each of the kneeling figures put a hand in the flame.

'The Dark Flame has chosen you, and you have taken the oath,' said the one who had opened the book and was clearly their leader. 'More will rally to our cause once it is known that the book is open. Until then, use the concealing potion to hide the firemark.'

Archie woke up covered in sweat and gasping for air. For a while he lay awake, his heart still racing. He tried to tell himself that it was just a bad dream. But he knew that it was more than that. *The Book of Night* had been opened and the Pale Writers released. They had sensed him watching.

His new firemark was glowing an angry red. The tears falling from the eye had turned black.

Fifty miles away, Horace Catchpole examined the package tied with leather twine on his desk. He had retrieved it from the Folly & Catchpole cellars, the place known as the dungeon. Now he sat looking at it, trying to make up his mind what he should do.

He reread the entry in the ledger.

> Property of Fabian Grey.
> Do NOT remove.
> Owner will collect.

Horace had been working with the magical realm long enough to know who Fabian Grey was. He had a feeling that whatever was inside the package was important.

This put him in a difficult position. Should he obey Folly & Catchpole's first principle and mind his own business? Or break the centuries-old tradition and tell someone about the package – and if so, who?

The instruction was very clear: the owner would collect. Since the owner had left that instruction over three hundred and fifty years ago, in the normal run of things he should be long dead and therefore unable to collect. But a number of Folly & Catchpole's best clients were deceased. And Horace knew from experience that ghosts could get very cross if their instructions were ignored.

He was pondering this when his thoughts were interrupted by a sound at the window. *Tap, tap.*

Horace crossed the room and opened the blind. A raven was perched on the outside windowsill. As Horace peered at it, the bird tapped its beak on the glass again. *Tap, tap.*

Horace opened the window and the raven hopped inside. It landed on his desk. Horace wondered whether this was the same raven that had once collected a ring for Archie Greene.

'Who are you here on behalf of?' he asked the bird.

The raven cocked its head on one side. 'Fabian Grey,' it cried.

Horace glanced at the package. 'I'll need some proof,' he said.

'Its record says: "Property of Fabian Grey. Do not remove. Owner will collect",' the bird said.

'That doesn't prove anything,' stammered Horace.

'How else would I know the instruction?' said the raven, giving him a scornful glare.

Then, before Horace could respond, it grasped the leather twine in its claws and tried to fly away.

But the package was too heavy for it and it only succeeded in dragging it off the edge of the desk onto the floor. Fluttering down beside it, the raven seized the twine a second time.

But by now Horace had recovered himself. 'Not so fast,' he said, standing in front of the window. 'I'll need better proof than that!'

With a cry of frustration, the raven dropped the package. It fixed Horace with its beady-eyed stare. 'I'll send another,' it said. Then it flapped its wings once and arrowed past him out of the open window into the night.

11

The Green Bottle

When Archie arrived at the museum the next day, he went straight to Lost Books. He was desperate to tell Hawke about his dream. But Hawke wasn't there.

Archie decided to look for him in the archive. He found Morag Pandrama searching through some ancient texts. A severe-looking woman with olive skin and almond-shaped eyes, her pince-nez were perched on the end of her aquiline nose.

As Archie arrived she made a loud tutting sound and closed the volume she was examining, placing it on an ever-growing pile of discarded books on the left of the table. On the right was an even larger stack that she had yet to open. When she heard Archie come in she looked up with a frown, indicating she was very busy and didn't want to be disturbed.

When he asked for Hawke, she shook her head. 'I haven't seen him,' she said. 'Even he takes a day off once in a blue moon.'

She opened another book and buried her nose in it.

'When will he be back?' Archie asked.

Pandrama regarded him over her pince-nez. 'Tomorrow I expect,' she said, and carried on scanning the pages.

Archie was crestfallen. Hawke had said he was to let him know if he had any more dreams about Grey or the raven. He was sure that this latest one was important. But when he recounted it to Pandrama she shook her head.

'Sorry, Archie, I don't know anything about dreams. But I do know that I've got a lot of research to get through and very little time. Gideon has made it very clear that we have to find out what Grey saw. So unless your dream told you which of these texts to look at first –' she gestured at the shelves crammed with books and scrolls – 'then it's not much help to me.'

'But I dreamed about *The Book of Night*,' he said.

Pandrama smiled at him. 'Well, I'm not surprised. I think Gideon dreams of nothing else, but you need to talk to him about that.'

'I just thought I should tell someone, that's all,' said Archie.

'Tell someone what?' asked a sharp voice. Archie turned to see Aurelius Rusp standing in the doorway. Rusp was one of Archie's least favourite people. Ever since he'd discovered the fire in the museum thirteen years earlier, Rusp had become a real grouch. He didn't seem to have a kind word to say to anyone, especially Archie. Sometimes, though, he helped Hawke in Lost Books.

'It doesn't matter,' Archie said.

Rusp shrugged. 'Well, then, don't loiter, boy. Some of us have work to do.' He addressed Pandrama. 'Morag, I saw Gideon yesterday and he asked me to help you look through the records.'

Pandrama looked up. 'I see,' she said. 'I thought Faustus was meant to be helping me but he must be busy with something else. Perhaps he's at the Royal Society today. You can start with those,' she said indicating the untouched stack of books on her desk. 'I'll put the ones I've already been through away and get some more,' she added, scooping up the other pile.

She hurried towards one of the smaller rooms that adjoined the main archive. Rusp took her place at the table and continued thumbing through the texts where she'd left off.

They seemed to have forgotten Archie was even

there. He watched for a while and then slipped away. While he was here, he might as well do some research of his own.

He looked up drawing books in the reference book.

Drawing books: These are among the most dangerous of all magical books. They have the power to draw people into them. The most famous drawing books are *The Book of Yore* and *The Book of Prophecy*. Together with *The Book of Reckoning*, these are sometimes called the three Books of Destiny. But *The Book of Yore* is not concerned with destiny because it deals with the past. However, by revealing the past it may change the future.

A number of people who have consulted drawing books have gone missing. If the book is closed while someone is inside and the page is lost, then it is notoriously difficult to find the place again. In other cases, people have been unable to return because they have broken the natural lores of magic.

The Grim Grimoire had said that Alex Greene was trapped inside a book and that Arthur Ripley was involved in some way. What exactly did that mean? Had Ripley closed the book with his father inside it, deliberately losing his place so that he couldn't get out? And where were Archie's mother and sister? Were they trapped with his father?

He wondered again if *The Book of Night* was a drawing book and whether his family might be trapped inside it. It gave him a sick feeling in his stomach.

The very time that he needed to talk to Hawke and the head of Lost Books wasn't around. But he had to tell someone about his dream so he went to find Old Zeb. The bookbinder was a good listener.

When Archie told him about his dream, the old man looked alarmed. 'Oh dear, oh dear,' he said, covering his mouth with his hand.

'What does it mean?' asked Archie.

'You saw the Greaders opening *The Book of Night*,' the old bookbinder said solemnly. 'Which means either they have already opened it or they are about to. You must tell Gideon as soon as possible.'

Archie felt the knot in his stomach tighten another notch. It was just as he'd feared. He looked at his hand. His new firemark was glowing faintly.

'But why did I dream about it?' he asked.

Old Zeb shook his head. 'I don't know, Archie. What does Gideon say?'

'He says that magic comes more easily to me because I am a book whisperer.'

'You certainly picked up bookbinding very quickly,' mused Old Zeb, 'so he's probably right. But that makes you more sensitive to magic, too. You must be careful. You consulted the Books of Destiny. They are very powerful magical books. It can't be good for your mind. *The Book of Yore* is bad enough, but *The Book of Prophecy* . . .'

He shook his head again. 'That book has sent people mad. And now you're having bad dreams . . . dreams that seem to be prophetic. That's why Gideon has always said that consulting *The Book of Prophecy* should only be considered as a last resort. It's too powerful for mortal minds.'

Archie could see concern in the old man's eyes.

'I've wondered about that,' said Archie. 'Why didn't it affect me the way it affected Fabian Grey? I must have been protected by my retrospectre.' The guarding spell using the Emerald Eye enabled him to safely leave his physical body behind and enter drawing books.

'Perhaps,' said Old Zeb, but he didn't look convinced and avoided Archie's eye. 'That's something else you should ask Gideon about.'

I would if I could find him, Archie thought to himself.

On his way out, Archie was thinking about what the old man had said. Was it possible that because he'd consulted *The Book of Prophecy* he was dreaming about the future? He was just passing the second door, the blue one that was guarded by the stone griffins called the bookend beasts, when he felt an icy blast of air. He noticed that the door was slightly ajar. That was very odd.

For one thing, the door had an invisible handle, which made it difficult to open, but, more worryingly, it was also a secret entrance into the crypt where the other Terrible Tomes were kept.

Someone's been in here, thought Archie, nudging the door open and feeling the icy air catch in his chest.

He noticed two sets of footprints in the frost on the flagstoned floor; one set leading in and another leading back to the door.

Both sets of tracks looked like they were made by the same feet. The footprints going in were close together, but the ones coming out were much further apart.

Whoever made them had crept in slowly but left very quickly. The second set of prints was further apart because they were running. The good news was that it looked like whoever had tried to get into the crypt had failed.

It was something else to tell Hawke when he saw him. He hurried back to Lost Books.

Pandrama and Rusp were ploughing through more books. They mostly ignored him.

Archie wandered through the maze of rooms that made up the archive. He noticed the alcove he'd seen before. When he investigated, there was a small door that led into another room. He wondered what was in there.

'What are you up to?' growled a voice behind him.

Archie spun round to see Rusp glaring at him. 'Erm, nothing,' he replied, startled. 'I was just exploring.'

'Well, you're wasting your time there,' said Rusp. 'That's Fabian Grey's cloakroom. It's got a locking spell on it. People have been trying to open it for centuries but no magic seems to work.'

Archie glanced at the door again. He'd had a funny feeling about the place. Perhaps that was why.

'Grey was arrested here in the archive after the Great Fire of London,' Rusp continued. 'He was taken by surprise – didn't even have time to get his cloak.'

'Now, take these texts through to Morag. She's waiting for them,' he added, indicating a pile of heavy-looking books.

Archie did as he was told. For the next hour or so Rusp kept him busy carrying books to Pandrama. But after a while, they were both too preoccupied looking through the records to pay him much mind.

As the afternoon wore on, Archie decided to see if Hawke was back. He went to his office and knocked. When there was no answer he tried the door. It was unlocked so he let himself in.

He looked around the study. There was no one there. A thought occurred to him. This was a chance to find out about Hawke's mysterious green medicine bottle. He crossed to the desk and opened the drawer.

It was cluttered with all sorts of curious objects. The imagining glass with the black handle and silvery lens Hawke used to examine magical books was in there, and there was another broken one with a pink lens that Archie had retrieved from a break-in at the Aisle of White. But it was the green glass bottle that Archie was interested in. He picked it up and read the label. 'One teaspoonful to be taken twice a day.'

He took out the stopper and sniffed it. It smelled foul. So it was medicine!

He replaced the stopper and put the bottle back where he'd found it. Hawke was on some sort of medication. But what was it for?

'Looking for something?' asked a voice behind him, making him jump.

Archie looked up to see the tall, thin figure of Wolfus Bone standing in the doorway. The magic diviner looked even more emaciated than usual. His face was still badly bruised from the drubbing he'd had at the Royal Society and he was walking with a stick. The attack had obviously left him very frail.

'Erm, no,' said Archie, trying not to look as guilty as he felt. 'I was just tidying up.'

'Hmmm,' said Bone, giving him a knowing look. 'I've come to help with your divining lessons,' he added, his tall frame hunched over his walking stick.

Archie spent the rest of the afternoon practising delving spells with Bone.

As he walked home from the museum that night, his mind turned back to the green bottle. If Hawke was ill, what was wrong with him? He was still thinking about this as he passed the entrance to the Bodleian Library in Broad Street.

He didn't notice the pale figure that followed him along the road. It slipped from one pool of darkness to the next, moving closer and closer to Archie as he made his way home to Houndstooth Road.

When Archie opened the gate to number 32, the white spectre stole up on him like mist. Archie felt a shiver run up his spine as if someone had walked over his grave. The air around him turned cold and something dark entered his mind like an unwanted memory. He heard a hoarse voice that seemed to come from inside his own head.

'What's it like to be so unloved and alone?' it whispered. 'Your parents abandoned you. They left you when you were a baby because they knew you couldn't be trusted with magic.'

Archie was startled. Where had that thought come from?

'My parents had to leave,' he said to himself, correcting the stray thought. 'They had no choice. They left me with Gran because they wanted to keep me safe.'

'Really?' the cold voice persisted. 'Then why did the old woman leave you, too, as soon as she could?'

Archie was shocked by the thought. But now he came to think of it, Gran had seemed relieved to send him away to stay with the Foxes. That was because she wanted him to meet his cousins, he reassured himself. It was true that she had gone away immediately afterwards . . . but maybe she'd always wanted to travel, and who could blame her?

But then again, what if the voice was right and

she couldn't wait to get away from him? She hadn't asked to raise him after all. She had been lumbered with him when his parents disappeared.

Perhaps Gardenia Greene hadn't really wanted him! Archie suddenly found himself doubting everything.

'She doesn't even visit you,' whispered the voice in his head.

'That's because she's been travelling,' Archie thought, trying to convince himself. But he wasn't so certain as he had been.

'Don't you wonder why, though?' persisted the voice. 'Why does she choose to travel instead of visiting you?'

'She's told me in her letters – she's searching for . . . answers.'

'Ha! That's convenient. Searching for answers to what? Searching for excuses to stay away from you more like!'

Archie felt hollow inside. The whispering voice sensed his uncertainty and pressed home its advantage. 'Your parents and sister were happy until you came along. If it hadn't been for you they would still be together. You are the reason that your family broke up.'

No, that's not true! Archie thought. The voice was wrong. It was just bad timing that his family had disappeared soon after he was born. It wasn't his fault. If Arthur Ripley hadn't trapped his father in a book, he'd still be around.

The voice in his head heard his thoughts. 'Bad timing?' it sneered. 'Yes, it was bad timing for them, all right! You brought ruin on your family. You can't blame Ripley. It's all *your* fault! Your cousins know it, too. They wish you'd never come to Oxford. They hide it well but they don't want you around. They know you're dangerous. You've nearly got them killed – twice. Third time they won't be so lucky.'

'No,' cried Archie, but the tears were welling up in his eyes. The voice was right. His whole life was one big mistake – one disaster after another. He felt himself falling into a dark hole. He still had his hand on the gate. The lights were on inside number 32. Bramble and Thistle were inside with Loretta and Woodbine, where they belonged. Archie didn't belong there. He was a cuckoo in the nest.

'They wouldn't miss you!' sneered the voice in his mind. 'They'd be better off without you. Everyone would be better off without *you*.'

Archie glanced at the lights in the house. He could see the Foxe family through the window. They looked happy. The voice was right. He knew it was right. They were perfectly happy without him. He felt the tears hot on his face and turned away. He ran blindly out into the road just as a car turned into the street. He saw a glare of headlights and heard a squeal of brakes as it nearly hit him. Then an angry voice bellowed from the car window.

'What's the matter with you, kid? Are you stupid?' An angry red face danced in front of Archie's eyes and then with another squeal of tyres the car roared off into the night.

Archie turned and tripped on the pavement. His head hit something hard and he landed on his back, the wind knocked out of him. His head was spinning. The voice was right. He was worthless.

Archie's eyes dimmed. He felt himself being pulled into darkness. He saw a pale figure bend over him. 'What's this?' it hissed. 'John Dee's scrying stone!' Its breath smelled like rotten fish. A ghostly hand reached for the Emerald Eye around his neck. Its long icy fingers closed around the crystal pendant.

The next thing Archie heard was someone running and then voices. Familiar voices.

He was aware of people leaning over him and the touch of warm skin on his hand.

'Is he breathing?' asked Bramble's worried voice. Archie felt someone put an ear to his chest.

He heard Woodbine's voice. 'Thistle, Bramble, take an arm each and help me get him into the house.'

'What is it?' cried Loretta. 'What's happened?'

'It's Archie. He's been attacked,' said Woodbine.

Half an hour later, Archie was sitting by the fire in the Foxes' living room with a blanket around his shoulders, drinking hot sweet tea.

'W-what happened?' he croaked.

'You were attacked. It's a good job you had your keepsafe on. It protected you from the worst of it.'

Archie felt the reassuring presence of the Emerald Eye on the silver chain around his neck. He clasped the gemstone – it was warm in his hand.

He looked up at his uncle. 'What was it?'

Woodbine glanced at Loretta. She nodded. 'Tell the boy,' she said gently. 'He deserves to know.'

'You were attacked by one of the Pale Writers,' said Woodbine. 'There are three of them. The first is Doubt, the second is Dread, and the third, their leader and the most deadly of all, is Despair. They attack their victims when they are vulnerable. It was the first of the three that ambushed you. Doubt is the weakest of their number. I don't like to think what would have happened if all of them had attacked you at the same time.'

'But what do they want with me?' asked Archie.

Loretta answered. 'They must be drawn to you

because you are descended from Fabian Grey. They must sense that you share his magical abilities.'

Archie lay awake most of the night thinking about what Woodbine and Loretta had said. Every time he thought he'd got it straight in his head about his connection to Fabian Grey, it seemed there was another layer to it. He couldn't help worrying about their similarities. Like him, Grey had a forked fate and the Golden Circle firemark.

What they also had in common was that they had both consulted *The Book of Prophecy*. But the book had only shown Grey how to save magic.

As he turned this over and over in his mind, an idea was forming in Archie's head. Everyone who consulted *The Book of Prophecy* seemed to be badly affected by the experience. Fabian Grey had lost his mind for a while and Archie's father had disappeared under mysterious circumstances. Old Zeb had said the book's magic was too powerful for mortal minds.

But Archie had used his retrospectre. The spell had protected him from harm.

Perhaps he could do the same thing again! It might be the only way of discovering Grey's secret and stopping the Dark Flame. It might help him find out what had happened to his family, too. He was still brooding on these dark thoughts when he fell asleep.

12

The Oath

The next day was Friday. Archie was still feeling the effects of the Pale Writer attack. He was weak and listless. As they were about to leave the house, he glanced in the mirror in the hall.

'Do I look any different to you?' he asked Thistle.

'A little paler, perhaps,' said his cousin.

'I feel thinner, too,' Archie said. 'Less solid.'

'Mum's cooking will soon sort that out,' said Thistle, grinning.

Archie managed a smile, but he didn't feel reassured.

After breakfast, the three cousins walked into Oxford. Loretta had made them promise to stick together, especially after dark. Woodbine thought it unlikely that the Pale Writers would bother them in the daytime, but they should make sure they were safely indoors by nightfall.

Bramble had spent her evening researching the Pale Writers.

'They're creatures of the night,' she said as they walked into town. 'They prefer to get their victims on their own. They prey on their weaknesses and insecurities. They are drawn to anyone with the Golden Circle firemark because they want to corrupt all magic writers and turn them into darchemists.

'Make no mistake, Archie, if they can they will make you like them – a slave to the Dark Flame. You mustn't let them get inside your head. Fear feeds upon itself. If you can name your fear you can break its grip and turn it on itself.'

Archie thought about that all the way to Lost Books. When he got there, Hawke had already heard about the attack.

'So *The Book of Night* is open, just as we feared. The attack on you last night confirms it. How do you feel?'

'I've felt better,' said Archie, trying to play it down. 'It was as if that . . . thing . . . could read my mind. It seemed to home in on any tiny doubt.'

'Yes, that's exactly what it was doing,' said Hawke, 'using your doubts against you. That's their way. The Pale Writers delve inside your

148

memories to find your weaknesses. But they can only use real memories against you, not magical memories created by spells. Remember that.'

When Archie repeated what he'd told Thistle about feeling thin, Hawke looked concerned.

'I've never heard of anything like that before. I'm sure it's nothing,' he said, but Archie thought he avoided his eye.

'Zeb told me about your dream,' continued Hawke. 'What did you see?'

Archie explained about the Dark Flame and the oath. 'It sounded like some sort of spell,' he said.

Hawke's brow darkened. 'That's precisely what it was. The enemy is mustering its forces. The Flame is drawing the Greaders to it. It gets stronger with every new follower,' he said.

'There's something else,' said Archie. 'The one who opened the book seemed to be their leader.'

'A dark master,' said Hawke. For a moment he didn't speak. He looked straight through Archie as if he'd forgotten he was there, and then he gave a long sigh as if all the energy and life had gone out of him. 'I have to inform the magical authorities. They will need to act immediately. Thank you, Archie. You can go.'

And with that he picked up his quill and began to scribble a note.

*

That lunchtime, the Alchemists' Club minus Rupert held an impromptu meeting in Quill's. Arabella had already heard about the attack through the museum grapevine.

'So the Pale Writers are especially drawn to you!' she said. 'Remind me to walk home with someone else!'

It was meant as a joke to cheer him up but Archie couldn't manage a smile. He couldn't help thinking that the skin on his hands looked paler than usual. He had a moment of panic when he wondered if he was fading away. He needed some answers and he needed them quickly. He remembered his plan to consult *The Book of Prophecy*. It had seemed like a good idea the night before but now he wasn't so sure.

And when he told the others, they reacted with howls of protest.

'It's a crazy idea!' said Arabella. 'Everyone who's ever opened *The Book of Prophecy* has gone barking mad or disappeared!'

'Except me,' protested Archie. 'I consulted it before, remember, and my retrospectre protected me.'

The others weren't convinced, but it seemed the only way to find out what Grey had seen, and time was clearly running out. In truth, Archie was not completely convinced himself. His assertion that his retrospectre would protect him was mostly a show of bravado. He was beginning to have serious misgivings about the whole thing. But he didn't want to admit that, even to himself.

'If we can't talk you out of it then we need to be there in case something goes wrong,' said Bramble. 'When are you planning to do it?'

'As soon as I can,' said Archie, starting to wish he'd never thought of it. 'But I'll have to be careful. I can't afford to get caught,' he added.

'Shhhh!' hissed Arabella, rolling her eyes sideways at the next table where Peter Quiggley and another apprentice were sitting.

'What's up?' asked Bramble.

'I think they're listening to our conversation.'

Bramble glared at Quiggley. 'Are you ear wigging?' she asked.

'You don't really think I'm interested in your silly little club, do you?' sneered Quiggley.

With a self-satisfied smile he moved away.

'He's far too pleased with himself,' muttered Bramble.

'He's not worth bothering about,' said Arabella, tossing her hair. 'My parents know the Quiggleys and they haven't got a good word to say about anyone.'

When Archie went back to see Hawke that afternoon, his office door was closed and he could hear raised voices coming from inside.

After what Hawke had said about him listening at keyholes, he hesitated. He'd better not get caught eavesdropping again. He turned away.

But as he did he recognised Morag Pandrama's voice. She sounded defensive.

'There is no trace of Grey's vision in the archive, Gideon. Believe me, I have looked! If Grey wrote it down then it must be somewhere else.'

Archie was about to move away but something about Hawke's voice sounded different. He was usually so calm and reasonable. Archie had never heard him raise his voice before.

'Well, look again!' he growled. 'Grey must have left a clue somewhere.'

'I tell you: it's not here,' said Pandrama.

'Where then?' demanded Hawke, tetchily.

'Have you considered the fact that the museum isn't the only magical archive?' said Pandrama. 'There are others.'

Hawke grunted.

Pandrama's voice softened. 'You need some rest, Gideon. You are pushing yourself too hard. You'll make yourself ill again.'

There was a long sigh of frustration from Hawke. 'I'm so close to discovering Grey's secret, I know it. I can feel it in my blood.'

'Are you taking your medication?' asked Pandrama sharply.

'It doesn't help,' snapped Hawke. 'It blunts my mind.'

'But you know what they said at the asylum. You must take it – unless you want to have a relapse.'

Archie froze. So Hawke had spent time in the asylum. This was news. He wondered what had made the head of Lost Books ill.

'To hell with the asylum!' growled Hawke. Archie heard footsteps crossing the room. He managed to leap back just in time.

The door opened and Pandrama came out. She looked tired and shut the door behind her.

'He's having a bad day,' she said, seeing Archie's worried look. 'He's under a lot of pressure,' she added. 'The authorities are still blaming him for *The Book of Night* being stolen.'

'But it wasn't his fault,' said Archie, leaping to Hawke's defence.

'I know that,' said Pandrama. 'But they're looking for a scapegoat and he fits the bill.' She gave a loud tut. 'It doesn't help, of course, that he's refusing to take his medication. It's to calm his mind,' she added, seeing the question on Archie's face. 'When someone has a lot of magical ability like Gideon, it can be too much to handle. The medicine helps. I'll ask Motley to make a fresh batch.'

She gave Archie a resigned look. 'Try to

encourage him to take it,' she said. 'It's for his own good.'

Archie nodded and slipped through the door. Hawke was sitting at his desk holding his quill in one hand and staring into space. The head of Lost Books looked more ruffled than usual and Archie thought he could see a few grey hairs among the black. The stress must be taking its toll.

Archie was tidying Hawke's office, something he seemed to spend half his time doing. But no matter how often he picked up open books and stacked them neatly, the room never seemed to look any less cluttered. Archie wondered if it reflected Hawke's mind. The head of Lost Books seemed increasingly distracted, and Archie was starting to worry about his own health, too. Something was bothering him and he needed to get it off his chest.

'Why am I having these dreams?' he asked, trying to keep the desperation from his voice.

Hawke looked up and his face creased into a frown. 'You consulted *The Book of Prophecy*,' he said. 'What did you expect? That book nearly drove Fabian Grey mad. It's not wise to look into the future, Archie. It's a burden too great for mortals.'

'It may be the only way to find out what Grey saw,' said Archie.

Hawke looked up sharply. 'Consulting *The Book of Prophecy* should only be considered as a very last resort. It's too dangerous, even for a book whisperer.'

Archie felt his heart sink. That was what Old Zeb had said.

'Do you think it marked me in some way?' he asked, remembering what else the old bookbinder had said.

'It's possible,' said Hawke. 'It's a very powerful book and not one to be taken lightly. You were lucky.'

'But the Emerald Eye protected me,' said Archie, hoping it was true.

Hawke gave a long sigh. 'You fared better than most,' he agreed. 'The magic pendant shielded your mind from the worst effects, but your fate and that of Fabian Grey were already linked and now they are more tangled than ever.

'My guess is that when you consulted *The Book of Prophecy* you absorbed some of its powers. And it also made you more visible to the Pale Writers. They can sense your presence.'

Archie felt his blood turn cold. Hawke picked up his quill and resumed writing, a sign that the conversation was at an end. Archie closed the door behind him, leaving Hawke to his thoughts.

*

Archie agonised over what Hawke had told him for the rest of the day. What exactly did he mean about absorbing some of the book's powers? Archie wondered if he would ever be the same again. He was walking past a bookcase in the West Gallery when his thoughts were interrupted.

'Psssssssst!' hissed a papery voice. 'Over here.'

Archie glanced at the bookcase next to him.

'No, not there. Over here!'

He spotted the thick red cover of the mystery book on the next shelf.

'You again,' he said. 'You get about don't you? How do you do it?'

'Can't tell you that,' chuckled the book. 'Tricks of the trade. I've got some more information for you.'

'Do you know where my family are?' asked Archie, excitedly.

'Not exactly,' rustled the book, 'but I know someone who might be able to help you find them.'

'Who?'

The book dropped its voice to a whisper. 'The stone griffins,' it said. 'They are the keepers of magical secrets. They know more about magical books than anyone else. If your parents are trapped inside a magical book, they'd know which one.'

'The bookend beasts?' said Archie, remembering

the fierce stone griffins that could come to life if the magical items they protected were threatened.

'Yes,' said the book.

Archie swallowed hard. He'd been lucky to escape with his life both times he'd encountered the beasts. Now, if he wanted to find out what had happened to his family, it looked like he'd have to take his chances a third time.

There was no time to lose. He knew that if he told his cousins they would want to come with him, but it was too dangerous. This was one thing he had to do on his own.

Archie took a flaming torch from its bracket and held it aloft in the passageway under the Aisle of White. The bookend beasts' lair was behind the second door, the blue one. He reached out and felt for the invisible door handle, grasping it in his hand and turning it.

He took a deep breath and opened the door. On the previous occasion when he'd entered their lair he had no idea what he would be facing. But this time he did, and it wasn't reassuring.

As he pushed the door open and stepped inside the frozen chamber, a cold blast of air hit his face. The icy air made him gasp as it hit his lungs. On the ground all around him, frost glittered like tiny diamonds scattered on the flagstone floor, and his feet crunched on the ice crystals as he edged his way forward.

Archie held up his torch and the light reflected off the high-ceilinged room. Somewhere he could hear water dripping, and icicles like stalagmites and stalactites had formed on the floor and the ceiling. Thin ribbons of grey mist swirled around his feet, created by the warmer air coming into contact with the frozen ground. Immediately ahead of him Archie could see a very large stone griffin.

The bookend beast stood motionless. It was eight feet tall and carved from a single slab of grey stone. Its giant eagle's head had a vicious hooked beak and staring eyes. Below its neck it had the body of a lion with chiselled fur on its chest and flanks, and two huge feathered wings folded across its back.

As Archie stepped closer, the griffin's eyes lit up with an amber light. With a noise like stone grinding on stone, the beast turned its head and fixed Archie with its steely gaze. A ripple of light pulsed through the creature and its body turned from cold stone to living flesh. Archie had seen the bookend beast come to life before but his legs still turned to jelly at the sight of it.

He swallowed hard.

'Greetings, mighty bookend beast, guardian of

magical books and keeper of secrets,' he cried in a loud voice that echoed in the cold stone chamber. He knew that this was the correct way to address the ancient magical creatures. He'd read about it in his father's magical reference book.

The beast's voice when it spoke was a deep rumble that boomed off the walls.

'Who are you who wakes me from my sleep and disturbs me in my lair?' it thundered. It sniffed the air.

'Another human!' it roared angrily. 'Have you come with your cloaking magic to try to steal from me again? I warned you last time that I would kill you if you returned!'

Archie remembered the footsteps in the frost. Whoever had crept into the beast's lair had left very quickly and in fear for their life.

Archie realised he was in grave danger. The bookend beast could kill him with one blow from its mighty claws or freeze him with one blast of its icy breath. The griffin flexed its huge, razor-sharp talons.

'Wait,' cried Archie. 'There's been some sort of mistake! I'm Archie Greene. I'm an apprentice at the museum. I haven't come to steal from you!'

'Hmmmm,' rumbled the griffin, bowing its head to get a better look at him. 'Well, I can see you this time so perhaps you aren't the thief after all.'

It fixed him with its amber eyes. 'You look familiar. We bookend beasts have very long memories. You came here before seeking answers. You are the one that John Dee told us to expect.'

'Yes,' cried Archie, his voice breaking with relief. 'I'm the book whisperer.'

The beast eyed him suspiciously. 'Well, book whisperer, I remember you now. You were in a hurry then and I sense you are in a hurry now. My brother and I let you pass last time because you guessed the password the old magician gave us, but we warned you then about the foolishness of humans. We told you that it is dangerous to come here. Why have you returned?'

'Mighty bookend beast, guardian of magical books and keeper of secrets,' Archie said. 'I was told that the bookend beasts know more about magical books than anyone else in the magical realm,' he added, deliberately flattering the creature.

The griffin looked pleased. Its tone softened. 'Who told you this?' it enquired.

'A magical book,' replied Archie. 'Is it true?'

'Hmmm,' considered the beast, nodding its huge eagle head. 'I believe it is. For centuries my brother and I have kept watch over the magical books for humans. We guarded them in Alexandria. We were the ones who saved many of the magical books when the Great Library burned. Humans and their infernal fire!' it added, bitterly.

Archie sensed that the creature was angered by the memory of the fire that had destroyed the Great Library.

'I know that you don't put much store in humans,' he said, trying to soothe the creature. 'But I need your help to find my father.'

'Do not speak to me of humans!' it thundered. 'I would not waste my time on most of them, like the thief who came here to steal my very breath. I sent him running for his life. If you would know about my breath, I told him, then feel its cold upon your skin, for it will freeze your blood and stop your heart.'

'Who was this thief?' asked Archie. 'What did he look like?'

'I did not see his face. He used cloaking magic to make himself invisible, but I would recognise his smell again. And if he returns he will not leave this place alive!'

The griffin's amber eyes glowered in the gloom. It was getting angry again.

'Leave now and you may live – if you remain I will pass judgment on you.'

'But I need your help,' said Archie. 'My father was trapped in a magical book. His name is Alex Greene, do you know anything about him?'

The griffin put its head on its giant lion paws. It closed its eyes for a moment in thought. 'If your father is imprisoned in a magical book, then it must be a drawing book.'

'I know that already,' said Archie. 'But which one?'

The beast opened one amber eye. 'You humans are very impatient!' it declared. 'I know of one drawing book that might do such a thing: *The Book of Yore.*'

Archie gasped. Could this be the answer to what had become of his father? His mind was racing, but the bookend beast was still speaking.

'*The Book of Yore* has a treacherous nature. But your father would have to have done something to deserve such a punishment.'

Archie thought for a moment. 'Well, he was expelled from the museum because he took a book from Arthur Ripley's collection. Perhaps that's why Ripley trapped him in the book!'

The griffin shook its head. 'Ripley might have closed the book with your father inside, but even *The Book of Yore* could not imprison him without a very good reason. Your father must have broken one of the natural lores of magic.'

The only magical lores Archie knew about were the ones introduced after the Great Fire of London. 'You mean the Lores of Magical Restraint?' he asked.

The griffin grew angry again. 'Those petty rules! Never,' it thundered. 'Those lores were invented by foolish humans! No, I mean the natural rules of magic – the ones that protect the universe from chaos. They are the lores of time and destiny. No one can cheat their fate.'

Archie remembered that *The Book of Prophecy* had told him that before.

'But how could my father have broken them?' He demanded, his voice urgent.

'That is for you to discover. This audience is at an end,' said the beast. 'Now leave while you can.'

'But I don't understand,' cried Archie.

'You will in time,' said the beast. 'John Dee said we were to help you if we could, for magic's sake!' And with that it turned back to stone.

13

The Book of Prophecy

L oretta tutted and shook her head. She was reading the magical realm's newspaper, the *Crystal Ball*, at the breakfast table. Archie read the headline across the table.

STOLEN TOME IS *BOOK OF NIGHT*

The Magical League today confirmed that the book stolen from the Royal Society of Magic two weeks ago is *The Book of Night*, the most feared of all the Terrible Tomes.

It is widely believed that *The Book of Night* has been opened. There have been several reports of sightings of the creatures called the Pale Writers, which serve the Flame of Pandemonium, the so-called Dark Flame.

The release of the Pale Writers could herald the start of a dark age of magic.

The head of magical enforcement at the Magical League, Uther Morgred, refused to comment on claims that a growing number of followers had taken the Dark Oath, pledging allegiance to the Dark Flame. But one source close to the Royal Society of Magic admitted: 'Frankly, we are running out of options. If we don't find a way to stop the Dark Flame then we might as well all take the oath.'

Calling for calm, Morgred dismissed this as scaremongering: 'There is no need for panic,' he said. 'We are doing everything in our power to recover the book.'

'Nonsense!' exclaimed Loretta. 'They've done absolutely nothing since the first proclamation. People want reassurance and instead we get this rubbish!' She shook the newspaper. 'And the Royal Society is no better. If they hadn't been hoarding books it would never have been stolen in the first place.'

'They're waiting to see which way the wind is blowing,' growled Woodbine. 'They're scared to take action until they know how many have taken the oath in case they end up on the losing side.'

The news that *The Book of Night* was open had

already cast a dark cloud over the museum. The elders and apprentices were edgy.

Even more worrying, ever since the attack by the Pale Writer, Archie had had the feeling that someone was following him. Inside the museum he was sure he could hear stealthy footsteps behind him sometimes, but when he turned round there was no one there. It was all very unsettling and he hoped he was just imagining things.

Almost a week had passed since he'd told his friends that he would consult *The Book of Prophecy* at the first opportunity, but in reality he kept putting it off. So when Bramble had another idea he leaped at it.

'I've been thinking,' she said, as they were drinking hot chocolate in Quill's. 'If Fabian Grey wrote down his vision, then whatever he did with it would be recorded in *The Book of Yore*.'

Archie started at the mention of the book.

She was right! *The Book of Yore* contained the history of magic. Such an important moment would have to be in the book.

The Book of Yore could be treacherous – Archie knew that from his own dealings with it and from what the bookend beast had told him. After all, it had been *The Book of Yore* which had trapped him in the burning Library of Alexandria. And according to the bookend beast it could have trapped his father, too.

But on the occasions Archie had consulted the book since his scare, his retrospectre had kept him safe. As long as he used the spell again, he should be all right. He'd rather take his chances with *The Book of Yore* than *The Book of Prophecy* any day. Besides, he might find out what had happened to his family once and for all.

'That's brilliant!' he cried. 'Bramble, you're a genius. Why didn't I think of that?'

Bramble smiled. 'Because you're not a genius?'

Archie grinned back.

'But I meant what I said about you consulting *The Book of Prophecy*, Archie. Don't try anything on your own this time. You need the club's help.'

Archie got his chance to put Bramble's idea into action sooner than he expected. The next day was Saturday and the museum was quiet at the weekend. Archie had been in the archive and was walking past the Scriptorium. There was no one around.

It was too good an opportunity to miss. He knew Bramble had said he should wait to have someone there to help him, but he was sure she would understand when he explained later. After all, she'd made him promise not to risk *The Book of Prophecy* and he wasn't going to. He pushed the door open. The magic torches on the wall blazed with light, illuminating the room. Archie slipped inside.

At the far end of the room he could see the glass dome that contained *The Book of Prophecy* and *The Book of Reckoning*. He climbed the wooden stairs to get a view of the two Books of Destiny. *The Book of Reckoning* was open as always, the blue bennu quill dancing in the air as it kept the tally of life and death.

The Book of Prophecy was closed. It had whispered to Archie before to warn him about the Alchemist's Curse, but today it was silent and Archie was relieved.

Stepping off the wooden platform, he turned his attention to *The Book of Yore*. A thick brown bruiser of a book, it was in its usual place at the other end of the Scriptorium.

The last time he'd tried to consult it about his father, the book had been unable – or was it unwilling? – to help. He didn't understand why that was but he realised that he had to be careful what he asked. *The Book of Yore* was tricky and capable of twisting his words.

Archie clutched the Emerald Eye in his hand and felt its reassuring warmth.

He closed his eyes in concentration. 'Gadabout,'

he said, pronouncing the magical name that allowed him to cast the retrospectre spell. The crystal pendant began to pulse and Archie felt the shadow of his soul slip out of his body as he had the previous times.

He took a step, his ghost-like retrospectre leaving a trail of silvery light. He glanced back at his physical body, a look of concentration frozen on his face and his hand still gripping the Emerald Eye. It was a weird sensation to see himself like that, one that he would never get used to.

He approached *The Book of Yore*. 'I wish to consult the past,' he said, trying to strike a commanding tone.

He was concentrating so hard that he didn't notice the door to the Scriptorium open and close behind him, or hear stealthy footsteps as someone crept into the room.

Archie heard the raspy sandpaper voice reply. 'The past is gone. Those who disturb it may not change it, *but they may be changed by it.*'

'I understand,' said Archie, his heart beating faster. 'But I need to know if Grey wrote down his vision. I need to know how he was meant to defeat the Dark Flame.'

There was a long silence, as if *The Book of Yore* was deciding. Archie wondered if it was going to refuse him again, but it suddenly flipped open.

'The past is full of surprises, book whisperer. Are you ready to face the truth?'

Archie swallowed hard. 'I am ready,' he said.

The pages turned as if a wind blew through them. 'Your page is marked.'

The book fell open to where a bookmark had appeared. The page rippled like the surface of a lake. The date at the top of the page was 2nd September 1666, the night of the Great Fire of London.

Archie hesitated.

'What's the matter, book whisperer?' asked the voice. 'Afraid of what you might discover?'

'I've seen this night before,' said Archie. 'You're tricking me.'

'The past has many rooms, book whisperer.'

Archie thought he heard the voice laugh. But it was too late for him to resist. There was a rushing sound in his ears and he was drawn into the page like smoke up a chimney.

He recognised the scene outside Thomas Farrinor's bakery in Pudding Lane immediately.

Through their magical experiments, the original Alchemists' Club had started the Great Fire of London. They had succeeded in making azoth, which it seemed Grey had intended to use to rewrite *The Opus Magus* and restore the magical books. But the plan had gone disastrously wrong – one of the group's members, Felicia Nightshade, had tried to complete the Unfinished Spell in *The Grim Grimoire*. When Grey had tried to stop her, the *Grimoire* had cursed him and the other alchemists and set fire to the bakery.

But Archie already knew all this, so why was *The Book of Yore* showing him again? What had he missed before?

As he observed the scene, a man in a scarlet cloak appeared and entered the building. From the white streak in his hair, Archie recognised him as Fabian Grey.

Archie followed him down to the cellar as he'd done before and watched in fascination as the same scene played out. He saw the five members of the original Alchemists' Club making azoth, and the showdown between Grey and Felicia Nightshade that caused the blaze. Roderick Trevellan, Angelica Ripley and Braxton Foxe fled from the burning building, up the stairs to the street.

Felicia Nightshade followed them through the choking smoke to the safety of the street above. Only Grey remained behind, desperately trying to put out the fire.

As Archie watched, the alchemist tried to beat out the flames but he was losing the battle. He sank to his knees and then slumped forward, overcome by the smoke. With a shock Archie realised that Grey would die in the smoke-filled cellar. But this couldn't be right! Archie knew that Grey had survived.

The fire was burning fiercely and there were groaning sounds from the wooden structure, signalling that the building was about to collapse. Archie felt his heart beating fast. He had to do something to save Grey.

And then Archie saw him, the man in the blue cloak. It was the same man Archie had seen the last time he'd consulted *The Book of Yore*. Archie remembered that the man had passed him before on the stairs and it suddenly struck him as odd that he should be racing into a burning building when everyone else was trying to escape.

The man plunged into the smoke-filled room. Covering his face with his sleeve, he forced his way through the flames until he reached Grey's slumped figure. With a mighty effort he hoisted Grey up onto his shoulder in a fireman's lift. Then he seized *The Grim Grimoire* in his other hand and stumbled from the blazing cellar.

Archie hadn't seen any of this before. He'd assumed that Grey had managed to escape on his own when he realised he couldn't put the fire out. But now Archie saw that without his mysterious rescuer Grey would have died.

The smoke was so thick now it was hard to see. The stranger climbed the stairs and staggered out into the street. By now Pudding Lane was thronged with people.

A woman stepped forward. She had a scarf tied around her face to keep out the smoke. 'Let them through,' she cried. The crowd parted and Grey's rescuer, still carrying Grey over his shoulder, passed through.

'Is he all right?' asked the woman.

'He's alive,' said the man in the blue cloak, 'but we need to get him away from here.'

He set Grey on his feet and the woman helped support him as they made their way down Pudding Lane away from the fire.

Archie watched for a moment and then he raced after them, his retrospectre casting a silvery light as he ran. But at the end of the street, he stopped. They'd disappeared. The streets were full of frightened voices as people raised the alarm. A pall of black smoke from the burning baker's shop hung in the air, making it hard to see.

Archie ran up a side street and down another lane. By now the fire was travelling fast. The wind had caught the flames carrying the burning embers from thatched roof to thatched roof, setting the houses ablaze. There was no sign of the woman or the two men. For a moment, Archie thought he'd lost them, but then he caught a glimpse of them through the smoke. Grey was able to walk supported by the other two.

Archie ran after them. The smoke was so dense now that he could barely see them in front of him. The woman was hurrying away from the fire, calling out a warning to the people still inside their houses. The two men had stopped and were talking earnestly.

'It's the only way,' said Grey's rescuer. 'You must write down what has happened or you will forget it all.'

'I *wish* I could forget tonight!' cried Grey. 'It is the worst day of my life!'

He sank to his knees, coughing and wheezing as he tried to catch his breath.

'Listen to me,' urged the other man. 'In a few days you won't remember any of this. The *Grimoire* has cursed you to lose your memory. That's why you must write down what you saw while it's still fresh in your mind.'

'The curse!' cried Grey, staring at him in horror. 'So that's what it is.'

'Yes,' said the other man, 'and there's another part to it.' He hesitated, as if afraid to go on. 'At the first new moon you will transform into the first beast you see.'

Grey looked up at him, confusion on his face.

Then his expression changed to a look of horrified recognition. 'The raven!' he exclaimed. 'The raven from my vision!'

Archie stopped in his tracks. So there was a raven in the vision that Grey had seen in *The Book of Prophecy*. Could it be the same raven that had delivered Grey's ring to him? Archie was desperate to find out more.

'You remember it now, but you won't remember it later,' said the man in the blue cloak. 'You must write it down for safekeeping.'

For the first time Archie could see Grey's rescuer's face clearly.

And with a shock he recognised his own father – Alex Greene.

So that was how Fabian Grey had escaped from the blaze that night. Alex Greene had saved his life!

At first Archie was so surprised he just stared. Then he cried out – perhaps his father would be able to hear him? But his voice was lost in the roaring sound of the fire. He stumbled on, desperate to reach his father, but it was useless. He had lost them in the smoke.

Then he heard an urgent, raspy voice in his ear. 'Book whisperer, you are in great danger. The Scriptorium is under attack – leave now or you will be trapped here forever.'

For a moment he hesitated, trying again to

locate his father through the smoke. He must be so close to him! Then he heard the voice rasp again. 'Flee! Flee for your life!'

Archie had no choice. 'Gadabout!' he cried, and a sound like wind filled his ears.

He fell out of *The Book of Yore*, coughing and choking. He was back in the Scriptorium, but there was still smoke all around him. He was shocked to see flames leaping from the glass dome where the Books of Destiny were kept.

A cloaked figure was moving across the room.

'Stop!' Archie cried.

But the hooded figure was already at the door. With a last glance at the burning *Book of Prophecy*, the figure opened the door and vanished into thin air. Archie raced to the open door and looked out, but there was no one there.

He turned back towards the glass dome. Inside, *The Book of Prophecy* was blazing with a black flame, giving off a vile-smelling plume of dense smoke. Archie felt nauseous, every sinew in his body ached and his head was spinning. The fumes were overpowering.

He heard the door to the Scriptorium open and was suddenly aware of other people in the room. Bramble, Thistle and Arabella were there, with Gideon Hawke, Feodora Graves and Faustus Gaunt.

'What manner of dark magic is this?' cried Gaunt.

'There must be something you can do?' coughed Archie, weakly.

Gaunt shook his head. 'It is too late,' he said. 'The spell is too far advanced.'

The other elders looked shocked by what they were seeing, but Hawke looked devastated. His face was leaden and he stared in horror as the flames consumed *The Book of Prophecy*, devouring it until all that was left was a pile of ash.

When she heard what had happened, Loretta insisted Archie be brought home immediately. Woodbine was dispatched to collect him.

Pink had mixed him a sleeping potion to help him rest and as soon as he got back to Houndstooth Road Loretta made him take it and go to bed. Archie's brain was still trying to take in what had just happened. He couldn't get his head around the fact that *The Book of Prophecy* was no more.

Whatever secrets the book might have been able to tell them about *The Opus Magus* and Fabian Grey were lost forever.

14

The Traitor

When Archie woke the next morning, it was already ten o'clock. The memory of what had happened came flooding back to him. He couldn't quite believe that one of the Books of Destiny had been destroyed and it was his fault. Then he remembered what he'd seen in *The Book of Yore* about his father saving Fabian Grey's life. He had to tell Hawke straight away!

He leaped out of bed. His clothes were in a pile on the floor where he'd left them the night before. They stank of smoke from the fire but he was in too much of a hurry to care.

He tore down the stairs. Bramble and Thistle had already left for the museum.

'Is that you, Archie?' called Loretta from the

kitchen. But the only reply was the sound of the front door slamming as he raced down the garden path.

Bramble and Thistle were talking to Arabella when Archie caught up with them in the Great Gallery of the museum. When he recounted what he'd seen in *The Book of Yore*, they were shocked.

'So your father saved Fabian Grey's life!' exclaimed Thistle.

Archie nodded. 'Yes, but he told Grey that he wouldn't remember anything about it because the *Grimoire* has cursed him to lose his memory. So he had to write down the vision he saw in *The Book of Prophecy*. And there's something else. At the first new moon he said that Grey would turn into the first beast that he saw. By then Grey was in the Tower of London so the first beast he saw would be—'

'A raven,' said Thistle.

'Yes,' said Archie. 'And Grey said something about there being a raven in the prophecy.'

'That could be a really important clue,' said Bramble. 'You have to tell Hawke immediately.'

'I know,' said Archie. 'I'm on my way now.'

When Archie arrived at Lost Books, he found Hawke distracted. His normal calm manner had been shattered. He was pacing up and down in his study like a caged animal. His face was pale and he was muttering to himself as he walked up and down. Was he unravelling under the pressure?

Archie noticed the glass bottle with the medication on the desk. It didn't look as if it had been touched. Hawke stopped pacing and turned to him.

'Tell me what you saw in *The Book of Yore*,' he demanded. His voice was sharp.

Archie repeated what he'd just told the others. When he got to the part about his father saving Grey from the cellar, Hawke stared at him.

'Your father?' he said, his eyes wide with surprise. 'Alex Greene saved Fabian Grey? How is that possible?'

'I don't know,' said Archie. 'He must have used *The Book of Yore* to reach him.'

'But it is forbidden!' exclaimed Hawke. 'No one may interfere with the past. It is one of the natural lores of magic.'

Archie remembered that the bookend beast had said the same thing.

Hawke studied him intently. 'Did you see anything else?' His voice was shrill and accusatory.

Archie had never seen Hawke like this before. Archie felt himself wither under his gaze. He couldn't think straight. 'I don't remember,' he said, shaking his head.

Hawke had crossed the room and his face was only inches from Archie's. His eyes were wide and staring.

'You must remember,' he said. 'It's very important. Did Grey say anything about what he saw?'

'Only that there was a raven in the vision,' said Archie. 'My father was trying to get him to write down what he'd seen in *The Book of Prophecy*.'

'*The Opus Magus*!' cried Hawke. 'I knew it would be written down somewhere! No one believed me, but I knew it!'

'I don't know if it was *The Opus Magus*,' said Archie. 'And I didn't see whether he wrote it down or not.'

Hawke slammed his hand on the desk in frustration, making Archie jump.

'We have to know what it was! It holds the key to defeating the Dark Flame!' exclaimed Hawke, thumping his hand on the desk again. 'Without that knowledge we are completely blind. We are so close,' he said. 'I feel like I am chasing my own tail.'

Hawke glanced over his shoulder at the door. Then he lowered his voice.

'If you remember anything else, tell me and no one else. Trust no one. Is that clear, Archie?'

Archie nodded. Hawke was becoming increasingly paranoid.

'I've just remembered something else,' said Archie. 'I saw a hooded figure in the Scriptorium.'

'Did you see who it was?' asked Hawke, his eyes burning into Archie's.

Archie shook his head. 'I only saw him for a moment and then he seemed to disappear into thin air.'

'It must be some sort of concealing magic,' mused Hawke. He looked into the fire in the hearth. 'So there's a traitor in the museum,' he breathed. 'I thought as much. When they realised you were consulting *The Book of Yore* they must have feared you'd try *The Book of Prophecy* next. They destroyed it so that we could not discover its secret.'

Archie pondered all that he'd heard. So Hawke was convinced that there was a traitor working inside the museum, but who could it be?

The newest arrival was Faustus Gaunt. Could it be him? Surely not. After all, Gaunt had been brought in by Hawke to help him with Dee's prophecy and discover how to defeat the Dark Flame.

Thistle suspected that Gaunt was their secret informer, FG, but there had been no more messages. The mystery seemed more baffling than ever.

*

News of the destruction of *The Book of Prophecy* was greeted with shock in the magical realm. The Books of Destiny were among the most powerful and significant of all the magical books, and *The Book of Prophecy* was symbolic of the future of magic. People were stunned that an act of such wanton destruction could occur inside the museum – a place dedicated to the preservation of magic.

'**BOOK OF PROPHECY MEETS ITS DOOM,**' declared the headline in the *Crystal Ball*.

The Book of Prophecy, one of the three Books of Destiny, was destroyed in a fire at the Museum of Magical Miscellany last Saturday. Foul play is suspected.

This is not the first security breach at the museum in recent months, and the theft of *The Book of Night* from the Royal Society of Magic just a few weeks ago raises concerns that information has been leaked to Greaders. The latest disaster will fuel rumours already circulating of a traitor operating inside the museum.

Uther Morgred, the head of magical enforcement at the Magical League, said: 'This was an act of magical vandalism that wilfully ignored the Lores of Magical Restraint. It calls into serious question the security and competence of the museum elders, and there will be a thorough investigation. We will find the perpetrator of this heinous crime and they will be punished.'

Everything the museum stood for seemed to have gone up in flames with the book. Its destruction added to the rumours already circulating about the Dark Flame. If ordinary magical households were concerned before, now they were really frightened.

What made matters worse for those inside the museum was that the act of vandalism appeared to have been carried out by one of their own number. There were no reports of an intruder getting inside the museum which suggested that Hawke was right and there was a traitor in their midst.

Archie blamed himself for what had happened. By consulting *The Book of Yore* he had forced the traitor's hand. And he wasn't the only one who thought it. Some of the other apprentices were whispering behind his back.

When he passed Enid Drew in the Great Gallery he heard her say to Peter Quiggley pointedly, 'If a certain person hadn't poked his nose in, *The Book of Prophecy* would still be safe. Some people don't know when to leave well alone!'

15

Back to the Asylum

The end of May brought damp weather and a general feeling of melancholy.

Summer still seemed a long way off. The air was chilly. Almost a week had passed since *The Book of Prophecy* had been destroyed and Archie was making his way to Lost Books one morning when Faustus Gaunt intercepted him.

'Archie, can I have a quick word,' he said, steering him to one side, his expression serious. 'You mustn't take the destruction of *The Book of Prophecy* personally. It wasn't your fault.'

'Hawke thinks it was,' said Archie.

'Yes, well, Gideon has his reasons. He's taken the loss of *The Book of Prophecy* badly. Consulting it was always a last resort for him. But it was an option if all else failed. Now, well . . .' His voice trailed off.

Archie felt terrible. 'So it is all my fault,' he said. 'I shouldn't have acted without discussing it with him.'

Gaunt twitched an eyebrow. 'You acted rashly,' he agreed. 'But what's done is done and can't be undone. And besides, you didn't destroy the book, someone else did – someone inside the museum,' he added, grimly. 'I think that's what has upset Gideon more than anything else. He feels the museum has been betrayed. Of course, it doesn't help that he's not been taking his medication. Gideon is very gifted magically, but he's also very highly strung. Magically talented people often are. There have been a couple of . . .' He paused, picking his words carefully, '. . . incidents in the past.'

'Incidents?' asked Archie. He waited for Gaunt to explain.

'Yes. On a couple of occasions Gideon used magic outside of magical premises and the authorities found out about it. It's on his record and it looks bad. The Magical League takes a very dim view of such things. And there have been other . . . episodes. The last time was thirteen years ago, just before the first Greader plot. Gideon got it into his head that someone was trying to poison him. It was nonsense, of course, but he spent

187

some time at the asylum. They calmed him down and helped him understand that he was being paranoid. He's been absolutely fine since then. It's not a problem as long as he takes his medication!'

'And the medication – what's in it?' asked Archie suspiciously. Hawke didn't seem the sort of person who would imagine things. If he thought someone was trying to poison him then Archie was inclined to believe him.

'It's all natural magic,' Gaunt replied, 'a calming tonic that Motley Brown mixes for him. Personally, I favour something stronger,' he added, with a wry smile. 'But the way Gideon has been behaving lately, I'd say he's not taking it as regularly as he should.'

Hawke could be a bit intense sometimes, but Archie liked him. He found it hard to believe that he was dangerous. It all sounded very suspicious to him. Was Hawke really ill or was it another attempt by the Magical League to blame him for the disappearance of *The Book of Night*?

Gaunt saw the disbelief on his face. 'Archie, your loyalty is commendable. Gideon is a great man, but he has his flaws like everyone else. You must see that. And that's why the museum has been forced to take the steps that it has.'

Archie gazed at him uncomprehendingly. Gaunt continued. 'Gideon's behaviour has been erratic of late. It could indicate that his judgement is impaired. Under the circumstances, we had to report our suspicions that he wasn't taking his medication. And it was inevitable that the Magical League would want to investigate.'

Archie was still not getting his point. But at that moment it became crystal clear. Striding towards them was the imposing figure of Uther Morgred, the Magical League's chief enforcer.

Morgred was dressed in black with a long leather coat trimmed with black fur. His face looked even more severe in person than it had in the oculus, if that was possible. His dark eyes glared at anyone who came into his field of vision.

'Ah, Uther,' said Gaunt. 'I trust that you have all you need?'

Morgred's eyes flashed. 'I have just come from the Scriptorium,' he said. 'Frankly, I am astonished at the lack of security. I understand that the room was left unlocked and that some of the apprentices have been allowed to dabble with writing magic?'

Archie was about to protest but one look from Gaunt silenced him. He knew that the museum elders hadn't informed the Magical League about the Alchemists' Club rewriting the magical books. He wondered why. Perhaps the museum elders thought the authorities would try to stop them. From what Archie had seen, they were probably right. The Magical League seemed more concerned with suppressing magic than restoring it.

'Who told you that?' asked Gaunt, twitching his other eyebrow.

'Dr Brown, the head of Natural Magic, informed me,' said Morgred. 'He also tells me that dangerous magical materials and creatures have disappeared from the mythical menagerie.'

Both Gaunt's eyebrows twitched. 'Snufflings are hardly dangerous, Uther.'

'But salamander blood could be!' said Morgred, his dark eyes boring into Gaunt. 'I understand that one escaped and was on the loose for a while.'

The head of Mortal Magic looked awkward. 'Yes, well, that's a different matter. But I don't see what any of that has to do with *The Book of Prophecy*?'

'Lax security. Sloppy supervision,' said Morgred, and Archie detected his voice had turned even colder. 'It's part of a pattern – an accident waiting to happen. And now it's happened. First *The Book of Night* is stolen and now an irreplaceable Book of Destiny has been destroyed. Both happened on Hawke's watch. It makes you wonder whose side he's on!'

Archie felt himself flush with anger. 'Hold on a minute, that's not fair!' he exclaimed. 'It wasn't Hawke's fault, it was . . .'

Gaunt glared at him. He managed to bite his tongue.

'The boy is right, Uther. You are jumping to conclusions,' Gaunt said. 'If the Royal Society hadn't kept *The Book of Night* secret all these years it would still be safe.'

'Would it?' demanded Morgred. 'Even if *The Book of Night* had been brought to the museum, from what I've seen it would have been at risk here. And now *The Book of Prophecy* has been destroyed! You can't blame that on anyone else.'

His eyes bored into Gaunt's. 'I will get to the bottom of this even if I have to tear the museum down one book at a time to get to the truth.'

'But that's ridiculous,' said Gaunt. 'It's obvious that someone has managed to infiltrate the museum ...' His voice trailed off as he realised the implications of what he'd just said. The magic enforcer seized on his words.

'So you agree that there is a traitor inside the museum? It's just as I suspected. Well, when I find them they'll wish that they'd never been born. And make no mistake about it, I will find them. There will be a full investigation and Gideon Hawke's name is at the top of my list of suspects.'

With a final hard stare, he turned and strode back towards the Great Gallery leaving Gaunt speechless.

*

After what Gaunt had said about his medication, Archie watched Hawke closely for the next few days. There was no sign of the green medicine bottle so Archie assumed he wasn't taking it any more.

And the head of Lost Books was definitely not his usual self. His appearance reflected his state of mind. He looked more dishevelled than normal. Archie wondered if he knew that Morgred suspected him. If he did, he didn't show any signs of slowing down. He spent most of his time in the archive poring over ancient texts.

'Archie,' he said one day, doing his best to compose his face into a smile. 'I think it's time we found out what's really going on at the Royal Society of Magic. But first we need to pay a visit to the asylum.'

Archie looked up. Perhaps Hawke realised he needed help. Perhaps he was going to ask for some stronger medication. But Hawke's next statement suggested otherwise.

'Katerina Krone is there,' he said. 'She is recovered enough from the *Grimoire*'s spell to be able to speak. She was part of the last plot so she might have knowledge of this one.'

So he wasn't going to the asylum on his own account. He thought Katerina might have information about the Dark Flame. It seemed to Archie that Hawke was clutching at straws. Perhaps he really had lost the plot. All that Archie could do was keep his eyes and ears open for clues.

The next day, Hawke and Archie caught the train to London, and then a bus before walking the last part of the journey to the asylum. Archie found himself gazing at the red-brick building with its spiky iron railings outside. He looked up at the bars on the windows.

He had been here once before with Hawke. On their previous visit they had come to question Arthur Ripley to find out what he knew about the Alchemists' Curse. Shortly after that, Ripley had escaped from the asylum and he was still on the run.

Archie wondered whether they were wasting their time. The last he'd seen of Katerina Krone she'd been under the *Grimoire's* curse and completely spellbound – frozen like a statue, unable to move or speak. He doubted whether she would be much different now. Even if she was, what could she possibly tell them?

The sign on the door read: THE ASYLUM. RESPITE FOR THE MAGICALLY ILL.

Hawke grasped the large brass doorknocker and

knocked three times. A small hatch slid open and two eyes peered out.

'Gideon?' said a surprised voice. 'We weren't expecting you!'

'Good morning, Rumold. I took the liberty of dropping by without an appointment,' said Hawke.

Rumold seemed momentarily at a loss, but then he recovered himself.

'Of course, Gideon. We are always pleased to see you. Whatever the circumstances . . .'

The door opened and Rumold stood in the doorway. He was a tall man with iron-grey hair. On his previous visit, Archie had wondered how the two men knew each other. Thanks to Gaunt, he now knew the answer. Hawke had once been an inmate at the asylum.

'Ah, and I see you have brought young Archie Greene with you again,' said Rumold, his eyes alighting on Archie.

'Is it for yourself that you've come to see us? Or perhaps Archie is in need of our help? I understand that it was because of him that *The Book of Prophecy* was destroyed?'

Archie felt a momentary panic. Was this some sort of trick? Had Hawke brought him here under false pretences as a punishment?

'Nonsense,' said Hawke. 'I trust the boy

completely. I have never doubted him and he has no reason to doubt himself.'

So he didn't blame Archie for the loss of *The Book of Prophecy* after all. That was a relief.

'We have come on another matter entirely,' continued Hawke. 'I would like to see one of your ... patients. Katerina Krone. I understand that she's sufficiently recovered to talk?'

'Katerina is making good progress,' said Rumold in a guarded voice. 'I'm not sure that it would be helpful for her to see you, though. It might prove too much of a shock and set her recovery back.'

'I'm afraid I'm going to have to insist,' said Hawke, his eyes narrowing. 'I believe she may have important information concerning the Dark Flame.'

Archie thought that some of the friendliness had gone from his voice. He sounded curt, almost dismissive. Rumold noticed it, too.

'Are you all right, Gideon?' he asked solicitously. 'You don't seem yourself. Have you been taking your medication?'

'I am absolutely fine,' said Hawke. 'And now if you don't mind I would like to see Katerina.

'I'm under strict instructions that she's not to see anyone,' said Rumold, holding out his hands apologetically and blocking the doorway.

'From whom?'

'From the Magical League,' said Rumold.

Hawke's brow clouded. 'But I am the head of Lost Books at the Museum of Magical Miscellany and this investigation concerns the disappearance of a very dangerous book. So I believe, in this instance, I have authority over the Magical League.'

A look of irritation flickered on Rumold's face. 'Well, yes, I suppose so,' he muttered. 'Look – there's no reason for us to fall out over this. Why don't you come back tomorrow when I've had a chance to clear it with them?'

'There's no time for that,' snapped Hawke. 'Take me to Katerina or I will find the way myself!'

Archie was shocked at the change in Hawke's manner. He'd always been so polite before, but now there was a real edge to his voice. His eyes bored into Rumold's like a challenge. The two men glared at each other for a moment and then Hawke said, 'Step aside, Rumold. You are out of your depth.'

Rumold's eyes flared. He spoke slowly as if it took all his concentration to control his anger. 'It is you who is out of his depth, Gideon. You are out of order. When the Magical League hears about this they will not let it go unpunished.'

Hawke shrugged. 'I'll take that chance,' he said. 'There's too much at stake here to let them bully me out of doing my job. Now are you going to step aside or will I have to move you?'

An angry scowl momentarily flashed across Rumold's face, but then he replaced it with a thin smile. 'Very well, Gideon. But you must face the consequences of your actions.'

He threw the door open and they stepped into a large, white hallway. 'Follow me,' he said, leading them through another door and along a white corridor.

Archie and Hawke did as he said. 'Are you sure about this?' Archie whispered as they fell into step behind Rumold. Hawke gave him the faintest of smiles. 'Yes,' he said. 'I have never been more sure.'

Archie studied Hawke. He realised he didn't even know where the head of Lost Books had trained. Old Zeb had said that it must have been at one of the magical academies because the old bookbinder hadn't taught him. Archie wondered which academy. Could it have been in Prague, the same academy as Katerina?

They followed Rumold through a maze of identical-looking corridors. Archie could hear the sounds of inmates moving around in their cells or shouting out. The place made him feel uneasy. He tried to imagine what it would be like to be shut up in one of the small rooms with no way out.

They passed the cell where Arthur Ripley had

been locked up. It was deep inside the building and Archie wondered how Ripley had managed to escape from such a secure place. When he mentioned this to Hawke, the head of Lost Books nodded.

'That's what I keep asking myself,' he said in a low voice. 'And the answer I keep coming back to is that he must have had some help.'

He glanced at Rumold walking in front of them. Archie nodded. Hawke's actions were beginning to make some sort of sense. If he suspected that someone inside the asylum had helped Ripley escape, that would explain his impatience with Rumold. On the other hand, if Hawke wasn't taking his medication then that could also explain his paranoia . . .

Archie gave Hawke a sideways glance. He preferred to believe the first explanation. He trusted Hawke and although his behaviour was a little odd of late, Archie had no grounds to doubt him. Not yet anyway. And until he did, Archie would remain loyal.

Finally they turned into an isolated corridor and Rumold unlocked a thick iron door. He showed them into a room with a table and two chairs. There were no windows.

'Wait here and I will get Katerina,' he said. He turned abruptly and closed the door behind them.

Archie heard the sound of a key being turned in the lock. He saw Hawke flinch and felt his own heart start to beat faster.

Hawke's eyes were roving all around, as if he was fighting to stay in control. Archie was relieved to hear the sound of halting footsteps in the corridor outside and then the sound of a key being turned in the lock. The heavy iron door swung open and Katerina stood in the doorway. She was thinner than Archie remembered and her flowing auburn hair had been cut short.

'You have visitors,' Rumold said, ushering her towards one of the chairs. Katerina stared ahead blankly. She stumbled forward.

Her once piercing blue eyes were dull and she moved slowly as if she was drugged. But she still looked a lot better than the last time Archie had seen her. Then, she'd been frozen like a statue.

Katerina sat in the chair, her elbows on the table, wringing her hands constantly as if she was washing them. Archie noticed that she did this for almost the entire interview.

'Thank you, Rumold,' Hawke said, dismissing him.

Rumold closed the door with a loud clang and the key turned in the lock. Archie could sense that Rumold was still there, watching them through the grille.

'Hello, Katerina,' Hawke said gently, sitting in the other chair. 'Do you remember who I am?'

Katerina flicked her eyes at him and looked away. She nodded.

'And do you remember Archie?' Hawke asked.

Again she flicked her eyes and nodded. This time Archie thought he detected some other emotion. He couldn't be sure what it was. Was it fear, or anger perhaps?

Hawke was speaking again. 'It's good to see that you are recovering from the *Grimoire*'s curse,' he said. 'Perhaps there is hope for all those the book cursed.'

Katerina stared at him with lustreless eyes.

'I want to ask you about something,' Hawke continued, his voice still gentle but more urgent. 'We know that you exchanged letters with Arthur Ripley. He was the one who told you about the *Grimoire* being in the Darchive at the Museum of Magical Miscellany, wasn't he?'

Archie knew it was true because Katerina had told him so herself. She nodded. So she remembered what had happened.

'Good,' said Hawke. 'What else do you remember about Arthur Ripley's plans? What was meant to happen once you had the *Grimoire* in your possession?'

'I was to inherit Hecate's powers,' said Katerina.

Her voice was flat and lacking vitality, but she spoke clearly.

'And what was Ripley's part in all this?' asked Hawke. 'What did he want from you?'

'Ripley wanted a darchemist,' said Katerina. 'He had big plans for a dark magic writer.' Her glassy eyes stared straight ahead.

'What plans?' asked Hawke.

Silence.

'Katerina, what was Ripley going to do with a darchemist?'

Katerina stopped wringing her hands for a second. Her eyes shone with a sudden intensity. 'Rewrite *The Opus Magus*, of course!' she said in a mocking voice that reminded Archie of the *Grimoire*. She threw back her head and laughed manically. 'That's been his plan all along!

'Welcome to the dark age of magic!' she screeched. 'And there's nothing that any of you can do to stop it. Only Fabian Grey can do that, and he's dead! And Archie Greene doesn't even know about his part.'

'What part?' exclaimed Archie. 'What are you talking about?'

A smile flickered across Katerina's lips. 'See,' she said, her eyes shining with malice. 'He doesn't know.' She looked at Hawke. 'And you don't know either.'

Katerina's eyes smouldered with madness, and a secret. 'My ancestor Felicia Nightshade said that when Grey escaped from *The Book of Prophecy* he was babbling like a madman. Most of what he said made no sense but he kept repeating the same phrase: "Only the Greys can save magic." Plural, you see – more than one Grey!'

Archie stared in bewilderment. 'But I was born three hundred and fifty years later!'

'Yes,' said Katerina, 'but your fate and Fabian Grey's are connected. Whatever Grey saw in *The Book of Prophecy*, it involves you as well!'

Archie stared at her in shock. His heart was pounding. Was this the final part of his forked fate? Was he supposed to save magic by defeating the Dark Flame in place of Grey? He felt light-headed.

The iron door opened and Rumold was in the room. He seized Katerina by the shoulders and shook her.

'That's enough,' he cried. 'Drink this.'

He held a flask to her full lips and Katerina drank from it, and immediately calmed down. She started to wring her hands again. Fast to begin with but slowing as the potion took effect until she sat quietly clasping her hands together as if one might comfort the other.

'You have upset her, Gideon,' Rumold

reprimanded. 'You shouldn't have asked about Ripley. Her mind is too fragile. She doesn't know what she is saying.'

Hawke glared at him. 'But I disagree, Rumold. I think she knows exactly what she's saying.'

Before Rumold could stop him, Hawke snatched Katerina's right hand in his and turned the palm to face him. Archie gasped. There was a black firemark on it: the Black Dragon.

'Another one who has taken the Dark Oath,' said Hawke. 'I wonder how many more are in this building.'

Rumold glanced at the door as if he was expecting someone. The door remained closed. Hawke didn't seem to have noticed. He fixed Rumold with a stare and his mismatched eyes bored into him with such intensity that Archie worried that the head of Lost Books might have lost control.

Rumold swallowed hard. His eyes flicked to the door again. Just then it opened and a tall, gaunt man entered the room.

'Gideon, I understand you've been distressing the patients,' he said in his cold voice with an undercurrent of menace.

Hawke swung around in his chair. 'Uther,' he said. 'What an unpleasant surprise.' His eyes returned to Rumold's face. 'So you called in reinforcements. I might have guessed you would.'

Rumold shrugged. 'It's for your own good, Gideon. You are confused. You haven't been taking your medication. We cannot allow you to leave like this.'

At a nod from Morgred, two burly men in white coats stepped into the room and stood on either side of Hawke.

Morgred gave a thin smile. 'Gideon Hawke,' he said, 'I am relieving you of your duties as head of Lost Books, with immediate effect.'

For a moment Archie thought that Hawke was going to resist, but he saw a look of resignation in his eyes.

'Very well, Uther,' he said, wearily. 'If that is what the Magical League orders, I will return to Oxford and pack my things.'

Morgred glanced at Rumold, who shook his head once.

'That won't be possible, Gideon,' Rumold said, the self-assurance returning to his voice. 'It will be better for you to spend some time here. That way we can monitor your progress. We want to help you.'

Hawke's brow furrowed. 'I see I have no choice,' he muttered. 'Very well, can I have my old room then?' he asked. 'The one with the window so I can see the birds?'

Rumold nodded. 'If it pleases you, Gideon, then yes.'

Hawke gave a thin-lipped smile. His eyes narrowed as if he was trying to calculate something. 'And what about Archie?' he said. 'I hope that he'll be allowed to continue his apprenticeship at the museum.'

Morgred nodded. 'Yes, the boy will be allowed to continue with his work.'

Archie felt a mixture of relief that he was free to leave and carry on with his apprenticeship, and alarm for Hawke who would have to remain at the asylum. He felt a sudden panic. Had he allowed Hawke's paranoia to cloud his own judgment? Whose side was Hawke really on?

He felt Morgred's hand on his shoulder.

'Come along, Archie. Gideon needs to get some rest.'

The magical enforcer steered Archie towards the door, but as he passed him Hawke caught his arm.

'May I give my apprentice a final piece of advice?' he asked.

'Very well,' Morgred said. 'But make it brief.'

'Thank you, Uther,' said Hawke. 'Very thoughtful of you.' He leaned forward and whispered into Archie's ear so that the others couldn't hear him.

'Remember the Torchstones.'

Aloud he said, 'Keep practising the delving spells I showed you. You're making excellent progress.'

Archie gazed at him quizzically. Hawke's eyes looked tired but he managed a thin smile and a wink.

'And Archie – trust no one.'

It was with a heavy heart that Archie caught the train back to Oxford. He felt deeply sad for Hawke, but when he thought about it, he realised that Hawke's erratic behaviour had started earlier, when *The Book of Night* was stolen.

He tried to convince himself that Hawke would be looked after in the asylum, but he couldn't shift a nagging feeling that something was very wrong. He didn't trust Rumold or Morgred. If someone wanted to get Hawke out of the way, this was a very convenient way to do it.

Archie got off the train and headed home. He wondered what was really going on. It seemed like some sort of power struggle was occurring in the magical realm. One thing seemed certain: with Hawke gone, the Alchemists' Club would have to discover what Grey saw on their own.

Back at the Foxes', Loretta was distraught to hear the news about Hawke.

'He's been under enormous pressure. It must have been too much for him. That's the price you pay for magical ability like his!' she exclaimed, and then burst into tears.

'There, there,' consoled Woodbine.

'I can't believe they've done this. Relieved him of his duties at the very time we need him most!' sniffed Loretta.

'Did Morgred say who would be taking his place as head of Lost Books?' asked Woodbine.

Archie shook his head.

'They'll have to appoint someone in the next couple of days,' said Woodbine. 'It will be one of the museum elders I imagine.' He looked grim.

16

Mixed Messages

The next morning, Archie called an emergency meeting of the Alchemists' Club. Rupert was in London but the others agreed to meet in the usual place later that evening.

When Archie arrived at the laboratory he spotted the message on the bench immediately. It was in a white envelope as before and in the same firm handwriting. But this time it was addressed to Archie Greene care of the Alchemists' Club. He opened it and read the note inside.

Gideon is as sane as you or I. Someone wanted him out of the way. You must tread carefully. With Hawke gone, the museum is no longer safe for you and your friends. The enemy has spies inside the museum and at the Royal Society.

The Dark Flame is rising. The fate of magic is at stake. I will help you if I can, but you must help yourselves now.

FG

Archie stared at the message. Once again it was signed FG with a picture of a raven. Whoever had sent it obviously knew all about Grey's secret laboratory and about the Alchemists' Club. Archie wondered again if it could be Fabian Grey himself trying to help them.

When the others arrived he showed them the note and Arabella echoed his thoughts.

'I know this sounds ridiculous,' she said, 'but could it be Fabian Grey? Is it possible that he's still alive after more than three hundred and fifty years?'

'Grey would know about the laboratory, so that part makes sense,' reasoned Thistle. 'But realistically my money is on Faustus Gaunt. The messages started at about the same time that he arrived at the museum.'

'But why all the secrecy?' asked Archie.

'Perhaps he thinks he's being watched?' said Thistle.

'We have to get a message to Rupert,' said Bramble. 'We need to warn him. He may not be safe at the Royal Society.'

But as it turned out, Rupert was trying to get a message to them.

The next day, Archie was in Hawke's study tidying up when he noticed that the oculus was glowing with an eerie orange light. Approaching the desk, he peered into the glass orb. He was surprised to see Rupert's earnest face looking back at him. His hair was standing up and he looked a little more dishevelled than usual.

'Hello, is that you, Archie?'

'Yes, it's me,' said Archie. 'But how did you know I'd be here?'

'I didn't,' said Rupert, smiling. 'I heard what happened to Hawke. Everyone at the Royal Society is talking about it. I needed to get hold of you so I thought I'd take a chance.'

'Well, it worked. But we can't talk for long – someone could be listening on one of the other oculuses.'

'Oculi,' said Rupert. 'When there's more than one oculus, the plural is oculi.'

Archie smiled. 'Well, someone could be listening on the other oculi. So what did you want to tell me?'

'Yeah, right, good point,' said Rupert, glancing over his shoulder. 'Well, the thing is, I think there's something going on here at the Royal Society. The other day Gloom hinted that the stolen book wasn't the only secret kept here.'

Archie felt his curiosity growing. 'What do you mean? What kind of secrets?'

Archie saw Rupert glance over his shoulder again as if he was worried he might be overheard. Then he leaned in closer so that the glass magnified his features, making his nose look big and his lips seem extra thick.

'I think there's a secret library hidden inside the Royal Society,' he whispered. 'There's a reading room here with one door and no windows, and the other day I saw Gloom go into it, but when I followed him he wasn't there. He'd vanished.'

'He can't have vanished,' said Archie, his eyes wide. He remembered now that Gloom had mentioned some other books being kept at the Royal Society when he'd overheard him talking to Hawke.

'That's what I thought,' said Rupert, 'but he definitely wasn't in the room. He reappeared a little while later carrying an old book under his arm. My guess is that there's a secret entrance into another room. And that's where *The Book of Night* was being kept.'

Archie was catching on fast. 'So there could be other secrets stored in there as well,' he said. 'Morag Pandrama said there were other magical archives as well as the one at the museum. Perhaps the secret library at the Royal Society contains the book in which Fabian Grey wrote down what he saw?'

'The only way we're going to know is if we can get in there and have a look for ourselves,' said Rupert.

Archie's brain was working overtime. The latest note from FG had warned them about spies inside the Royal Society. Hawke had had his suspicions, too. It was time to find out what was really going on at the Royal Society, he'd said. That was what he was planning to do after he'd visited Katerina in the asylum. But he never got the chance.

'Can you get us inside the Royal Society?' asked Archie.

Rupert nodded. 'Yes, that's actually easy enough. But then what, once you're inside?'

'If you can get us into the reading room, then we can use Thistle's curiosity compass to locate the secret entrance. If there are magic books concealed there, the compass will pick up on their power.'

Rupert ran his hand through his hair. 'All right,'

he said. 'I'll find a way. Can you come down to London tomorrow night?'

Archie nodded. 'We'll be there,' he said. He had another thought. He realised he didn't actually know where in London the Royal Society was. 'You'd better tell us where the entrance is.'

'Oh, that's easy,' said Rupert. 'It's opposite the British Museum in Great Russell Street. There's an antiquarian bookshop called the Inkwell. The entrance to the Royal Society is inside the bookshop. Just tell Matilda the password.'

Archie raised his eyebrows. 'Password?'

'Oh, don't worry, it's easy. It'll be written on the blackboard. And make sure you come at seven because everyone will be at dinner so we'll have the place to ourselves.'

Archie grinned. 'Good, that's a plan then. I can't wait to tell the others. And Rupert . . .'

Rupert's chiselled features peered back at him from the oculus. 'What?'

'Be careful,' said Archie. 'There are spies inside the Royal Society. If they find out you're spying on them it could be dangerous for you.'

'Spying on the spies, eh?' grinned Rupert. 'Don't worry, they won't suspect a thing. I'm too careful for that.'

Archie hoped Rupert was right. But he knew that his friend had already taken a big risk by contacting him with the oculus. Perhaps he'd be more careful from now on.

When Archie told his cousins about the plan to go to the Royal Society they were as excited as he was. Bramble and Thistle both agreed that if there was a secret library there then they had to investigate. But Arabella had reservations.

'What if we get caught breaking into the Royal Society?' she said. 'We could get expelled from the museum and have our apprenticeships revoked.'

'It's a risk we have to take,' said Archie. 'Time is running out – and besides, we're not breaking in, we're visiting Rupert. But first there's something we need to do in the archive.'

Archie approached the glass case containing the Torchstones. Bramble and Arabella were just behind him. Thistle was acting as lookout by the door.

'I've never seen them before,' said Bramble, looking over Archie's shoulder. 'They're beautiful!'

Archie opened the case and carefully grasped one of the golden orbs. It was cold to his touch. He could feel its magical energy sending a tingling sensation up his arm. The two protective bands of silver gleamed in the light from the overhead lanterns.

'What happens if someone realises there's one

missing?' asked Arabella, gazing at the Torchstone in his hand.

Archie shrugged. 'The only people who come in here are Hawke, Gaunt and Pandrama,' he said. 'Hawke's locked up in the asylum and I think he would approve anyway, and the other two are far too interested in the texts to notice.'

'What about Rusp?' asked Thistle. 'You said he has been helping out. He has it in for you. He'd love to get you into trouble.'

'That's true,' said Archie. 'But it's a chance I'll have to take. As long as he doesn't catch us red-handed. Now, come on.'

He slipped the Torchstone into his pocket and headed back towards the door followed by Arabella. Bramble was still gazing at the second Torchstone in the case.

'Hurry up, Bram!' urged Archie over his shoulder. 'We don't want to be caught in the act.'

'I'm right behind you,' called Bramble. 'We can't afford to leave any obvious clues that Rusp might notice.'

Archie opened the door and the two boys and Arabella slipped out.

Bramble appeared a moment later.

'All done,' she said, smiling.

'Good, now let's get to the Word Smithy.'

*

When they reached the Aisle of White, the bookshop was closed up for the night. Archie let them in with his key and they made their way down to the mending workshop.

Old Zeb used a glove when handling the Word Smithy. It was on the bench so Archie slipped it on and opened the door. The Flame of Pharos was burning low.

'It doesn't look very healthy,' said Bramble, peering into the furnace.

'I know. It's been like that for a while,' said Archie. 'Even more reason to activate the Torchstone.'

He held the egg-shaped object between the thumb and forefinger, as Hawke had done, and gently squeezed. The case sprang open to reveal the hidden chamber within. Bramble gasped with delight.

Archie reached inside the Word Smithy with his gloved hand and took out a glowing ember. Very carefully he tipped the embers into the hollow compartment. Then he recited the spell engraved on the silver casing.

'I carry the flame
To light the dark
Let shadows flee
My sacred spark.'

As he did, the two halves of the Torchstone snapped shut. It felt suddenly warm in his hand and the amber-coloured crystal gave off a golden glow.

All four of them gazed at it for a moment and then Archie slipped it back into his pocket where it nestled warmly against his leg.

'Right, let's get of here,' he said.

Arabella moved to open the door to the workshop and she and Thistle stepped out into the passageway.

Bramble was still staring at the Flame of Pharos in the Word Smithy.

'Come on,' said Archie. He was used to seeing the Flame every day. But he knew how mesmerising it was to watch. He took off the glove and gave it to Bramble.

'Don't forget to close the furnace,' he said gently.

17

The Royal Society

The following day, Archie, Bramble, Thistle and Arabella went to the museum as usual. No announcement had been made about who was taking over from Gideon Hawke in Lost Books so Archie didn't have much to do.

He tidied Hawke's office again, but the room remained stubbornly messy. It was almost as if there was an anti-tidy spell on it. That would have been just like Hawke, Archie thought, and he smiled at the idea. He wondered how the former head of Lost Books was getting on at the asylum. For all its clutter, the office seemed empty without him.

Archie moped around the rest of the day, staying out of the way of Pandrama and Gaunt, and especially Rusp, who were still poring over the old texts. He was relieved that none of them noticed that one of the Torchstones was missing.

At five, Archie met up with his two cousins and Arabella, and they made their way to Oxford train station to catch the five-thirty to Paddington station in London. From there they caught the tube to Holborn and walked the short distance to Great Russell Street.

Ahead of them, on the right, they could see a huge building set back into a large courtyard.

'That's the British Museum,' said Archie. 'The bookshop is up here somewhere on the left,' he added, indicating a row of buildings on the other side of the road. 'We just have to find it.'

'What's the name again?' asked Thistle.

'The Inkwell,' replied Archie. 'Rupert said we have to tell Matilda the password. It'll be written on a blackboard.'

'Not much of a password then!' said Bramble. 'Who's Matilda anyway?'

Archie shrugged. 'No idea, but I'm sure it will all make sense when we get there.'

'I hope so,' said Arabella. 'Otherwise we've had a wasted journey!'

Just then there was a cry from Thistle who was walking ahead.

'Look!' he cried. 'Here it is.'

He was pointing excitedly at a brass sign on the door of a dingy, rundown building. It was dull from many years of London weather and the writing was hard to read, but they could still make out the words.

The Inkwell
Antiquarian Books
Established 1666

'This is it all right,' said Archie.

The paint on the door was battleship grey and peeling. It didn't look very encouraging. Archie stood back to examine the bookshop. It was built of sandstone that had been eaten away by traffic fumes and other pollution, leaving black stains in the crevices. The shop windows on either side of the door had faded red curtains drawn across and the glass looked like it hadn't been cleaned in years.

'It looks a bit rundown,' said Bramble.

'Just a little,' scoffed Arabella, turning up her nose. 'What a dump! You could walk straight past it and not even notice it's here.'

'We almost did!' agreed Archie. 'It was only Thistle's sharp eyes that spotted it. How *did* you spot it, by the way?'

'It was the peeling paint on the door,' Thistle said, grinning. 'It reminded me of home!'

'Well, I suppose we'd better go in,' said Archie, a note of reluctance in his voice. It had seemed so simple when Rupert had suggested it, but now that they were actually here he wasn't so sure. What if this Matilda person wouldn't let them in? What if she reported them to the magical authorities?

But Archie knew there was no going back. There was no sign of a doorbell, so he pushed on the door. To his surprise it swung open and the four of them slipped inside.

They found themselves in a large, dark room. The light from outside struggled to get past the dirty windows and curtains. The only illumination came from some flickering gas lamps that smelled faintly of paraffin. The carpets were threadbare with the occasional rip that had been repaired with black tape.

The Inkwell didn't look like any bookshop Archie had ever seen before. It was even stranger than the Aisle of White, and that was saying something! The floor was littered with piles of old books and stacks of yellowing newspapers.

Thistle raised his eyebrows. 'It seems a little dated,' he whispered.

Archie glimpsed the front page of the newspaper on the top of the pile. 'Titanic Sinks On Maiden Voyage,' it read. It was dated 15th April 1912.

'Just a little!' he agreed, smiling.

On the far side of the room a desk barred their way. As they approached it they could hear something: *Click! Click! Clickety-click! Click! Click! Clickety-click!*

A croaky voice accompanied the clicking sounds. 'Knit one, purl one, drop one. Knit one, purl one, drop one. Knit one . . .'

The four children looked at each other with wide eyes.

'What on earth is that?' Bramble mouthed.

'I don't know!' Archie mouthed back.

Just then the clicking and the counting both stopped and the voice said, 'I can lip-read, you know.'

Sitting behind the desk was a very old woman. They hadn't noticed her before because her dark clothes were camouflaged by the gloom. Now that they were closer they could see that she was dressed from head to foot in black. She wore a starched lace collar that came up to her chin. Her hair was grey and covered by a lace bonnet. She looked like she had stepped straight out of a Victorian photograph.

Hanging on the wall behind her was a blackboard with what looked like the menu of the day.

'What do you want?' she asked. 'I'd like to get back to my knitting, you see. Are you lost?'

'Erm ... no,' said Archie, stepping forward. 'We've come to see Rupert Trevallan.'

'Young Master Rupert?' the old woman said with a note of surprise. Her face was small and deeply lined. It resembled a shelled walnut.

'And you're Matilda?' Archie guessed.

'Yes,' said the old woman suspiciously. 'Well, this is most irregular. Young Master Rupert doesn't usually have visitors. Have you got an appointment?'

'Not really an appointment as such,' said Archie, unsure what to say to this. 'But he is expecting us.'

'No appointment?' said the old woman. 'That is *most* irregular.'

Archie tried to give her a confident smile, but his smile got stuck in his teeth.

'No appointment!' the old woman said again. She thought about this for a moment, and then plucked a feathered quill from an inkwell and began to write in a large leather-bound book on her desk.

'Name?'

'Archie Greene.'

The old receptionist scratched down the words in the book.

'And this is Bramble and Thistle Foxe. And Arabella Ripley.'

Matilda gave them a cursory glance and recorded their names as well.

'Password?'

Archie looked around for inspiration. Rupert had said the password would be on a blackboard, but the only blackboard he could see was the one with the menu on it. He glanced at the dishes of the day.

'Parsnip soup?' he said hopefully, reading out the first thing that caught his eye.

Matilda shook her head firmly.

Archie tried again. 'Beef Wellington?'

Again she shook her head, an exasperated look on her face.

Archie tried one last time. 'Treacle pudding?'

The old receptionist nodded. 'Welcome to the Royal Society of Magic,' she said. 'Follow me.'

Rupert's office was a scene of devastation. There were pieces of paper and books everywhere. Filing cabinets had been left half open, with files spilling out onto the floor. There were boxes of documents stacked precariously on top of each other.

In the midst of this confusion, two feet were parked on the desk. Rupert was slumped in a chair with his feet up.

Matilda put her head round the corner.

'Master Rupert?' she said. 'Your visitors are here!'

Rupert swung his feet off the desk and sat bolt upright.

'Archie!' he cried. 'Bramble, Thistle, Arabella. He leaped from his chair and shook each of them energetically by the hand. 'I'm so glad to see you.'

Then he caught sight of the ancient receptionist hovering in the background.

'Thank you, Matilda,' he said. 'You can get back to your knitting ... er ... I mean back to your work.'

The old woman seemed reluctant to go. 'Should I let Mr Gloom know that you have visitors?' she asked.

'No, no, that won't be necessary,' said Rupert. 'Thank you, Matilda. I wouldn't want to put you to any trouble.'

'But Mr Gloom gave strict instructions that he wanted to be kept informed about any visitors, after, well, you know what ...' Matilda said.

'Yes, well, he's only just got back from his trip. He'll be at dinner now. It is treacle pudding, after all!'

Rupert flashed her his most charming smile. 'And Matilda, make sure you get some this time,' he said kindly. 'Can't have you missing out on pudding again!'

Matilda gave him a grateful look. 'Thank you, Mr Rupert. I wish everyone was as thoughtful as you.'

She retreated back along the corridor.

Rupert undid his top button and loosened his collar. He beckoned his four visitors into the cramped office, pushing several piles of documents onto the threadbare carpet to make space.

'Come in, come in,' he said, smiling. 'Sit down. Make yourselves comfortable. Don't mind Matilda – she's been here a long time, virtually part of the furniture.'

'We can see that,' said Thistle. 'She must be a hundred if she's a day.'

The four other members of the Alchemists' Club shuffled awkwardly into the room.

Now that they came to look at him properly, they could see that Rupert was very dishevelled. Gone was the neat and tidy boy they remembered as an apprentice. His jacket hung limply on the back of his chair and his shirt was a disaster zone. It was creased, had two buttons missing and what looked like coffee stains all down the front. His shoes were scuffed and undone.

'You look . . .'

'Yes . . .?' Rupert said.

'Tired,' Archie said, diplomatically.

'Well . . . I've had a lot on,' said Rupert. 'I've been researching the properties of different magical creatures. Well, their blood actually. Motley Brown told Gloom there was a way to make azoth from the blood of the larger magical creatures, dragons and griffins and so on. That's why I'm here. The supply of azoth is running very low, you see, so we need to find an alternative source.'

'Griffin blood?' said Archie, thinking of the bookend beasts. 'That sounds dangerous.'

'Yes,' said Rupert, 'that's why we haven't managed to get hold of any yet! Brown was here earlier today but he's been unable to lay his hands on any so far.'

He ran his hand through his hair. 'Anyway,' he added, attempting a smile, 'it's good to see you.'

'Is everything all right, Rupert?' asked Bramble.

Rupert hesitated. 'Well, erm ... not really,' he said resignedly. 'There are some very odd things going on here and they are connected with the reading room. I'll show you what I mean, but we'll have to be quick or they'll have finished their dinner. Come on, follow me.'

He led them out of his office and along a corridor with a thick red carpet until they reached some dark wooden doors.

'It's through here,' he said, pushing the doors open. 'Welcome to the Royal Society of Magic!'

It had the air of a gentleman's club. After the shabbiness of The Inkwell, it was like stepping into another world.

They were in a high-ceilinged room, with an

imposing green marble staircase running through the centre. The stairs led to a landing halfway up, with two smaller flights of stairs off to the left and right. Sweeping balustrades curved up and then round in a wide arc.

The carpets were purple with gold coronets woven into their pattern.

'The king's atrium,' explained Rupert as he led them up the stairs. 'It was built for King Charles II. He founded the Royal Society to further the understanding of magic. It was the king's way of controlling magic after it had almost destroyed London in the Great Fire. The Royal Society's mission is to promote excellence in magic and to encourage its use for the benefit of humankind,' he added grandly.

'The dining hall is on the other side of the building so we won't be disturbed. Now, come on, the reading room is this way,' he added, leading them up the small flight of stairs on the left-hand side.

They followed him along another corridor, which ended abruptly in a single door.

'This is where Gloom went the other day when he disappeared,' Rupert said.

'But won't it be locked?' asked Bramble.

Rupert held up a key and smiled. 'Yep, thought of that. I told Gloom I wanted to do some late-night research so he let me borrow his key.'

'Well done,' said Bramble, admiringly.

Rupert fitted the key in the lock and turned it. The door swung open and they stepped into a small, square room. There were no windows and the only door they could see was the one they had just entered by

The room resembled a very small library, with book-lined walls and two desks with overhead lights. Three large mirrors were set into the bookcases at even intervals, reflecting the light and making the room appear larger than it really was.

'The queen's reading room,' announced Rupert. 'It was Queen Victoria's favourite room at the Royal Society. Apparently she spent hours in here.'

In the middle of the room, taking up far too much space, was a statue of a man holding out his hands as if in welcome. There was a silver ring on one of his fingers. 'That's Dawlish Hooke,' said Rupert. 'He was the first president of the Society. He was famous for making magical jewellery. He got the idea from Fabian Grey.'

'And this is where Gloom disappeared?' asked Archie.

'Yep. I saw him let himself in with the key.

I came in straight after him but the room was empty,' said Rupert. 'As you can see, it's not a big room so there aren't many places to hide. And there's only one way in and out,' he added, indicating the door. 'So where did he go?'

'Well, let's see what the curiosity compass says,' said Thistle, taking the magical instrument from his pocket and flipping it open. The needle immediately began to spin.

'There's some serious magical energy in here,' said Thistle. 'But where's it coming from?'

He began to move around the room holding the compass in both hands, his eyes trained on it for any change. He made a slow circuit, pausing as he passed each of the mirrors. There was no change in the needle as he held the compass up to the first two mirrors. But when he reached the third, the needle began to spin madly.

'It must be behind the mirror,' said Archie.

Rupert ran his fingers along the sides of the mirror trying to get it to move but it wouldn't budge. 'Nope, there's no door here,' he said.

'Hold on,' said Archie. 'I've just had an idea. If there's a secret library, I think I know another way to find it.'

He spoke the delving spell Hawke had taught him.

'Secret volumes
On hidden shelves
Books of magic
Reveal yourselves!'

For a moment nothing happened. Then just as he was beginning to think the spell hadn't worked there was a sound like books sliding across a flat surface. Archie scanned the books on the shelves on either side of the mirror but he couldn't see any change.

'Look!' cried Arabella, pointing at the mirror. 'There, the books in the mirror have moved.'

Sure enough, when they looked at the reflection of the bookcases, they could see that several books had eased forward so that their spines stuck out proud on the shelves.

'Where are they?' asked Rupert.

'They must be on the bookcase behind us,' said Thistle, turning round to look.

But Archie had noticed something else. 'Where are our reflections?' he said.

'Archie's right,' said Bramble. 'Our reflections have disappeared. And the bookcases in the mirror aren't the ones in the reading room.'

Now that they looked more closely, they could see that the bookcase in the mirror didn't match any on their side. Where a moment before they could see the reflection of the room behind them, now when they looked into the mirror they could see a different room altogether.

'It's not a mirror we're looking into – it's a window!' exclaimed Archie. 'There's another room behind it!'

Rupert reached forward. His hand touched solid glass. 'So how do we get in?'

Archie glanced at the statue of Dawlish Hooke with the silver ring on his outstretched hand.

'That's odd,' he said. 'Statues don't normally wear rings.'

'I told you, Hooke was famous for his enchanted jewellery,' said Rupert. 'He made that ring for the king himself.'

Archie glanced at the gold ring on his own finger, the one that had belonged to Fabian Grey and contained his magic quill.

He examined the statue more carefully. By the look of the wear on Hooke's finger the silver ring had been removed many times

'I wonder,' he said, reaching forward to pluck the ring from the statue. He slipped it on to his own finger next to Grey's ring. Then approaching the mirror, he reached out his hand with the ring to touch the glass. It passed straight through.

'It's a permission wall!' he exclaimed. 'It's operated by the ring. Come on!'

18

The Hidden Library

Archie stepped through the mirror and found himself in the secret room on the other side. From where he was now he could see into the reading room he'd just left, where his friends were goggling at his sudden disappearance.

He passed the ring back through the mirror to Rupert who slipped it on to his finger and stepped through. One by one each of the others followed, taking it in turn to pass the ring to the next one until all five of them were safely on the other side of the mirror.

The room on this side was bigger than the one they had just left. The walls were lined with polished wooden panels. On a desk in the middle was a stack of ancient books.

'What is this place?' asked Thistle.

'I think it's the secret library that Gloom accidentally told Hawke about,' said Archie.

'I knew it!' exclaimed Rupert, triumphantly.

'Well done, Rupert,' said Bramble. 'So ... I wonder what they're keeping here that is so secret they didn't even want the museum elders knowing about it?'

Archie was already scanning the spines of the books on the desk. 'Listen to these titles,' he said, picking up a book in each hand. '*Darke Deedes and Broken Promises*,' he said, reading the first title. 'And this one is called *Curses to Kill and Maim*.'

'Charming!' said Thistle. 'And here's another to warm your heart: *Treachery and the Art of Betrayal*.'

The others were looking at the book titles now. 'They're all dark magic,' said Arabella. 'Every single one of them.'

'Yes,' breathed Archie. 'It's a library of dark magic!'

He glanced at the title of another book that was open on the desk. It was called *Powerful Blood Magic*.

'That's odd,' said Rupert, looking over his shoulder. 'I'm researching magical bloods but Gloom didn't mention anything about this book ...'

Some pages were marked. Archie started to read.

Hare's Blood: the blood of a hare can be used to make a potion that produces the symptoms of madness. The blood must be taken from a March hare on the night of the spring equinox and mixed with henbane, the plant known as White Dragon. When administered on a regular basis, the maddening potion destabilises the victim's mind, so that they show the early signs of insanity.

There were more pages marked.

Snuffling Blood: the blood of snufflings can be used to make an invisibility potion ...

Archie turned to the next marked page.

Dragon's (Dracus) Blood: Although it has many useful applications, the most powerful property of the blood of a dragon is its ability to extinguish a magical flame. The blood must be taken from a freshly slain dragon and administered within twenty-four hours with the following quenching spell:

Blood of Dracus
Newly slain
Beast of darkness
Quench the Flame.

Archie remembered that Old Zeb had said that dragon's blood was one of the only ways to put out a magical flame. His thoughts were interrupted by Thistle.

'But who would want a library of dark magic?'

'Greaders!' said Bramble.

'You'd be surprised how many people in the magical realm are interested in dark magic,' agreed Arabella. 'That includes my family. The Ripleys have their own hoard of dark magical books and artefacts at our house in Oxford. Not that I approve, of course,' she added hastily.

'Do you think Gloom is a Greader?' asked Rupert.

Archie shook his head. 'No. From what you said it looks like he knows about the secret library. But I think he only found out about it recently. He was the one who told Hawke about *The Book of Night* being kept here – he wouldn't have done that if he was a Greader.'

'But why didn't he tell me about the blood magic book?' said Rupert.

'He may not know it's here,' said Archie. 'It

looks like someone's been reading it very recently. You said that Gloom only just got back from a trip?'

'Yes,' said Rupert. 'He got back this evening.'

'So if it wasn't Gloom, who was reading the book?' asked Bramble.

'We've had several visitors today,' said Rupert, thoughtfully. 'Uther Morgred was here earlier and Faustus Gaunt was here yesterday. They're both fellows of the Society. Morgred was asking about security at the Royal Society. I don't think he was very impressed with our password system.'

'I wonder if Morgred knows about the dark library?' said Bramble.

'Maybe. Perhaps the books are locked away here by him to keep them out of the wrong hands?' suggested Rupert.

'Or maybe to get them into the *wrong* hands, if the Royal Society is full of Greaders!' said Archie.

The five members of the Alchemists' Club looked at each other. The full significance of their discovery was just starting to sink in.

They heard a sound coming from the direction of the mirror.

'Shhhhhhhhh!' hissed Rupert, putting his finger to his lips.

Holding their breath, they peered through

the mirror. The door to the reading room had just opened and they could see the bald head of Orpheus Gloom.

Archie's mind raced. If Gloom checked the statue he would see that the ring was missing. He would guess that someone had used it to get into the hidden library and they would be discovered.

Watching from their hiding place, the members of the Alchemists' Club exchanged anxious glances. But just as they were beginning to fear the worst, they heard someone speak to Gloom.

'How long have you known about the dark library, Orpheus?' Archie recognised Uther Morgred's cold voice.

'Not long at all,' replied Gloom defensively. 'I only discovered it by accident a few weeks ago. I was appalled at the books it contains.'

'Including *The Book of Night*?' pressed Morgred.

'Yes, yes,' said Gloom. 'I knew what it was immediately, of course. I've been a magic assessor for thirty years, after all, and it is the most infamous of all the seven,' he added. 'Though it was quite a shock, I can tell you, to find it here at the Royal Society. To think it was right under our noses all this time!'

'What did you do then?'

'I reported it to Gideon Hawke in Lost Books and he arranged to have it collected. A book like that should be in the crypt at the Museum of Magical Miscellany, under lock and key with as many guarding spells as possible!' declared Gloom hotly.

'And Hawke didn't think it important enough to collect it himself?'

'I hadn't thought about it that way,' admitted Gloom. 'But no, I suppose not, because he sent Wolfus Bone and Woodbine Foxe.'

Morgred sounded displeased. 'Bone and Foxe! Woodbine Foxe doesn't even work for the museum any more. He was expelled.'

On the other side of the mirror Archie felt Bramble and Thistle bristle.

'Well, Gideon said he trusted them,' Gloom said. 'It wasn't up to me.'

'This is most unsatisfactory,' said Morgred. 'And what happened when they arrived?'

'Well, the Greaders must have found out about the book being moved. They snatched it when Bone and Foxe came to collect it.'

Morgred sounded even more displeased. 'This is a very serious breach of security.'

'Yes, well, I can see that,' stammered Gloom. 'But you can't seriously think that I am to blame? I informed Hawke as soon as I knew *The Book of Night* was here. I couldn't have done any more. Could I?'

Gloom sounded frightened now. His bald head glistened with sweat.

The door closed revealing the sallow face of Gloom's inquisitor. Morgred had closed the door so that he was shut in the room with Gloom. He leaned in close, his dark eyes searching Gloom's.

'I don't know, Orpheus. *Could* you have done more?'

Gloom's lip trembled. 'No, Uther, I couldn't. You must see that?'

'Show me your palm,' demanded Morgred.

'You won't find the Black Dragon on me, Uther,' Gloom said, but his hand was shaking.

'We've just discovered that the Greaders are using an invisibility potion to conceal the firemark,' said Morgred, rubbing Gloom's palm with his thumb. He inspected it closely.

'You're clean,' he said, sounding slightly disappointed. 'But I will be watching you very closely. No one is to use the dark library without my express permission.'

Gloom swallowed hard. 'What will happen to Gideon . . . I mean, Hawke?' he asked.

Morgred swept his dark hair off his forehead and considered. 'Hawke made a serious error,' he said. 'Sending Bone and Foxe on such an important mission was a misjudgement. To make matters worse he tried to interrogate Katerina

Krone at the asylum. His health issues have always been a worry. When he was given the job we were told his problems were behind him but he has obviously had a relapse. It raises fresh concerns about his suitability as head of Lost Books. He will be spending some time at the asylum. Resting.'

Gloom looked alarmed. 'But who will take over at Lost Books? We can't afford to have the position empty now. We are in crisis!'

'Yes, precisely,' said Morgred, his dark eyes flashing. 'And that is why we have appointed a new head of Lost Books.'

'Good! Who?' gasped Gloom, his face flushed.

'Motley Brown,' said Morgred. 'I've just seen him and informed him of his new responsibilities. Let's hope he does a better job than Hawke.'

He turned on his heel and strode out of the room. Watching through the mirror, the children saw Gloom standing with his mouth open. He gathered himself and hurried after Morgred.

They heard his voice down the corridor. 'Is that wise? Motley's a nice enough chap but he doesn't have Gideon's magical ability . . .'

'Nonsense,' said Morgred. 'Besides, magical ability is overrated . . .'

Their voices trailed off as they receded down the corridor.

'Quick,' whispered Archie. 'Let's get out of here before they find us.'

He put on the silver ring and stepped back through the mirror. Then he tossed the ring to Rupert, who did the same. Thistle was the last one out and he slipped the silver ring back onto the statue's finger.

'Thanks, Dawlish,' he said, patting the statue on the back.

'Hurry up, Thistle,' said Rupert. 'I need to get you down the stairs and out.'

'How long have we got?' asked Archie, glancing at the clock on the wall, which showed just after eight.

'They'll probably be in supper for another ten minutes,' said Rupert. 'As I said, they like their puddings!'

The children raced back down the stairs and along the corridor where they had come in. They were not a moment too soon, as they heard loud voices approaching.

'I'd better go,' said Rupert. 'You know the way out.'

They said their goodbyes to Rupert and sped down the corridor.

When they got back to The Inkwell, they could hear the clicking sound of knitting needles. They slipped past Matilda in the gloom and headed for the door. They were just on their way out when they heard her cracked voice say, 'Goodnight, Master Archie, Master Thistle, Mistress Bramble and Mistress Arabella.'

On the train on their way back to Oxford, it was clear to Archie that Morgred needed to blame someone for the theft of *The Book of Night* and Hawke was an easy target.

And then there was Gloom. What if Gloom had deliberately used the theft of *The Book of Night* to discredit Hawke? He could easily have arranged to have the book snatched by some Greader accomplices when Wolfus Bone and Woodbine came to get it. Even if he had started out good, or at least neutral, he might well have changed sides to save his skin.

These same thoughts kept occupying his mind as he and his two cousins walked along Houndstooth Road and up the path of number 32. The three children opened the front door and let themselves into the house.

At the sound of the door, Loretta called out. 'Bramble? Thistle? Archie? Is that you?'

'Yes, Mum,' Bramble replied. 'We're back,'

'Come into the kitchen,' Loretta called. 'I've got a surprise for you.'

'Uh-oh,' said Thistle. Loretta's surprises were usually of the culinary kind. Archie sniffed the air suspiciously. He was quietly dreading that his aunt had been baking again. But he couldn't smell cooking. He put his head round the door.

'What sort of surprise?' he asked.

'The best sort,' said Loretta, beaming a big smile.

Archie's mouth dropped open. His gran, Gardenia Greene, was sitting at the kitchen table.

19

An Unexpected Visitor

'Gran!' cried Archie, giving her a big hug. 'You're back!'

'It would certainly appear so,' said Gardenia with a twinkle in her eye. She gave him a massive hug. 'Now where are my other two grandchildren?'

Just then there was a whoop from Bramble and Thistle as they came into the kitchen and caught sight of her. They came rushing forward.

'Steady now,' said Gardenia, a big smile on her face. 'Or you'll knock me over. I'm not as young as I was, you know.'

'Nonsense,' said Bramble. 'You look great. Travelling obviously agrees with you but we're very glad to have you back!'

*

A little while later, they were all seated around the kitchen table at 32 Houndstooth Road: Archie, Bramble, Thistle, Loretta, Woodbine and Gardenia.

'More cake, Mum?' asked Loretta.

'Did you make it yourself?' enquired Gardenia, holding a half-eaten piece of cake and chewing thoughtfully. 'I can't quite place the flavour.'

'Yes,' said Loretta, proudly. 'Victoria sponge with pilchard filling – it's my own recipe.'

'I thought it might be,' said her mother.

'I'll have another piece,' said Thistle, holding out his plate hopefully.

Loretta cut him another slice and Thistle crammed it into his mouth whole.

'Where are your manners, Thistle Foxe?' said Loretta, shaking her head in despair. Thistle flashed a smile, his teeth covered in cake, which Loretta tried to ignore.

'Well, now you've eaten something, Mum, let's hear about your travels,' Loretta continued. 'Where have you been all this time?'

'Yes, come on, Gran,' said Bramble. 'You promised to tell us all about your adventures.'

'I did,' said Gardenia, her eyes lighting up. 'And what an exciting time I've had!'

She looked pleased to have a reason to leave the rest of her cake and pushed her plate to one side. The Foxes stopped chewing and paid attention.

'I've been following in the footsteps of Fabian Grey,' Gardenia said, looking at Archie. 'Your father told me to find out everything I could about him. I went to the Himalayas first because that's where Grey headed straight after escaping from the Tower of London.'

Archie remembered the first postcard Gran had sent was from Kathmandu.

'High up in the mountains there's an ancient library with some very old magical records. I tracked Grey to that place. It was clear that he went there looking for *The Opus Magus*.'

'And did he find it?' asked Thistle, excitedly.

Gardenia shook her head. 'No, but he stayed in the mountains for a while studying the old records for clues about what had happened to it. Those clues led him to India and then to China, and eventually to Alexandria.'

'How do you know all this?' asked Woodbine.

'Because I followed his trail.'

'But after three hundred and fifty years I'm surprised there was a trail to follow,' said Loretta.

'Ah, I knew what to look for,' said Gardenia. 'Everywhere I went I heard the same story again and again. It had been handed down from generation to generation. The local people spoke of a wild-looking man with a streak of white in his hair seeking a magical book. And everywhere he went a large, black, talking bird appeared soon after – a raven.'

'A raven!' exclaimed Bramble, her hand flying to her mouth.

'A raven delivered Grey's ring to me!' said Archie, holding out his hand so Gardenia could see it on his finger.

She nodded, knowingly. 'Yes,' she said. 'Wherever Grey went, the raven went, too. But they never appeared together at the same time – it was always one or the other.'

She looked around at their curious faces. 'Some of the tales went further, saying that the man and the raven were one and the same. At first I didn't believe it. But as I learned more, I began to wonder. And it was then that I realised how Fabian Grey had escaped from the Tower of London.'

'He turned into a raven!' gasped Archie, suddenly remembering something he'd heard before. 'That's what Arthur Ripley said when I saw him in the asylum. It didn't make any sense at the time, but Ripley must have heard the stories, too, and made the same connection.'

Gardenia smiled. 'That's right. It seems that Grey was able to turn into a raven. That's how he escaped.'

'But that's impossible,' cried Loretta. 'Isn't it?'

'Not impossible,' said Woodbine, rubbing his chin. 'There are shape-shifting spells and Grey was very gifted magically. Brilliant in fact.'

Gardenia's eyes gleamed. 'Yes, he was, but I don't think it was something he did on purpose. It wasn't his spell, you see. I believe it was the curse *The Grim Grimoire* put on him.'

'Yes,' said Archie, remembering what his father had said to Fabian Grey in *The Book of Yore*. 'Part of the curse was that he would turn into the first beast he saw. And in the Tower of London the first animal he would have seen was a raven.'

Gardenia nodded. 'The other members of the Alchemists' Club met with accidents,' she said, 'but the *Grimoire* saved its cruellest curse for Grey because it hated him the most.'

'According to the stories, the raven always appeared at the same time of the month – when there was a new moon. That's the darkest night of the month because the moon is at its weakest. On those nights I believe that Grey became a raven for a few hours.'

'But you said the *Grimoire* kept its cruellest curse for Grey. There are worse things than turning into a bird once a month!' said Loretta. 'And at least it meant he could escape from the Tower.'

'Ah, but that's not the worst part,' said Gardenia. 'The curse also took away his greatest magical gift, his bibliographical memory. In fact, it gradually took away *all* memories of his former life. So after a while he was searching for *The Opus Magus* without knowing why.'

'How awful, to forget who you are and what you've been,' Bramble said. 'But what became of him?'

'Eventually, his search brought him back to England. By then he had lost his identity so completely that no one knew who he was – not even himself.'

'So he came home. I'm glad about that,' said Bramble. 'I wouldn't like to think of him wandering the world lost and alone. Do you know what happened to him in the end?'

Gardenia smiled knowingly. 'I know where his grave is, and I plan to take Archie there if he is willing.'

'Yes, of course,' said Archie. 'But how sad to think that he died so alone.'

'But I'm not convinced that Grey is in it,' said Gardenia. 'That's the other strange part of the story. Grey's travels took him all over the world and lasted many years. But the descriptions of his appearance barely change. He never seemed to age. Or at least he aged very slowly – a year for every ten years of a normal life. Three hundred and fifty years would be like thirty-five years to him.'

…ian Grey were linked: that you had great magical …lity and would become a magic writer, and that …e Grey, too, you had a forked fate. The first fork …uld be meeting Barzak, and if you survived that, …e second fork was connected to Grey himself.'

'That was the Alchemist's Curse,' said Archie.

'Yes,' said Gardenia, 'and the third fork is also …nnected to Grey.' She paused. 'You see, Archie, …elieve that you have a part to play in fulfilling …rey's destiny.'

…Katerina had said as much already. Archie felt …e knot in his stomach tighten another notch.

…He had so many questions but Gardenia was …ill speaking.

'Your father was very shaken by what the book …owed him. None of us could imagine how you …ight survive an encounter with a darchemist like …arzak. Surely he would either kill you or enslave …ou with his dark magic.

'We should have had more faith,' she said, …queezing his arm. 'But we feared the worst. That's …hy your father made me promise to keep you …way from magic. He hoped against hope that …ou might be able to avoid the first fork.'

'But it didn't work,' said Archie.

'No.' She shook her head. 'In my heart of hearts …never believed it would.' She gave Archie a …ad smile.

'Wait a minute,' said Archie. 'Are you saying that he might still be alive . . .?'

Gardenia nodded.

'But that really is impossible!' exclaimed Loretta.

'No,' said Gardenia. 'Grey discovered the formula for azoth. One of its properties is that it can extend the life of mortals.'

Archie pictured the scene in the cellar in Pudding Lane. 'I remember now!' he said with a shock. 'When the experiment went wrong, Grey was showered in azoth. It must have prolonged his life.'

'The azoth must have affected him,' said Gardenia. 'It would have slowed down his ageing. Who knows, perhaps he realised what had happened and started taking it himself deliberately in order to stay young.'

'But if he's cursed to turn into a raven every new moon and he doesn't even know who he is, why would he want to prolong his misery?' asked Loretta.

'I think I know,' said Archie. Something had suddenly clicked in his mind. 'If Grey is still alive it's because somehow, in spite of all that happened to him, he knows there's something he desperately needs to do.'

'What could he possibly need to do after three hundred and fifty years?' asked Loretta.

'Save magic,' said Archie. 'Whatever it was that he saw in *The Book of Prophecy*, he needs to finish it.'

Gardenia nodded. 'That's right. It's his destiny.'

'But what is it he's meant to do?' cried Thistle.

'Ah, that is the cruellest part of all,' said Gardenia. 'I don't think he knows. Thanks to the curse, he has no memory of it.'

'You have got to be kidding me,' cried Thistle. 'Are you saying that Fabian Grey doesn't know what he has to do? So even if we find him, he still can't help?'

Gardenia nodded sadly. It was such a strange story. Not only was Fabian Grey quite possibly still alive, he was cursed to turn into a raven every new moon. And the next day he would have no memory of it. Strangest of all, he did not even know his real identity.

The whole family sat up late into the night talking. One by one they crept off to their beds until it was just Archie and Gardenia left. The fire was burning low. Now that they were alone, Archie asked her the question that had been on his mind all evening.

'Gran, why did you never tell me about magic and about the museum and everything?'

She gave a long sigh. 'It all seems like such a long time ago now,' she said, putting her hand on his shoulder. 'When you were born it was a very happy time for all of us. But a few v father came to see me. He told me h By then we could all see that y different colours, making you the have magician's eye since Fabian Gre we wondered whether you might tal

'But is that so bad?' asked Archie.

Gardenia shook her head. 'No, you have to understand that no one about him then. We had all grown up started the Great Fire of London. He for blackening the name of magic a underground. As far as we knew, it wa Fabian Grey that magic had been out

'So you see, when your father t might have inherited some of Gre ability, he was worried that people wou worst of you. He set out to discover ev could about Grey. Eventually that ques *The Book of Prophecy*.'

She shook her head. 'Everyone wh consulted that book has paid a terr including your father. And now I under the book is destroyed. Perhaps it is for t

'How can you say that?' cried Archie.

She gave a wan smile. 'It's unwise to lo into the future. Your father found that ou way. The book showed him that your fate a

'No one can cheat his fate,' said Archie, repeating what *The Book of Prophecy* had told him.

'That's right,' she said. 'But a promise is a promise, so I kept you away from magic and that meant I had to keep you away from Oxford. That was the hardest part of all. It was the only way to prevent you finding out about the museum, but it broke my heart that you had to grow up apart from Bramble and Thistle.'

'And I found out anyway,' said Archie.

Gardenia smiled, and this time it was a real smile. 'Yes, you did. When the book arrived on your twelfth birthday I knew the game was up and you had to make your own way. Of course I had no idea what the book really was. I thought it was from someone at the museum. If I had thought for one second it was Barzak's book . . .' She shivered.

'So you let me take the book to the Aisle of White knowing that I would find out about the museum.'

'It couldn't be helped. The book came with a special instruction so ignoring it would have meant breaking the lore. I had to trust Loretta and Woodbine to keep you safe. But it also meant that you were finally reunited with Bramble.'

'And Thistle,' said Archie.

'Yes,' she said. 'Of course. And it also left me free to keep the other part of my promise – to discover everything that I could about Fabian Grey. So that's what I did.'

Archie was quiet for a while. He was still digesting all this. Some of it he already knew or had guessed, but other parts were new to him. He had not understood all his connections with Fabian Grey. No wonder everyone had been so concerned about his magical abilities, his book whispering and the unusual firemarks. No wonder they had been so alarmed about his forked fate.

He wanted to ask Gran why she had lied to him about his parents' disappearance. But this didn't seem the right moment. He was angry that she had deceived him. But he was fascinated by the new information she had managed to gather.

'In all your travels did you ever find out what Grey actually saw in his vision?' asked Archie.

'No,' said Gardenia. 'That is the one thing that eluded me. But tomorrow I will take you to see his gravestone. Perhaps there will be a clue there.'

In a house on the other side of Oxford, a single candle was the only light in a downstairs room. The flickering flame illuminated a dead rat on the table. A boy sitting in the shadows picked it up and bit into it. The rat's blood trickled down his chin like a red stream.

'Swallow it!' said his master. 'Use the rat's life

power to extinguish the candle and command the darkness. If you can take the darkness from a rat's blood, one day you will be able to take it from a dragon's.'

The boy closed his eyes and swallowed. Concentrating very hard he uttered the words of the spell.

'Blood of Ratus
Newly slain
Beast of darkness
Quench the Flame.'

The candle guttered and went out, plunging the room into total darkness.

'Good,' said the man. 'You are almost ready!'

'But where will we get dragon's blood?' asked the boy.

'Leave that to me,' said the man, relighting the candle. 'There is more than one way to bleed a dragon.'

He opened his left hand to show the boy the firemark there.

20

The Memorial

The lychgate groaned open and Gardenia Greene stepped into the churchyard. The wind whispered in the tall trees that stood like sentries guarding the graves. Was it a welcome or a warning?

Archie swallowed hard. Gran beckoned him forward. He wanted to follow but his feet felt like they had turned to stone. It was just a country graveyard like many others in England, but something about this place unnerved him.

'Come along, Archie,' she called over her shoulder. 'You won't see anything from there.'

That was what Archie was rather hoping. It had seemed like a good idea when Gran had said they were going to visit Fabian Grey's grave. The Greys – his mother's side of the family – had been buried in the churchyard for hundreds of years. The village was named after them – Grey's End.

Archie had thought it would be exciting to see the place. But now he was here he felt a strange reluctance.

Gardenia walked slowly on, glancing from side to side at the gravestones as if reacquainting herself with old friends. Archie took a deep breath and followed.

'Generations of Greys are buried here,' she pronounced solemnly when he caught up with her. 'That's your great-uncle Thaddeus Grey,' she added, indicating a crumbling tombstone shaped like a horse.

'Lost most of his money on the horses. And that's Aldous Grey, over there. And his wife Gertrude is next to him.'

Archie peered at the gravestones. The names were chiselled in Gothic letters, discoloured with green moss. 'In loving memory of Aldous Grey,' it read. '1792 to 1863. And his loving wife Gertrude, 1795 to 1869.'

'The Greenes are buried near Oxford,' said Gardenia. 'I often visit the churchyard. I never knew most of them when they were alive, of course. But we're quite close now.'

Archie nodded, sympathetically. Then her words

sank in. He glanced at his grandmother. There was no trace of humour on her face.

'But how can you know them if they died before you were even born?' he asked.

She saw his confused expression. 'It's the echo,' she said, as if the word explained everything. 'Magic doesn't disappear immediately, Archie. It lingers. Our most precious memories, the ones we seek to leave behind for our loved ones, remain. Memories reverberate. When you throw a stone into a pond it makes the ripples on the surface, and the ripples continue long after the stone has gone. Memories are the same. You can feel a person's echo very strongly in a place they once loved – or in a graveyard.'

She smiled. 'Our most cherished memories linger like a dream. Or a nightmare,' she added under her breath. 'If someone lives an evil life then that remains behind for a time, too. But the good outlives the bad. Always remember that.'

She moved on down the line of graves until she reached the end of the row.

'This is what I brought you to see,' she said, indicating the very last gravestone.

The other gravestones caught the sunlight shining through the trees. But this one was in shadow. The name of Fabian Grey was chiselled into the flat stone face. The moss had grown thick on its surface, obscuring what was written there.

'But if his grave was here all along ...' said Archie.

Gardenia shook her head. 'I don't think it is a real grave, just a memorial erected by his family. Read the inscription.'

Archie read the words carved into the stone, speaking them aloud.

'Lost but not forgotten
Precious are the memories of Fabian Grey.'

'It doesn't make sense,' he said.

At that moment, something snapped inside him. Something had been gnawing away at him. He could bear it no longer.

'Why did you let me think that my parents and sister were all killed in a ferry disaster?' he demanded.

Gardenia froze as if she'd been shot. For a moment she didn't move. When she turned to face him her face looked more lined than ever.

'Let's sit for a moment,' she said, indicating an old wooden bench beneath a yew tree.

She sat down and patted the seat next to her. Archie wanted to be furious, to punish her for deceiving him for all these years, but now that she was there with him it was hard to stay angry. He sat down beside her.

She touched his hand. 'I needed to give you some kind of a reason for why they'd disappeared. I couldn't tell you the truth without explaining about magic, and I certainly didn't want you to think they had abandoned you. A ferry did sink at about the same time so I linked the two things together.

'You lied to me!' said Archie.

'It was a little lie that grew into a big lie,' said Gardenia. 'At first I told you they were lost at sea because I hoped they would come back. But as the years passed it seemed kinder to let you believe they'd drowned. I didn't know what else to do.'

Archie nodded. He understood her reasons but he still felt betrayed. He turned away.

'I'm sorry, Archie. I didn't mean to hurt you.'

Archie's eyes prickled with tears. He pulled his hand away.

'One day perhaps you'll understand,' said Gardenia. She stood up wearily and started back towards the lychgate. Archie remained behind.

Dusk had fallen suddenly. The graveyard was full of shadows now. Archie could see her walking ahead, her bony shoulders hunched as she retraced the way they'd come.

He wiped his eyes with his sleeve and called after her. 'Why did they leave me behind?'

But she was too far away to hear him. The

gravestones seemed to swallow up his voice in their ancient rock. He started after her.

The lychgate was a pool of darkness. He'd just reached it when he heard something behind him and thought he saw something out of the corner of his eye. But when he turned to look, the churchyard was quiet and still.

Then, as he opened the gate, he felt the hairs on the back of his neck stand up. A bird landed on a gravestone beside him and cried out what sounded like a warning. Turning his head he saw a white face with two dark eye sockets appear from behind a gravestone. The cheeks were sunken and the skin so thin it was translucent. Archie recognised it – it was another one of the Pale Writers!

The Pale Writer reached out a wizened hand and Archie saw it had long, yellowed fingernails. He jumped back but the creature lunged at him, its nails biting into his wrist. He felt a sharp pain and looked down, expecting to see blood where it had torn his flesh. His skin was whole but he felt gripped by a paralysing dread. His entire being had turned rigid with fear.

Archie's heart was pounding so fast that he thought it would burst. He felt like he was surrounded by unknown danger on all sides. The gravestones loomed menacingly. The Pale Writer

gripped him with its other withered hand and the terrible dread seized him again.

Archie's senses were working overtime. He could smell the creature's rank breath, a sickly stench of decay. Archie couldn't move, his body immobilised by fear. But somehow his mind was still alert. He remembered that the second Pale Writer was Dread. Bramble had said it would attack him when he was vulnerable.

The skull-like face moved closer. Archie felt its disgusting breath on his face and heard it hiss. It had spotted the Emerald Eye around his neck, and its clutching hand reached for the pendant. But as it tried to take his keepsafe, something glowed with an amber light. The hand recoiled as if it had been burned with acid.

It was the Torchstone, still safe in his pocket! The Pale Writer was staring at its shrivelled hand, its skull-like features twisted with hate.

'You recognise it, don't you?' Archie cried. 'It's the Flame of Pharos.'

The amber glow lit the darkness. The Pale Writer shrank from its light. Archie tried to remember what Bramble had told him. Fear feeds upon itself. Name your fear and you can break its grip and turn it on itself. And when he realised how simple it was, he felt Dread's grip loosen.

'You're just fear!' he cried. 'That's all you are. If I

decide not to be afraid then you have no hold over me. Your power is broken!'

The Pale Writer looked at him with loathing in its black eyes. It raised its claw-like hands to strike again. But as it did, Archie held up the Torchstone. The Pale Writer hissed and backed away, covering its face.

'You fear the Flame,' Archie cried. 'You can't bear its light!'

The Pale Writer hissed again and lunged at him, knocking the Torchstone from his hand.

Archie tried to catch it, but it fell to the ground. He felt Dread's shadow loom over him.

Archie heard the lychgate open. He heard a voice call out a banishing spell.

'Flame of Pharos
Sacred light
Shade of darkness
Put to flight!'

'Be gone, you creature of darkness. Leave the boy!'

Gardenia Greene stepped out of the gloom. With an angry hiss, the Pale Writer fled into the night.

'Are you all right, Archie?' Gardenia rushed over to him, picking him up.

'Yes, I'm okay,' he managed to murmur. 'Has it gone?'

'Yes, it fled when I arrived. The Pale Writers are cowards. They like to get their victims alone. It must have been lying in wait in the graveyard. The first one was watching the museum and followed you home. This one was waiting in ambush because it knew we would come here eventually.

'We're lucky it didn't have time to summon the other two. One Pale Writer on its own is bad enough, but all three together – that would be a different story.'

She studied Archie. 'You look like a wraith yourself, your face is so pale,' she said. 'Can you walk?'

Archie got to his feet. He felt dizzy and his head was pounding, but he managed to stand. His legs were weak and he felt a horrible gnawing empty feeling inside.

Gardenia held his face in her hands. 'So far, you have faced the two lesser Pale Writers, Doubt and Dread. The third is Despair. It is their leader and is the most deadly. We need to find a way to protect you.'

'I have the Emerald Eye,' said Archie, clasping the magic pendant around his neck and trying to sound more assured than he felt. 'It wards off dark magic.'

'That is why Dee gave it to you as your keepsafe,' said Gardenia. 'But it's not strong enough to protect you from them completely.'

'The Pale Writer tried to snatch the Eye,' said Archie. 'The first one tried to take it, too.'

Gardenia shook her head gravely. 'They would,' she said. 'They were darchemists once. They crave powerful magic and the Emerald Eye is too much for them to resist. They know that it is protecting you like an amulet. If they could separate you from it then you would be totally vulnerable to their magic. And make no mistake about it, Archie – they are utterly ruthless. Now, let's get out of here,' she said, striding back towards the lychgate.

Archie suddenly remembered the Torchstone. He searched for it among the gravestones, but he couldn't see it anywhere. He could hear Gardenia calling.

'Come along, Archie!'

'I'm just coming,' Archie called back, frantically feeling in the dark. He had to find the Torchstone! He should never have let it out of his sight. He tried a delving spell, but there was no magical energy. The Torchstone had gone. The Pale Writer must have somehow taken it, he thought.

This was a disaster! He'd promised Hawke that he would be a flame carrier and now he'd lost the Torchstone. What was he going to do?

'Archie, come on!' Gran's voice sounded urgent. 'We need to get away from here. Before they come back!'

The thought of the Pale Writers returning was enough to persuade him. Abandoning his search, he ran after her.

21

Bed Rest and Buns

At Loretta's insistence, Archie spent the next two days in bed. He needed to build up his strength again, she said. He tried to appeal to his grandmother, but she stood firmly behind Loretta.

'Archie, you can't expect to face the Pale Writers without being affected. I don't think you can take many more of their attacks. Every time they touch you a little part of your spirit is extinguished. You need time to recover.'

Archie reluctantly conceded. In truth, he knew they were right. His second brush with a Pale Writer had left him very weak. More worryingly, the unpleasant hollow feeling he'd felt after the first attack was back, and much worse. It was as if the vile creature had taken some of the very essence he was made from.

He felt thinner and less substantial somehow, despite Loretta's best efforts to feed him up with marmalade omelettes and her own special recipe for cherry buns. It didn't help that Loretta had substituted curry for cherry in her recipe so the buns were filled with curry powder. But it was more than Loretta's cooking that had left a bad taste in his mouth. He couldn't shake off the feeling that he was more vulnerable than before.

He brooded over what Gran had told him. The Pale Writers had once been magic writers. They had surrendered their souls to the Dark Flame when they summoned it from Pandemonium. Given half a chance they would steal Archie's soul, too, and make him a servant of the Dark Flame. It wasn't a very comforting thought.

On the second day after the attack, Archie had some welcome visitors. Rupert was back in Oxford for a few days and dropped in at 32 Houndstooth Road with Arabella.

The Alchemists' Club crowded into the boys' bedroom where Archie was sitting up in bed with a pile of pillows plumped up behind him.

'You do look a bit pale, Arch,' said Rupert. 'Sorry, bad choice of words!'

'Thanks!' said Archie.

'How are you feeling?' asked Arabella.

'Much better,' said Archie. 'In fact, I feel well enough to hold a meeting of the Alchemists' Club. Even if Rupert thinks I don't look it,' he added, managing a smile.

'We're all here, so why not?' said Thistle.

The others agreed. They took it in turns to repeat the pledge.

Archie, Bramble and Thistle filled in the other two on what Gardenia had discovered on her travels.

'I have some news, too,' declared Arabella when they had finished. 'Last night there was a Greader meeting at my parents' house, and I overheard them talking about *The Opus Magus*. The rumour among the Greaders is that Grey did hide it somewhere, but that it may not be a book. It may be in some other form.'

'Like what?' asked Bramble.

'I couldn't hear everything they were saying, but it sounded like a place to store memories. And they think they know how to find it.'

'We have to find it before they do,' said Archie. 'What else has been going on while I've been stuck in here?'

'Brown has officially taken over from Hawke in Lost Books,' said Thistle. 'So when you go back to the museum, you'll be reporting to him.'

Archie pinched his lip thoughtfully. 'What's he like?'

'He was all right with me when I worked in the mythical menagerie,' Rupert said. 'But I always got the impression that he was a bit bored with the Natural Magic Department, and wanted to do something else. Now he's got his chance.'

'He's under a lot of pressure, though,' said Arabella. 'Graves says that it was the strain of trying to find out what Grey had to do to fulfil the prophecy that pushed Hawke over the edge. Now Brown is in the hot seat.'

'What's he doing about it?' asked Archie.

'Not much so far,' said Bramble. 'He seems to spend all his time going through Hawke's things. It's as if he's looking for something.'

'Grey's account of what he saw in his vision,' said Archie. 'That was what was driving Hawke so hard. He was convinced that Grey must have written it down.'

'Well, whatever it is, Brown has torn Hawke's office apart trying to find it. When I took a book in the other day, the place was completely trashed. He's even thrown out Hawke's favourite sofa.'

'I loved that sofa!' said Rupert.

'So did Hawke,' said Archie, angrily.

After the others had left, Bramble stayed behind.

'Are you okay?' she asked. 'You really don't look your usual self.'

'I just feel so helpless,' groaned Archie. 'The Greaders are closing in on *The Opus Magus* and we still don't know how to defeat the Dark Flame. And to make matters worse, I'm stuck here.'

'Not for much longer,' said Bramble. 'Pink sent you a present.' She crossed the room and took something from her bag.

'What is it?' asked Archie.

'It's a thickening potion,' said Bramble. 'Guaranteed to put some colour back in your cheeks! Now drink it down and I'll bring you some more tomorrow.'

The potion tasted of strawberries and cream and all sorts of other deliciously rich ingredients. Archie could feel his skin glowing.

'That's more like it,' said Bramble, smiling. 'Now what else is bothering you?'

She knew him too well to be fobbed off.

'I've been thinking about my family,' confided Archie. 'I've been trying to find out what happened to them. I've done some digging and it seems they were trapped in a drawing book. It might be *The Book of Yore*, but what if it's *The Book of Night*, or . . .' His voice trailed off.

'*The Book of Prophecy*?' asked Bramble.

Archie nodded. He felt himself choking up. 'I may never know what happened to them. And I don't understand why they didn't take me with them. That's all I really want – to know why they left me behind.'

Bramble touched his hand. 'Your dad was a good man,' she said. 'He would have done anything for his children. Your mum, too.'

Archie looked at her in astonishment. 'I didn't know you met them?'

Bramble's brow clouded. She looked as confused as he was. 'I have strong memories of them,' she said, slowly. 'I think I must have stayed at their house when I was little. It's strange, I feel like I knew them well.'

She smiled. 'And I know that wherever they are, they would want you to be brave and try to be happy.'

Archie smiled and wiped his eye. He suddenly felt very drowsy. 'And I'm sure they would want me to try to defeat the Dark Flame and save magic!'

'Yes,' said Bramble, squeezing his hand. 'They definitely would, and that is what we are going to do. Now get some rest – we have work to do tomorrow and you're going to need your strength.'

'That reminds me,' she added. 'Pink said to tell you that the thickening potion has a strong sleeping tonic in it, too.'

But Archie didn't hear her because he was already fast sleep. Bramble tucked him in and put out the light.

22

The Book of Reckoning

The next day Archie was feeling much stronger. Whatever magic was in Pink's thickening potion it seemed to be working. Loretta agreed to let him out of bed as long as he took it easy. He spent the day skulking around the house, but was desperate to go outside.

When Bramble and Thistle returned from the museum, Bramble brought some more of the potion and Archie swallowed it down in one. When Loretta saw him she remarked on how much more colour he had in his cheeks.

'I must ask Pink for the recipe,' said Loretta.

Bramble winked at Archie and Thistle grinned. It was unheard of for their mother to follow any recipes.

They pleaded with Loretta to let Archie out for a stroll.

'We won't let him out of our sight,' Bramble promised.

Eventually Loretta agreed, on the strict understanding that they were back before nine o'clock.

As soon as they were outside, the three cousins made a beeline for the museum. Archie kept an eye out for any suspicious-looking shadows lurking around.

On their way to Oxford city centre, they discussed the message on Fabian Grey's memorial.

'"Lost but not forgotten. Precious are the memories of Fabian Grey",' repeated Thistle.

'Well, he was famous for his bibliographical memory,' said Bramble. 'Perhaps that's what it's referring to?

'Gran thinks he's still alive,' said Thistle. 'But is that really possible?'

A thought struck Archie like a lightning bolt. It was so obvious that he slapped his forehead. 'Of course,' he groaned. 'How could we have been so stupid?'

'What are you talking about?' asked Thistle.

'*The Book of Reckoning*! It's been staring us in the face all this time,' said Archie. 'Come on!'

*

Pink mixed them a motion potion and they took the box seats to the museum, then made their way to the Scriptorium. Sure enough, Gideon Hawke's battered old sofa was standing in the passageway on its side where it had been discarded. Archie felt a sudden anger.

'I can't believe they'd just throw Hawke's things out like that!' he said.

'I know,' said Bramble. 'But Hawke is gone. It's Brown's office now and he's stamping his authority on the place.'

'What do you think will happen to Hawke?' asked Archie.

Bramble shrugged. 'It depends on whether they think he's well enough to leave the asylum.'

'Even if they do let him out, Dad says it's very unlikely that he'll get his job back,' said Thistle. 'He challenged the Magical League, so the magical authorities have got it in for him now.'

Archie looked thoughtful. 'Yes, I saw how they treated him. It wasn't very nice. I don't like Uther Morgred, or the man at the asylum, Rumold. I think they're in this up to their necks.'

'If you're right,' said Bramble, 'then we really do need to watch our backs.

They slipped into the Scriptorium. The magical torches blazed with light, illuminating the room as they stepped inside.

At night, the Scriptorium had an eerie feeling about it. For a moment Archie stood still, contemplating the silence. Bramble and Thistle stood on either side of him for moral support.

The Book of Yore was in its usual place against one wall, its ancient brown cover closed. At the far end of the Scriptorium where the two Books of Destiny had been there was just one book now. *The Book of Prophecy* was no more.

The Book of Reckoning recorded every birth and death in the magical realm. It was the size of a table and raised up at an angle of forty-five degrees so that its pages were visible. Suspended in its centre was an ornate crystal hourglass. The hourglass was protected by a silver case, which formed part of the spine. The pages of the book were shaped around it so that it could be seen even when the book was open.

'I don't know why we didn't think of it earlier,' said Bramble. 'Of course *The Book of Reckoning* will tell us if Grey is still alive.'

The magic Bennu bird quill floated in the air just above its open pages. It was constantly updating the names and dates.

Archie had forgotten just how amazing the book was. For a moment he gazed at it in wonder. The silver hourglass kept a tally of the time that was left until the books in the museum released their magic into the world. According to legend, that day would mark either the beginning of a new golden age of magic or the start of another dark age.

'Look!' cried Thistle, pointing at the sand running through the crystal hourglass.

'Time is running out,' said Archie.

He walked up the short flight of stairs to the raised wooden viewing platform that overlooked the book. His eyes roved across the open pages.

'Each and every one of us will pass through its pages,' Bramble had told him the very first time he'd visited the Scriptorium. Everything had seemed so new and exciting back then. He'd just met his cousins and was discovering the museum and the magical realm. With a jolt he remembered that all of that was in danger. The Dark Flame threatened everything he cared about.

His attention returned to the *Book of Reckoning*. Column after column of names filled its pages. Beside each entry was their date of birth and another space to record their death.

He watched as the magic quill wrote out a new name, *Jason Flinch*, and the date. A new baby had been born to a magical family. But then, immediately, the pages flicked backward. The quill hovered over an earlier entry – *Millicent Speckle, born 9th June 1930* – and added the word *died* and the date. Then it struck a single line through the name.

Archie glanced at Bramble and Thistle, standing on either side of the glass dome so they could see what was happening. He gathered himself.

'Fabian Grey,' he said, and held his breath.

At the sound of the name, *The Book of Reckoning* started to glow with a yellow light. The pages turned backwards, gathering speed until they were just a blur, and then suddenly stopped. The blue quill hovered above a faded entry.

Fabian Grey: Born 18th August 1649

There was no date for Grey's death. The three cousins gazed at each other in wonder.

'So Gran's right,' exclaimed Archie. 'Grey is alive!'

23

Echoes of the Past

Archie lay awake that night. His mind kept running over the same questions. Where had Grey been all these years? And where was he now? Most importantly, whose side was he on?

When he eventually fell asleep, Archie had the strangest dream so far. It was also the most vivid. He was in the Scriptorium and he heard a gentle voice calling him. Archie knew that it was *The Book of Prophecy.*

'No one may cheat their fate, book whisperer,' it said.

'You said that before,' Archie said. 'What does it mean? Who can't cheat their fate?'

Another thought struck him. 'How can you be talking to me when you were destroyed?'

'Magic is not destroyed so easily,' said the voice. 'It fades but it lives on in our memories. I am the echo of all those whose lives were touched by the prophecy.'

Then Archie realised – the book had shown Grey what he had to do to defeat the Dark Flame, which meant it could show him!

'What did you show Fabian Grey that nearly drove him mad?' he asked.

There was a long silence before the book spoke again. 'To know the future is a weight too heavy for most to carry. It has driven many to the edge of madness, Fabian Grey among them.'

'I understand,' said Archie, his heart beating faster. 'But I need to know. What did you show him about the future of magic? How do I defeat the Dark Flame?'

The Book of Prophecy towered over him; its cover had become a door with a large brass door knocker. Archie hesitated. He knew now that his retrospectre could not protect him. Everyone who had consulted *The Book of Prophecy* was affected by the experience. But he had to know what it had shown Grey.

He took a breath. Then he gripped the brass door knocker and gave three loud raps. The door swung open, and he stepped over the threshold into a large dimly lit room that he had been in once before, when he'd been desperate to lift the Alchemist's Curse. Bookcases formed a labyrinth.

'Welcome back to the Library of Lives,' said the voice. 'This way.'

Candles in sconces on the bookcases lit themselves to form a pathway through the maze. Each book had a name written on its spine.

Archie followed the trail of flickering flames. Every time he took another step another candle sparked into life to illuminate the shadows, urging him onwards. When he glanced back he could see that the candles behind him had extinguished so that he could not see the way out.

The trail led him further and further into the labyrinth until he came to a dead end. A bookcase blocked his path. The name on the spine was FABIAN GREY. Archie hesitated.

'You can still turn back, book whisperer,' said the voice. 'It is your choice.'

Making up his mind, Archie took the book from the shelf and opened it. At first the page was blank but as he watched, moving images appeared. He recognised the Scriptorium. He could see that both *The Book of Reckoning* and *The Book of Prophecy* were still intact inside the glass dome.

'This is not the future,' said Archie. 'It's the past!'

'These are the moments that shaped your

destiny, the choices that led you here. Watch closely and you will see how your future was made by others.'

The Library of Lives faded away and Archie found himself in a street that had been ravaged by fire. A thick cloud of smoke still hung in the air, making it hard to see. When he breathed in, it left a bitter taste in his mouth. The houses had been reduced to blackened stumps like rotten teeth. Only one building survived.

Archie read the brass plaque on the door.

FOLLY & CATCHPOLE
PRACTITIONERS OF MAGICAL LORE

A man approached. He looked familiar. With a shock Archie recognised his father.

Alex Greene checked his pocket watch. Archie wanted to call out to him but at that moment the door to the building opened and a second man emerged from inside. He drew his scarlet cloak up to cover his face but not before Archie saw the white streak in his hair.

The two men shook hands.

'It is done then?' asked Alex Greene.

Fabian Grey nodded. 'It is a strange tale but I have written it down as you asked and lodged it with the law firm. I have left instructions that I will collect it myself, although I have no idea when that will be. It is all here on this receipt,' he said.

He held up a piece of parchment for Archie's father to see and then tucked it inside his cloak.

'And your ring?' said Alex Greene.

Grey held out his hand to show that he no longer wore it on his finger. 'I have left it with a separate instruction as you asked. I informed them that it is to be collected by a raven when the Golden Circle firemarks start to appear.'

Alex Greene nodded. 'Thank you.'

Grey looked up and down the street and shivered. 'This part of the city is reduced to ashes.' He shook his head sadly. 'It's our fault that London burned. This building only survived because it has a magic charm on it and its contents, otherwise it would have been destroyed along with the rest.'

'What will you do now?' asked Alex.

'I will collect the *Grimoire* and take it to the Darchive at the museum,' Grey said. 'It will be safe there for a while at least. I owe you a great debt for saving my life. I know the price you have paid for it.'

'It was not for you that we made the sacrifice,' Alex replied.

Grey nodded. 'I understand,' he said. 'I will repay you in kind. Farewell, Alex Greene! We will not meet again.' He turned and disappeared into the pall of smoke that still hung over the street. Archie's father gazed after him for a moment and then turned and walked in the opposite direction.

Archie hesitated, unsure which of the two to follow, then he broke into a run.

'Wait!' he cried.

Alex Greene turned at the sound of his voice and Archie looked into his father's face. And then he heard a woman's voice.

'Archie! Is that really you? I can't believe it . . .'

He turned to see his mother. Amelia Greene was walking towards him with her arms outstretched. Archie ran towards her and would have run into her open arms, but he passed straight through her. He reached out for his father but he, too, was as insubstantial as the ribbons of smoke drifting around them.

Archie felt the sting of tears on his cheeks.

'I don't understand,' he said.

Amelia Greene looked into his eyes. 'My darling Archie, we are memories, an echo of the magic that brought you into the world.

'Your father and I set out to protect you. We consulted *The Book of Yore* and it told us that your destiny was linked to Fabian Grey's – your forked fates were intertwined. They always were. You both had three forks in your fate.

'Grey's first was when he looked in *The Book of*

Prophecy, and his second was what happened in the cellar in Pudding Lane when *The Grim Grimoire* cursed him.

'For you, the first was your meeting with Barzak, and the second was when you defeated *The Grim Grimoire*. The third for both of you is yet to come.

'We wanted to get a message to Grey to let him know this. But when your father tried to warn him, he was confronted by the fire in the cellar.'

She gave her husband a loving look. Archie's father smiled sadly.

'I could not stand by and watch a man die,' he said. 'So even though *The Book of Yore* had expressly forbidden us to change the future, I carried Grey from the burning cellar and your mother and I helped him to safety.

'Arthur Ripley shut *The Book of Yore*, thinking he had trapped us in the past. But the truth is that we could not have returned anyway because we broke the natural lores of magic. We interfered with the past and that is not permitted. The cost of saving Grey's life was our lives. But we have no regrets.'

'But I can save you,' cried Archie. 'I can bring you back with me.'

'No,' said Amelia Greene, and her gentle eyes smiled at her son. 'We cannot return after what we've done. We knew that at the time and we were happy to pay that price – though it will take another act of selflessness to defeat the Dark Flame.'

Archie felt the tears rolling down his cheeks.

'I won't leave,' he cried. 'I won't let you go again!'

'But you must, my darling,' his mother said. 'You have a destiny to fulfil, otherwise our sacrifice will have been for nothing.'

Alex Greene put his arm around his wife. 'We have missed you growing up,' he said. 'We have missed so many birthdays and good times with you. We couldn't have done it without the certain knowledge that we were leaving you with the most loving and caring family in your grandmother and your aunt Loretta and uncle Woodbine.'

Amelia Greene smiled. 'We set out to try to keep you safe, and we have never had a moment's regret. Not one. Not ever. We would do it all again in a heartbeat. So no matter how dark or desperate things seem, never doubt our love.'

Archie wiped his eyes and nodded. He felt his heart was breaking.

'Do not be sad for us,' his mother said, and she reached out her hand to touch his face but could not. 'We have been happy here. We have walked these streets together, and always we have thought of you and your sister, and knew that we might meet you once again in your dreams.'

Archie had a sudden thought. 'Rosie,' he gasped. 'Where is she? Isn't she here with you?'

'She is closer than you think, Archie,' said his father. 'She always was. You will find her. Now we must say goodbye.'

'Don't leave me!' cried Archie.

Amelia and Alex Greene smiled at their only son. 'Don't worry, Archie. As long as you remember us, we will never leave you. You are the love and the magic that we brought into the world, and we will meet again in your dreams.

'Now you must play your part. The future of magic depends on you. Your father asked Grey to leave something at Folly & Catchpole. It holds the key to everything. You must find the receipt and look for the raven's coming.'

As Archie watched, the scene began to fade like a mist evaporating in the sunshine and Alex and Amelia Greene with it. Archie found himself back in the Library of Lives.

As he turned away from the bookshelf, a candle ignited behind him and then another, guiding him back through the labyrinth. He followed the trail of lights retracing his steps until he could see the large door with the brass knocker standing open.

24

The Penfriend

When Archie awoke the next morning the dream was still vivid in his mind. When he told Bramble and Thistle about his mother and father, they all knew it was more than just a dream.

'It's *The Book of Prophecy*,' said Bramble. 'Somehow its magic is still working through you.'

She hugged him and Thistle put his arms around both of them. Archie felt the tears hot on his cheeks and buried his face in Bramble's shoulder. He felt his chest heaving with suppressed emotion, and then the tears flowed.

The three of them embraced until the sobs subsided. When Archie looked up, his cousins' cheeks were wet with tears, too, and he knew that he would never be alone as long as he had them in his life.

He wiped his face with his sleeve and sniffed. Bramble smiled and wiped her eyes.

'Grey left something at Folly & Catchpole,' said Archie, remembering what his mother had said. 'We need to find that receipt.'

The sky was dark with rain clouds as they walked into Oxford. It was still early when they reached the Aisle of White and they decided to check the laboratory for new messages. The bookshop wasn't open yet, so Archie let them in and they hurried downstairs. There was another note on the bench.

I have urgent news. Meet me here tonight (Thursday) at seven.
    FG

'Looks like we're finally going to meet our mysterious penfriend,' said Bramble. 'I'll let Arabella know.'

'What about Rupert?' asked Thistle.

'He won't be able to make it – he's in London,' said Bramble. 'We'll have to tell him what happens later. We can meet here at six thirty,' she added.

Archie nodded. 'There's something I need to do before then.'

When he passed the Scriptorium on his way to the Lost Books Department, Archie noticed that the old sofa that had been in the corridor the night before was gone. He shook his head. It didn't seem right. It felt as if all traces of Hawke were being erased.

When he reached Lost Books, there was a new sign on the door of the office.

Dr M Brown, Head of Lost Books

He heard voices. Faustus Gaunt was talking to Motley Brown.

'A third verse?' said Brown. 'But you said there were only two verses in Dee's prophecy.

'Yes, well I was wrong,' said Gaunt. 'The last verse was on a page that had come loose. We've only just found it now.'

Archie's heart quickened.

'And what does this third verse say?' asked Brown.

'I'll read it to you,' said Gaunt.

'To stop the dark
There is a price
A selfless act
Of sacrifice.'

'Oh dear,' said Brown. 'That doesn't sound good. What does it mean?'

'There's a price to be paid to defeat the Dark Flame,' said Gaunt. 'I suspect someone will have to pay with their life.'

His words hung awkwardly in the air. Archie swallowed hard. He had a sinking feeling.

'You have seen *The Book of Reckoning*. We are running out of time,' said Gaunt.

'I am well aware of that,' said Brown.

'You must do something,' urged Gaunt.

'I know what you are trying to do, Faustus. You are trying to force my hand, but I won't have it. If you continue with this I will have to inform Uther. There is only one Flame we answer to, and I think you have forgotten that. The time is coming when we must all stand up and be counted.'

'It is you, Motley, who have forgotten. The Dark Flame is rising and we can either join it or fight it. We must all choose which side we are on. I would hate to think that you were on the wrong side.'

'Are you threatening me, Faustus? My apprentice is a witness to this, you know.'

Gaunt swept out of the room, nearly bumping into Archie as he did.

Brown was sitting behind the desk peering at an open book through Hawke's imagining glass. Peter Quiggley was slouched in an armchair by the fire.

Archie knocked on the open door and Brown looked up.

'Ah, Archie,' he said, a smile flickering on his lips. 'Just the person I wanted to see. Come in. Sit down.'

He waved a hand absent-mindedly towards a stiff-backed chair that was in the place where the sofa used to be. Archie had to admit that the chair was a more sensible size for the room, but the study had lost some of its character. He wished he could relax into the soft embrace of the old sofa, but instead he perched on the uncomfortable chair.

Quiggley's eyes followed him from across the room.

'We heard you were attacked by another of the Pale Writers,' said Brown. 'Are you recovered?'

'I'm feeling much better, thank you,' said Archie.

'That's the ticket,' said Brown. 'Of course, you'll never fully recover from such an attack,' he murmured, more to himself than to Archie. 'But the important thing is that you fought it off. How did you do that exactly?'

Archie shrugged. 'Just lucky, I guess,' he murmured. He didn't want to admit that he'd used the

Torchstone. He felt terrible about losing it. He hadn't even told his cousins yet. His one consolation was that there was a spare. If he could get another ember from the Flame of Pharos quickly, no harm would have been done.

Brown peered at him through the tinted lens of the imagining glass, rubbing his chin thoughtfully.

'No matter,' he said. 'The thing is, Archie, as you know Gideon hasn't been himself lately and, well, I've been asked to step in and help out. Just for a while, you understand.'

Archie thought about the sign on the door. It suggested the appointment was more permanent. He glanced at Quiggley who was making himself at home in the chair by the fire with a big smirk on his face.

Archie gazed around the room. There were the signs of a hasty search. Books had been pulled off the shelves and dumped on the ground. The locks on Hawke's desk drawers had been forced and his things emptied on the floor.

Brown saw him looking. 'It's not pretty, I know, Archie, but there isn't much time and we can't afford to stand on ceremony. I need to know what Grey saw in *The Book of Prophecy* and I think Gideon was getting close. What did he tell you about it?'

Trust no one, Hawke had said, and as far as Archie was concerned that included Brown.

'Nothing,' Archie said. 'He never discussed it with me.'

'Never?' asked Brown.

'Well, he mentioned it in passing, but no more than that,' said Archie, guardedly.

'You're quite sure about that?'

'Yes,' said Archie, trying not to look too shifty.

Brown's face crumpled with disappointment. 'I thought he might have confided in you,' he said. 'Oh well, perhaps he didn't trust you with something so important. I'll just have to keep searching. If you think of anything, or remember anything Hawke said that might be a clue, you must tell me immediately.'

Archie nodded. 'What will happen now about my apprenticeship?' he asked. Brown gave him a distracted glance.

'Well, I haven't got time to teach you anything at the moment. I'm too busy trying to defeat the Dark Flame. What were you working on last?'

'Delving spells,' said Archie.

Brown looked more interested. 'Really?' he said thoughtfully. His eyes narrowed as an idea came into his head.

'Of course!' he said, speaking to himself again. 'With your book whispering and magic writing you'd be perfect. Hawke would have seen that. Why didn't I think of it before?' He suddenly seemed to realise he was speaking out loud.

Brown glanced at Quiggley. 'Perhaps you could show Peter what you've been learning.'

Quiggley sat up in the chair and glared at Archie. 'I don't think Greene has anything to teach me,' he said with a sneer. 'Not after what I've been learning recently.'

Archie wondered what sort of magic Quiggley had been taught. Hopefully, Brown had been teaching him how to care for the magical creatures in the menagerie.

'Yes, well, we can all learn from each other,' said Brown. 'Archie has some particularly rare talents. I want you to share what you know.'

Quiggley shot him a hopeful look, but Archie turned away.

That wasn't going to happen, Archie decided as he left the office. If Brown thought for a moment that he was going to share any of his secrets with Peter Quiggley he had another think coming! But right now he had other things on his mind.

He walked purposefully towards the archive. There was something he needed to do. He let himself in with his key and hurried through to the room where the Torchstones were kept. Now all he had to do was get another ember from the Word Smithy.

But the glass case was empty. The spare

Torchstone had gone.

Archie's heart sank. What was he going to do now? Hawke had asked him to be a flame carrier and he had managed to lose the first Torchstone. Now the second one had disappeared. He felt helpless. Who could have taken it?

He was beginning to lose hope. Then he had another thought.

'You have to find the receipt for Folly & Catchpole.' That's what his mother had said in his dream. If he could find that then everything might still be all right. But where could it be?

In the dream, Grey had shown the receipt to his father outside Folly & Catchpole's office. But what had he done with it after that? Archie had seen Grey put it in the pocket of his cloak.

Something stirred in Archie's mind. A light suddenly went on in his brain. Grey's cloak!

Grey had travelled to Oxford to hide the *Grimoire* in the Darchive. Rusp had said he was arrested immediately after: 'Taken by surprise – didn't even have time to get his cloak.' Perhaps the receipt was still in it!

Archie raced back through the archive to the alcove with the little door. Where better to leave a cloak than in a cloakroom?

Grey had locked the door with a magical spell. People had been trying to open it ever since but no one had discovered its secret. Archie examined the door. What kind of spell would prevent people opening a door?

He reached out to touch the door – and as he did he felt a strange tingling sensation in his hand. It was coming from Fabian Grey's ring on his finger. The mirror entrance to the secret library at the Royal Society was operated by Dawlish Hooke's magical ring. Perhaps the spell that Grey had put on the cloakroom used the same sort of magic?

The ring gleamed with a bright golden light and the lock that hadn't been turned in centuries clicked open. Grey must have put the spell on it when he was arrested knowing that it could only be opened by someone wearing the ring he'd left at Folly & Catchpole.

Archie was so excited he could hardly breathe. He pulled the little door towards him and peered inside.

There it was, hanging on a hook on the back of the door: Fabian Grey's scarlet cloak, just as he'd left it three hundred and fifty years ago. Archie felt goosebumps.

He fumbled with the material of the cloak, searching for an inside pocket. His hand touched a piece of parchment. It had a name and address printed on one side.

Folly & Catchpole, Gutter Lane, London.

Scarcely able to believe his eyes, Archie turned it over and read the words written on the other side.

Property of Fabian Grey.
Do NOT remove.
Owner will collect.

He'd found it! The clue that Hawke and Brown had been searching for! It had been in Grey's cloak all the time.

Now that he'd found it, what was he meant to do with it? What would Hawke have done with it? Trust no one, he'd said. Archie was sure he wouldn't have handed it over to the authorities and Archie wasn't about to either. Besides, that very evening they were meeting the mysterious FG. Maybe he'd get a chance to return it in person!

When Archie arrived at the Aisle of White, Bramble, Thistle and Arabella were waiting for him outside.

'Where've you been?' asked Arabella. 'And what's that?'

'Fabian Grey's cloak,' said Archie. 'It's a long story but I'm hoping that he might want it back. I'll explain later.'

'Do you really think the notes are from him?' asked Arabella.

'Only one way to find out,' said Bramble.

Archie let them into the bookshop and they crept downstairs. They could barely contain their excitement.

'If we wait in here,' Archie said, opening the door to the mending workshop, 'we'll hear whoever it is come down the stairs. They'll have to come in here to get the key to the lab.'

'But if it's Fabian Grey, he'll have his own key!' said Thistle.

'Good point,' said Archie. 'But in any case we'll hear them come past.'

They settled down to wait. The only light came from the Flame of Pharos burning in the Word Smithy. The Flame looked weaker than ever. Archie wondered what was wrong with it. Old Zeb had said that the Flame was hard to extinguish but it definitely looked like it was guttering.

Archie thought about the Torchstone again. If only he hadn't lost it! Arabella interrupted his thoughts. 'It's gone seven,' she said. 'He's late!'

'Shhhhhh,' hissed Bramble. 'I think I just heard something.'

They instantly fell silent, straining their ears for the slightest sounds of movement coming from the bookshop above them.

Then they all heard it, the cautious tread of footsteps on the spiral staircase. Someone was descending very carefully. The children glanced at each other. In the poor light from the furnace, their eyes were visible, glistening with excitement.

Archie had a sudden thought. 'What are we going to do if it is Fabian Grey?' he whispered. 'I'm not sure what you say to a three hundred and seventy year old alchemist!'

There were footsteps in the corridor. Someone was approaching stealthily. As they strained their senses to catch the slightest sound, the footsteps stopped outside the second door, the one that contained the bookend beasts.

The footsteps carried on down the passageway. Slowly they drew closer. Archie's mouth had gone dry. He felt goosebumps on his arms and the hairs on the back of his neck prickled.

The footsteps had almost reached the workshop now. Archie couldn't quite believe that after all this time he might be about to meet Fabian Grey, the most brilliant and infamous alchemist of all time.

The footsteps continued down the corridor and they heard a key turn and the door to the laboratory groan open.

'He's got his own key!' gasped Thistle.

'Quick, he's inside the lab,' said Archie. He opened the door to the mending workshop and crept down the corridor. Arabella hesitated at the workshop door, looking back up the passageway.

'What's the matter?' Archie whispered.

She shook her head. 'I thought I heard someone behind us. But there's no one there. I must have imagined it.'

When they reached the black door, Archie paused, with his hand on the handle.

'Ready?' he asked the other three. Bramble, Thistle and Arabella all nodded. 'On three. One, two, three . . .'

25

The Raven's Story

A rchie threw the door open and they all stared into the room expectantly with eyes as big as saucers.

'The Alchemists' Club, I presume!' said a familiar voice. 'Good evening, Archie, Bramble, Thistle and Arabella. It's a shame Rupert can't be here.'

Feodora Graves arched one eyebrow at them.

'Oh!' gasped Bramble. 'Feodora Graves – that FG!'

Graves raised her other eyebrow. 'You sound disappointed. Who were you expecting?'

The four children cast embarrassed glances at each other. Graves frowned. 'Don't tell me,' she tutted. 'You thought I was Fabian Grey!'

Archie looked sheepish. 'It was the initials,' he said lamely, trying to explain. 'FG?'

Graves allowed herself a rare smile. 'Well,' she said, 'I suppose I should be flattered.'

'How did you know about the laboratory?' asked Thistle.

'You didn't really think that all your comings and goings to the Aisle of White had gone unnoticed, did you?' said Graves. 'Old Zeb guessed what you'd discovered behind the black door. He told Gideon and I.'

'But how did you get in without the key?' asked Thistle.

She held out her hand and they saw she had another key. 'There were five keys, one for each of the original members of the Alchemists' Club. Zeb found this one long ago. It was easy for me to leave my messages on the bench for you to find.'

'And the picture of the raven?' said Archie.

'The raven brought you a warning when it delivered Grey's ring to you, and I was trying to warn you, too,' she said.

'But why all the secrecy?' asked Bramble. 'You could have talked to us any time you wanted.'

Graves' smile vanished. 'I suppose I do owe you an explanation for that,' she said. 'You'd better sit down.'

When they were all seated at the wooden bench, Graves told them that she knew all about the Alchemists' Club rewriting the magical books.

'Gideon told me what you were doing,' she said. 'All the heads of department knew but we agreed to let you get on with it. That way we didn't have to report it to the magical authorities and you didn't have the Magical League breathing down your necks. Writing magic is classified as a dangerous magical practice and against the Lores of Magical Restraint.

'Everything was fine until *The Book of Night* was stolen. That cast a huge shadow. I'd known for some time that we had a traitor inside the museum. Whoever it is has been spying on us for a long time. They seemed to know our every move. They were leaking information to the Greaders, even before Katerina Krone arrived.

'But I didn't know who it was. I still don't. That's why I sent you the cryptic messages. I wanted to warn you, but I didn't want the enemy to know what I suspected.'

She paused.

'Whoever is behind this wanted Gideon out of the way. He was following some line of enquiry that made them very uncomfortable, so they got rid of him.

'The reason I'm telling you now is that I believe they will try to get rid of me, too. That's why I'm leaving tonight. It isn't safe for me here any more. The Greaders are mustering their forces and soon they will be strong enough to try to take over the magical realm. They will be ruthless with those who oppose them.'

'Where will you go?' asked Bramble.

Graves gave a thin smile. 'I'll go into hiding. If the Greaders succeed in seizing power, the magical realm will need people like me to organise the resistance. I can do more to fight the Dark Flame if I'm still at liberty. And the Greaders are plotting something very dark indeed. Every day their ranks grow. The Black Dragon is spreading like an epidemic. People are frightened.'

'Why don't the museum elders do something to stop it?' asked Archie.

Graves shook her head sadly. 'I'm afraid it's beyond the powers of the museum,' she said. 'Any one of us who made a stand would be overruled and removed from office like Gideon. There are powers at work here that you don't understand.'

'The Magical League itself,' breathed Archie. The suspicion had been growing in his mind ever since Morgred had turned up at the asylum.

Graves nodded. 'I fear so,' she said. 'The Dark Flame is very powerful and very persuasive for any one who has Greader sympathies. And I'm afraid there are many of those in positions of power. The magical realm will be overcome by dark magic unless someone stops them. Grey's vision – it's the only hope!'

'We know,' said Archie. 'We've been searching and we're so close to knowing it. We think we've got the final clue—'

There was a creaking sound from the other side of the room near the door.

'What was that?' demanded Graves. 'I heard something.' She paused, listening. 'Over by the door! I can feel a presence.'

'There's someone there,' she cried. 'They're using some sort of cloaking magic!

'*Spell of Hiding*
Spell of stealth
Secret listener
Reveal yourself!'

As she uttered the last word they saw a cloaked figure standing by the door.

'A spy!' cried Graves. 'Quick, grab him!'

But it was too late; the hooded figure had already opened the door and darted into the passageway, slamming it shut behind them. By the time Archie and the others reached the door and opened it, the cloaked figure was gone. They heard footsteps running up the spiral stairs.

'Leave him,' cried Graves. 'You won't catch him

now – the revealing spell only lasts a few seconds. He's using invisibility magic and he'll have vanished again before you can catch up with him.'

'But how?' Bramble asked.

'Snuffling blood makes a very potent invisibility potion,' said Graves. 'I think we know where the snufflings have been going now.' She sighed. 'At least that explains how the enemy always seemed to know what we were doing.'

'I bet that's what the Greaders have been using to hide the Black Dragon firemark, too,' said Archie.

Graves' face looked drawn. She looked at each one of them in turn.

'The final battle of the flames is about to begin. I trust you to do what I have not – to find the secret to defeating the Dark Flame. I will do what I can to help you. By leaving tonight I will divert attention away from you. But it's up to the Alchemists' Club now. All our hopes rest with you.'

The four of them were thoughtful as they walked home. They felt the weight of responsibility on their shoulders. It was a new moon so there wasn't much light. They had just left the courtyard outside Quill's and were walking up Catte Street past the Bodleian Library when they heard a sound like crumbling masonry and some stones falling onto the pavement behind them.

Bramble looked up at the parapet. 'Where did they come from?' she said, leaning against the iron railings.

'Must have fallen off one of the statues,' said Thistle.

Bramble was still staring at the roof. 'Wait a minute,' she said, 'there's something missing. Look, up there, there's a gap. I'm sure there used to be a gargoyle there.'

Archie looked where she was pointing. She was right. 'It's the stone dragon,' he said. 'It's gone!'

'It can't have just gone,' said Arabella. 'Stone dragons don't just wander off!'

'You're right,' said Bramble, swallowing hard, 'unless they aren't stone any more. Look!'

They stared at the roof. Two angry red eyes stared back. They belonged to a large, heavily scaled reptile with a long snout and jaws full of razor-like teeth. Two wings were folded across its back.

'What on earth is that?' said Arabella.

'A medieval fire drake,' said Thistle, staring at the creature. 'A dragon to you.'

As they watched they saw something else on the roof, a dark shadow beside the creature.

'There's someone up there with it!' cried Arabella.

At that moment the creature opened its jaws and belched fire. They could see the cloaked figure crouching beside the beast. Something glinted in its hand. A knife. Archie recognised it.

'It's the Shadow Blade from Hawke's office!' he exclaimed.

'What's he doing?' asked Bramble.

They watched as the hooded figure plunged the blade into the dragon's chest. The wounded creature screamed with pain and launched itself off the roof.

The four children watched as it opened its wings, gliding through the air towards them.

'Its heading straight for us,' cried Archie. 'Run!'

Bramble and Thistle ducked out of the way, but Arabella stood transfixed, unable to take her eyes off the dragon as it hurtled towards her. The dragon opened its jaws, belching out a plume of fire. In another second it would have incinerated Arabella, but at that moment Archie rugby-tackled her to the ground. The dragon passed just over their heads, missing them by inches, its fiery breath making the iron railings glow red-hot. As it did, they could see the gaping wound in its chest near its heart.

With a few powerful beats of its wings, the dragon soared off among the towers and spires of the Oxford skyline. Then it wheeled around in the sky to make another pass. As they stared

after it, they saw a small dark shape of a bird dart in a circle around it. The dragon turned its head, its jaws snapping at the bird. But it was getting weaker. Its wing beats slowed and it began to fall out of the sky.

The children watched the dragon spinning out of control towards the ground, its fiery breath lighting the Oxford night like flashes of lightning. Down it tumbled until it disappeared from sight. With a final scream it crashed into the River Thames.

They were too stunned to speak for a few seconds. When they glanced back at the rooftop, the cloaked figure had vanished.

Thistle was the first to recover. 'What was that all about?' he said still staring in the direction that the creature had fallen into the river.

'Why bring it to life only to kill it?' asked Bramble.

'Someone is practising some very dark magic,' said Archie. 'And whoever it is is very nearby,' he added, looking around anxiously. 'And where did all these birds come from?'

A flock of black birds had landed on the roof of the Bodleian and were shrieking in their high-pitched voices.

'They're ravens,' said Thistle. 'You don't normally see this many all together.'

'Look for the raven's coming,' murmured Archie, under his breath.

One of the birds was sitting apart from the others.

The solitary raven ruffled its feathers and fixed him with its flinty-black eyes. It flew down and landed on the head of a statue nearby. Archie noticed that it had some white feathers among the black plumage of its head.

'We meet again, Archie Greene,' it said.

'You're the raven that brought the ring,' Archie said.

The bird gave him a haughty look, putting its head on one side. 'Yes, of course,' it replied. 'How many talking ravens do you know?'

A gentle breeze ruffled the raven's feathers. It turned its head on one side again and bowed. Now that Archie saw it up close, he thought its flinty eyes were slightly different colours, and some of the feathers on its head were definitely white.

'Gran was right – you're Fabian Grey!' exclaimed Archie, hardly able to contain himself.

The raven regarded him evenly. 'Yes,' it said, 'or at least I am one part of Fabian Grey – for that is the curse that was put on me. Poor Roderick, Angelica, and Braxton, their lives were cut so short. But the *Grimoire* wanted me to suffer. While the others were cursed to die young, I was cursed with another burden. This burden that you see before you.'

'Why didn't you say who you were before?' asked Archie.

'Would you have believed me?' asked the raven.

Archie thought for a moment. 'Probably not,' he agreed.

'I thought as much. That's why I was waiting for the right moment to reveal myself. I had to win your trust first.'

'Why are you telling us now?' asked Archie.

'The enemy has what it has been seeking,' said the raven.

'Dragon's blood,' said Archie.

'Yes.'

'It was you we saw flying with the dragon just before it fell from the sky.'

'I led it towards the river where it could do no more harm and I caught some of the beast's blood,' said the raven. Archie noticed it grasped a small silver phial in its claw.

The raven continued. 'Time is short. We have work to do. I bring a warning. The Flame of Pharos is in great danger. You must act quickly if you are to save it.'

'How do we know we can trust you?' asked Arabella suspiciously.

The raven fluttered into the air and alighted on

a ledge nearby. It ruffled its feathers and gave her a flinty stare. 'I give you my word,' it said. 'And my word is my mark.'

Archie recognised the phrase. 'That's what it says on the gold ring you gave me,' he said.

The bird bowed low to him, and then it bowed three more times to Bramble, Thistle and Arabella.

'What happened to you?' asked Archie.

'It's long story,' said the raven. 'But I will tell you what you need to know.

'When I was imprisoned in the Tower of London, I befriended the ravens that live there. They brought me food, and I told them my story. Without them I would have starved.

'As you see, I am cursed to spend part of my time as a raven. The change is brought on by the new moon, and lasts twenty-four hours. This I discovered when I was locked in the Tower. The *Grimoire*'s curse said that I would transform into the first creature I saw – and that was the raven that brought me my food. My raven form allowed me to escape from the Tower – but still I found myself in a prison of the flesh.'

The raven hopped closer. It fixed its flinty eyes on Archie.

'As a man I have no memory of my previous life. I do not even know myself as Fabian Grey – but as a raven I remember everything.'

The bird hopped a little closer still and looked into Archie's eyes. Archie could see the torment in its dark eyes. 'And so I am cursed to live this double life. Once a month I change into a raven and know that whatever I do, when I transform back into a man I will have no memory of it. Do you know what it is like to wake up in a strange city and not know how you got there? He thinks he's going mad, this other me. I leave him clues but he never knows what they mean or what he's meant to do with them!'

As the raven spoke Archie felt a terrible sadness for its predicament.

'Who is he this poor tormented man?'

'I know him only as Fabian Grey,' said the raven.

'Isn't there a spell that could lift the curse?' Archie asked.

'There is,' said the raven. 'I read it in a book a long time ago. It is a spell that would allow me to take on one or the other form permanently. But I cannot perform it as a raven and he does not remember.'

'When this is all over, we'll help you,' said Archie, struck again by the raven's sad plight.

'But how have you lived so long?' asked Thistle. 'Was it the azoth in the fire?'

'Yes,' said the raven appraisingly. 'I was drenched in it at the moment the *Grimoire* cursed me. It prolonged my life.'

Archie held up the scarlet cloak. 'I think this is yours,' he said.

The raven gazed at it in wonder. 'Is the receipt still in it?' it asked.

Archie took the piece of parchment from the pocket.

The raven's eyes glinted in the light from the street lamp. 'Thank you,' it said, and took the parchment from Archie's outstretched hand.

'What will you do with it?' asked Archie.

'I will deliver it somewhere my human self will find it, in the hope that it rekindles some deep memory in him.' The raven turned its head and looked at the roof of the Bodleian. 'And I will send the ravens to watch over you. They will carry the warning. The rest is up to you.'

It flapped its wings. 'Look for me when all hope has gone!' it said, and soared into the air.

26

Where Shadows Dwell

That night Archie slept fitfully. He dreamed that he was a raven flying over the rooftops of Oxford pursued by a great snarling dragon.

The next morning he awoke with a terrible sense of foreboding. He roused his cousins but he was too agitated to wait for them.

'I've got to go – sorry!' he said, dashing out of the front door while they were still getting up.

He ran all the way into Oxford. When he reached the courtyard outside the Aisle of White, he went to the bookshop.

He knew something was wrong the moment he stepped through the door. The bell didn't clang. Marjorie Gudge, Geoffrey Screech's assistant, was sitting behind the counter. She'd been crying.

'Where's Mr. Screech?' asked Archie urgently.

Marjorie blew her noise loudly into a handkerchief. 'Gone,' she sobbed.

'Gone where?' asked Archie.

'To tell the elders.'

'Why? What's happened?'

She blew her nose again and waved her hand towards the black velvet curtain behind her.

'It's too awful. See for yourself!' she wailed.

Archie's heart was beating fast. The last time he'd seen Marjorie this upset was when Greaders had broken into the bookshop. He pulled back the curtain and slipped through.

'Hello?' he said to the magical books that were usually there. But there was no reply. The bookcase was empty. There were always some magical books waiting to go to the museum. What could possibly have happened?

'Where are the books?' he called over his shoulder.

'Apparently they weren't safe here any more,' sniffled Marjorie. 'Motley Brown collected them an hour ago.'

Archie took the spiral stairs two at a time. When he reached the passageway at the bottom he raced past the first two doors and opened the third door. What he saw was almost too much to bear.

Old Zeb was sitting hunched over the

workbench with his head in his hands. His shoulders were stooped.

Archie shivered. The room was cold. He'd never known it be other than warm. He looked at the old bookbinder in bewilderment.

'What's the matter?' he asked. 'What's happened?'

Old Zeb looked up – his normally bright eyes had lost their sparkle. They looked dull and rheumy. He suddenly looked his age. He shook his head sadly from side to side.

'It's the Smithy.'

Archie crossed the room to the furnace against the wall. He touched it. It was cold. He opened the door and peered inside.

'The Flame!' he exclaimed.

Old Zeb shook his head again. He looked close to tears himself. 'Gone,' he said, his voice flat and breaking. 'The Flame of Pharos has been extinguished.'

'How?' asked Archie.

'Sabotage,' said Old Zeb. 'Someone deliberately put it out. Someone who knew how to quench it.'

'Dragon's blood!'

The old man nodded sadly.

So that was why the stone dragon had been brought to life and then killed – for its fresh blood. And that must have been why someone had taken Simon the salamander's blood as well – but clearly it hadn't been strong enough, perhaps because he wasn't a real dragon. The same person must also have entered the bookend beast's lair trying to get griffin's breath but had been scared off.

A lot of things were suddenly making sense and it all hit Archie like a punch in the stomach. He had another jolt of realisation.

'But if the Flame of Pharos is extinguished that means . . .'

'Yes,' said Old Zeb, 'that the Dark Flame is the only magical flame left in the world. We must choose between dark magic or no magic at all!'

The full force of the old man's words suddenly hit Archie. He felt utterly grief stricken.

Archie left the Aisle of White with his head in a spin. He couldn't quite believe what was happening. The Flame of Pharos that had burned for thousands of years and contained the spirits of the great magisters from the Golden Age of Magic was no more. Archie's world was shattered.

If only he hadn't lost the Torchstone! With the embers Old Zeb would have been able to rekindle the Flame. If only he had kept it safe. He'd let Hawke down. He'd let everyone down. He had failed magic and now there was only the Dark Flame left. And soon it would destroy all the good magic until there was only dark magic left in the world.

The only hope now was to destroy the Dark Flame as well. It would mean that there was no magic left in the world – but surely that was better than dark magic?

As he hurried across the courtyard he felt a drop of rain. A storm was coming.

He had to tell the Foxes the awful news. He pulled up his collar against the rain and trudged back to Houndstooth Road.

He reached the front door and let himself in. The house was quiet. He heard low voices coming from the kitchen. He closed the door behind him and made his way down the hall.

Bramble was sitting at the kitchen table with Loretta, Gardenia and Woodbine. From the looks on their faces they had been having a very serious conversation. Archie wondered what they'd been talking about but his news was too urgent to wait.

There was no easy way to break it to them.

'The Flame of Pharos has been extinguished,' he said.

He expected them to gasp with horror or for Loretta to burst into tears, but they didn't react.

'We know,' said Loretta. 'Wolfus told us. He came to the house to warn us that the elders are calling all the Flame-Keeping families together to defend the museum.'

Archie nodded. 'We'd better get down there, then,' he said. But no one moved. What was going on?

'Archie, sit down,' said Gardenia, gently. 'There's something you need to know. It's about your sister.'

Archie felt his heart leap into his mouth. 'Rosie? Do you know where she is?'

Loretta nodded. 'She's . . . here.'

'What?' cried Archie, staring from face to face. 'Where?'

Bramble stood up. 'Right in front of you,' she said. She had tears in her eyes.

Archie's mouth fell open. He stared at her, trying to take in what was happening. Could it be true?

Bramble was standing beside him, being brave like she'd always been. And suddenly he knew without any doubt that she was his sister not his cousin.

'You are Rosie!' he said, his eyes wide with wonder.

'Yes,' she said, 'though I didn't know it until just now.'

'I told her,' said Loretta.

Bramble reached out for Archie and hugged him, holding him so tight he could barely breathe. 'Welcome home, little brother,' she whispered in his ear.

Archie felt a dam of emotions burst inside him. He clutched her close and the tears streamed down his face. For a long moment they stayed like that – brother and sister locked together in an embrace.

'I was never very far away,' she whispered and kissed him lightly on the brow.

Archie felt a huge weight had been lifted from him. He looked over Bramble's shoulder and saw Gardenia and Loretta smiling lovingly at him.

Woodbine stood up. 'Well, then, young 'uns,' he said, trying to sound like his normal self but his voice catching with emotion.

Bramble threw her arms around him. 'Steady, girl!' Woodbine said, wiping a tear from his crinkly eye.

'It's all OK,' she said. 'Thank you for being my dad all these years!'

He coughed. 'You're very welcome.' He offered Archie one of his knuckle-crunching handshakes, but it turned into a hug.

'I've told Thistle, so he knows, too,' said Woodbine.

At the mention of his name, Thistle's freckly face appeared. 'I don't feel that I've lost a sister so much as gained a cousin,' he said. 'I always thought I was too good-looking to be your brother anyway.'

His face fell. 'But I don't know what to call you?'

'My name is Bramble,' she said. 'And don't

you forget it. And you are still my little squirt of a brother.'

Thistle smiled.

'Now,' said Loretta, 'I think we should all sit down.'

Loretta made a pot of tea and put out one of her cakes, but no one was hungry. They sat around the table talking.

Archie was still in shock. All this time he'd been trying to trace his family and his sister had been right under his nose. He wasn't sure whether he wanted to laugh or cry.

'Are there any more secrets in this family?' he said. 'Because I'm not sure I can take any more surprises!'

Loretta shook her head. 'No, that's everything now.'

Gardenia glanced at Loretta. 'It's been very hard on all of us. There wasn't a day went by when I didn't want to tell you that you had a sister, Archie. And it was the same for Loretta with you, Bramble. We couldn't even see each other because we couldn't take the risk of someone finding out.'

'We promised your mother and father that we would follow their wishes. They were adamant that we did everything possible to keep you both safe. This was their way of protecting you.

'When your father consulted *The Book of Prophecy* and discovered you had a forked fate, the two of them decided what they were going to do. It all happened so quickly that none of us had time to think it through. And then they were gone and we couldn't change it without breaking our promises. So we lived with it and hoped that it was for the best.

'When the book arrived on your twelfth birthday I was relieved that you could be together. Telling you that you were cousins instead of brother and sister seemed a small price to pay. You were together – and with Thistle, too. That was all that mattered. And we quickly realised that you were much stronger together than you were apart – and you looked after each other.'

'So why are you telling us now?' asked Bramble.

Loretta wiped her eye. 'Alex and Amelia said that if the Flame of Pharos was ever extinguished and we were facing the end of the museum and all that it stands for, then we were to tell you the truth. We were not to let you face your destiny without knowing who you really are to each other.

'That day has come. The final battle for the soul of magic is about to begin.'

It was raining when they crossed the courtyard. The Aisle of White was closed and shutters had been put across the window. The Flame Keepers had begun to gather at Quill's.

When Archie arrived with his family, Loretta's eyes were red but she had her best purple lipstick on and a steely look in her eyes. She was flanked by Gardenia and Woodbine, who looked equally determined.

Some apprentices were standing in the back of house. Pink was trying to calm them. When they came in, all eyes turned to Archie, Bramble and Thistle.

'So it's true,' said Meredith Merrydance, 'that the Flame of Pharos has been extinguished?'

Archie nodded once. He couldn't bring himself to pronounce the words.

The apprentices fell silent.

'Where are the Elders?' demanded Bramble. 'What are they doing?'

'Feodora has gone,' said Pink. 'She left last night. Took all her books of supernatural magic with her.'

But of course they knew this – Graves had told them what she intended to do. 'What about Gaunt and Brown?' asked Archie.

'Motley Brown took a load of magical books and left. I don't know where he's gone. Faustus is in the archive. He's still trying to figure out how Grey was meant to save magic. It's desperate now.

Wolfus and Morag are selecting which books they will try to save. Rusp is with them.'

The next hour passed in a blur. The rain was falling harder as the light faded and darkness fell.

Archie stared out through the permission wall at the gathering storm. Rain was lashing at the windows. A flash of forked lightning lit the courtyard and was followed by a rumble of thunder. He watched as people made their way through the downpour to be at Quill's.

The place was filling up. News that the Flame of Pharos had been extinguished had spread rapidly. Pockets of the magical community were gathering all over the country as they tried to make sense of what had happened.

The people who came to Quill's were Flame-Keeper families – descended from the defenders of the Great Library of Alexandria. Most of them were quiet, heads bowed like mourners at a wake. But they were resolute in their defiance of the Dark Flame.

Old Zeb and Geoffrey Screech were standing together. The old bookbinder looked frail but determined. Marjorie was with them and kept blowing her nose into a handkerchief.

But the one person Archie wanted to see most was missing. Gideon Hawke was locked up in the asylum. Archie wondered what he would do if he were there.

Gaunt, Bone and Pandrama arrived together. By the grim looks on their faces Archie guessed they had finally given up on the prophecy. He wondered if it was too late now anyway.

Bramble and Thistle stood beside him.

'So it's come to this,' said Woodbine, joining them.

'What's the plan?' asked Bramble.

Woodbine's eyes narrowed. 'We'll make our stand here at Quill's. Old Zeb has gone to wake up the bookend beasts. If the Greaders get into the museum then the magical books will be at their mercy. They will have complete control of the magical realm.'

'What are our chances?' whispered Archie.

His uncle dropped his voice. 'Without knowing what Grey was meant to do? All but zero. Now that the Flame of Pharos has been extinguished, the magic protecting the museum will start to fail. But we'll put up one hell of a fight! When the history of magic is written it will say that we went down with our heads held high, all spells blazing!'

Archie believed him. The Flame Keepers would defend the museum to the end. To the last man, woman or child. They would try to protect the magical books from the Dark Flame and the Greaders, no matter what the cost to them.

'See that?' whispered Woodbine, indicating Pandrama and Gaunt, who were carrying piles of books. 'They're taking the most precious books to a safe house!'

Even at this dark hour they were trying to smuggle some of the magical books to safety to keep fighting if the museum fell, as it surely must. Archie felt a wave of emotion well up inside him.

He was incredibly sad but proud at the same time. He was proud to be one of these people – a Flame Keeper. Some of them were standing around in their family groups, parents and apprentices together. The Merryweathers were there, and the Drews, and most of the other old families.

Rupert's family, the Trevallens, were there, too, but their son was not. Archie wondered if Rupert was safe. There were rumours of magical battles being fought in London.

Archie moved between the groups. The conversations were muted and people were stony-faced. The Flame Keepers were stoic but he could tell that most of them didn't hold out much hope.

He noticed that Arabella was standing alone. Archie remembered the first time he'd ever seen her in the Aisle of White with her mother. He could tell that she wasn't comfortable. She hadn't wanted to be there.

Arabella had always been an outsider. Perhaps that's why the two of them understood each other.

He tapped her on the shoulder.

'You okay, Arabella?' he said.

She managed the thinnest of smiles and a nod.

'I'm the only Ripley on the side of the Flame Keepers. Right now the followers of the Dark Flame are meeting at my parents' house. That's where they are mustering their forces. The place was pretty full when I left. I had to sneak out of an upstairs window and climb down a drainpipe to get away. Now the Flame of Pharos is extinguished, some people can't take the Dark Oath fast enough!'

The Ripley family had always had more than its fair share of Greaders. And they weren't the only ones. Archie knew from Woodbine that a lot of seemingly respectable members of the magical community secretly practised dark magic.

Others were just trying to save their own skins. They knew that once the Dark Master was in power he would be ruthless in punishing anyone who did not join him.

'Archie!'

He heard a cry behind him and turned to see Rupert striding towards him.

'I came as soon as I heard about the Flame,' he said. 'It's just too awful!'

'What's the news from London?' asked Archie.

'It's not good,' said Rupert. 'The Royal Society has been taken over by followers of the Dark Master. They've been taking the Dark Oath inside the building. I was lucky to get out before they sealed the doors.'

'And Gloom?' asked Archie.

'I don't know,' said Rupert. 'He said something about protecting the dark library, but I haven't seen him since.'

'Rupert, thank goodness you're okay!' exclaimed Bramble.

'What's the Magical League doing?' asked Thistle.

'Nothing. There have been attacks on other magical buildings, too, that have left some people dead. And the Unready know there's something going on. Their media is full of it, including radio and television reports of magical duels. The streets of London are empty. People are frightened.'

Rupert paused for breath. 'And Gideon Hawke has left the asylum.'

'What?' exclaimed Archie, and his heart skipped a beat. 'How did he escape?'

'That's just it,' said Rupert, shaking his head. 'The authorities there let him go. People are saying that he was in on the plot from the beginning.'

Archie's heart sank. He couldn't believe it. Not Hawke! He felt his anger rising.

'That's rubbish!' he said. 'It's all lies! Hawke wouldn't betray the museum.'

'Where is Fabian Grey when we need him!' snorted Arabella.

Grey may not be around to save magic, and who knew why Hawke had been released, but Archie Greene wasn't ready to give up just yet. Woodbine had said they would go down fighting. And that was what Archie intended to do!

He pulled the other members of the Alchemists' Club to one side. 'I think there's time for one last meeting,' he whispered. 'Come on.'

The five of them slipped through the door ray while Pink wasn't looking. They crossed the wet courtyard, let themselves into the Aisle of White and made their way down to Grey's laboratory.

Fifty miles away in London, Horace Catchpole stirred. He'd fallen asleep at his desk but something had just woken him. He'd been keeping a vigil at the Folly & Catchpole offices in Gutter Lane. The package for Fabian Grey was on his desk. Horace had heard about the Greader plot, but he still had a job to do.

Horace sat up and looked around him. His office was in darkness except for a thin sliver of light that entered the room through a gap beneath the blind. Sitting in the shadows he strained his hearing to pick up the slightest sound. Then he heard it again, the soft tread of footsteps on the stairs. Someone was approaching.

A floorboard creaked and Horace felt his heart beat a little faster. Glancing around the office, he thought about protecting himself from the intruder. He crossed to the small fireplace and picked up the poker. Then his eyes returned to the package on the desk.

The footsteps were getting closer now. They'd reached the top of the stairs and were moving down the corridor towards him. In another moment they would be outside his door.

Horace's eyes flicked nervously between the desk and the door. Very slowly the door handle began to turn. Horace took a breath and held it, his body taut. His mouth was dry. He had no idea what to expect. He'd known it was only a matter of time before the Greaders learned about the package and its whereabouts. When they did they would try to take it. But Horace wasn't going to let it go without a fight.

He gazed at the door as it slowly began to open, letting in a small amount of light from the landing, just enough for him to catch a glint of white hair. A dark figure was standing in the doorway. The tension was excruciating. A shadow fell across the desk. Horace swallowed hard.

'I suppose you've come for this?' he asked, indicating the package on the desk. The figure nodded and reached out a hand.

'Not so fast,' said Horace. 'You'll need to prove you are the rightful owner.'

The stranger took something from a pocket and slid it across the desk. As he did his cloak fell open revealing his face.

'Oh! It's you!' said Horace. 'But . . .'

'Perhaps it's best not to ask too many questions,' said the figure. 'After all, you are famed for minding your own business, and I have the receipt.'

Horace studied the slip of paper.

'Hmmm,' he said after a while. 'That seems to be in order.'

The man reached for the package a second time.

Horace put his hand on top of it. 'I have a duty of care to the magical realm,' he said. 'What do you intend to do with it?'

The man regarded him with new respect. 'I intend to use it,' he said.

'Use it. I see,' said Horace, as if he didn't quite trust his own ears. 'I'll have to ask you to sign the ledger. There are procedures to be followed.'

He spun the ledger around on the desk so that

it faced the visitor. 'At Folly & Catchpole we pride ourselves on not making mistakes ...'

'Yes, I remember,' interrupted the stranger. 'That's why you were chosen.'

The man grasped the pen tightly and Horace noticed that his hands shook when he tried to write.

The signature was little more than a squiggle.

'It's been in our cellar since 1666,' said Horace, unable to contain his curiosity. 'Why has it taken you so long to collect it?'

The man laughed. 'I couldn't remember where I'd left it. But it's all starting to come back to me now.'

He reached across the desk and took the package. 'Now, if you'll excuse me, I have something very important to do, something I've waited a long time for.'

Horace nodded and offered his hand. 'Good luck,' he said.

The man shook his hand. Then he turned and walked away. Horace listened as the footsteps receded down the stairs, then he loosened his tie and tried to breathe normally. It wasn't every day that he came face to face with Fabian Grey.

27

The Dark Master

The five members of the Alchemists' Club were standing in Grey's laboratory.

'We pledge to restore magic to its former glory,' they all repeated, but their words sounded hollow.

'What are we going to do?' asked Arabella, desperation in her voice. 'The Greaders will attack the museum any time now. They are just waiting for the signal. With the Dark Flame on their side, the Flame Keepers won't be able to resist them.'

'We have to destroy the Dark Flame,' said Archie. 'It's the only way to prevent a dark age of magic.'

'But even if we could, that would mean the end of magic,' said Rupert.

'And we pledged to restore magic to its former glory,' said Arabella.

'I know,' said Archie, 'but better no magic than that sort of magic!'

They heard footsteps on the stairs.

'Shhhh,' hissed Bramble, putting her finger to her lips. 'Someone's coming.' They crossed to the door and peered along the corridor.

The passageway appeared to be empty, but just then a hooded figure suddenly appeared from nowhere.

'Where did he come from?' whispered Rupert.

'An invisibility potion made from snuffling blood,' whispered Archie.

Rupert bristled with anger. 'He'll wish he could disappear when I get my hands on him!'

The figure pulled back his cloak and they recognised Peter Quiggley.

'The snake,' hissed Bramble.

Quiggley glanced up and down the passage to check the coast was clear. They stepped back into the shadows in time to avoid being seen by him.

Quiggley started down the passageway but stopped at the first door. 'Where's he going now?' whispered Thistle.

'He's using the Enchanted Entrance,' said Archie. 'He must be going to another magical building.'

Quiggley glanced over his shoulder again, then he fitted a key into the door and opened it. He stepped through, closing it behind him.

'He's left the key in the door,' said Archie. 'Come on!'

He raced along the passageway and grabbed the door handle.

'Door of mystery, door of grace,
Take me to my chosen place.'

He recited, using the spell that Old Zeb had taught him. The door opened and the five children stepped through it.

They didn't see Old Zeb standing in the shadows but he watched them go. Then he opened the blue door to the bookend beasts' frozen lair.

'Come on, my beauties,' he called, 'awaken now – there's work to be done.'

On the other side of the enchanted entrance, the five members of the Alchemists' Club found themselves in a long corridor.

'We're inside my parents' house,' whispered Arabella. 'This leads to the great hall. That's where the Greaders are gathering.'

Ahead of them they could see an open door. Archie took a step towards it.

'Wait!' whispered Arabella. 'Put these on.' She indicated some cloaks hanging on pegs. 'My parents use them for their Greader meetings.'

They slipped them on and pulled up the hoods to cover their faces and hurried along the corridor. As they stepped through the doorway, a flash of lightning illuminated a large room with a tall leaded window from the floor to the ceiling. Archie recognised it from his dream. It was where *The Book of Night* had been opened and he had witnessed the first Dark Oath ceremony. The last time he'd seen it he'd been watching through the window with the eyes of a raven.

The lightning was followed by a whip crack of thunder. Rain lashed against the tall window. Another flash of lightning lit the room. Archie was aware of cloaked figures all around him.

He pulled his hood closer and ducked in among the crowd, hoping they hadn't been seen. The others followed him.

'There's my parents,' whispered Arabella, covering her mouth with her hand. Archie spotted Veronica Ripley and her husband, Mortimer, watching the proceedings from a small balcony like a minstrels' gallery, smug smiles on their faces. They were gazing at the front of the room where a raised platform like a stage had been erected in front of the leaded window.

On a black plinth in the centre of the stage *The Book of Night* was open with a black flame burning in its pages.

Another flash of lightning lit the stage and Archie could see a group of shrouded figures standing around the flame. He counted five of them in all. One was very tall, two others were of medium height and the other two were shorter.

The tall figure raised its arms and spoke in a loud voice. 'My dark brothers and sisters, welcome to Ripley Mansion, the ancestral home of the Ripleys and the headquarters of our movement for many years. We are so glad that you could join us. Tonight we are celebrating the start of a new age of magic!

'We're expecting someone special and we will be meeting them very soon. First, let us all pledge our loyalty to the Dark Flame. Repeat the Dark Oath with me.'

Archie gazed around him at the swelling ranks of dark followers. More and more were joining all the time so that the room was full of them now. Archie had a horrible feeling that some of them were familiar. He was sure he recognised the stooped figure of Aurelius Rusp standing in front of him.

The crowd began chanting.

'Darkest of the two
We pledge ourselves to you
By the power of the Flame
We blacken magic's name!'

As the chanting grew louder the black flame burning in *The Book of Night* rose higher and burned more fiercely. Every new follower made the Flame more powerful. Archie was shocked to see how much bigger it had become since he'd seen it in his dream.

The chanting ceased and the room fell silent except for the driving rain against the tall windowpanes.

There was another eye-stabbing flash of lightning and rumble of thunder. Archie stared at the window where he could see a strangely shaped dark cloud was forming in the sky. He wondered what it was, but his attention was diverted back to the stage as the tall figure at the front pulled back his hood. Archie saw the sallow features of Uther Morgred.

No wonder the Magical League had been so useless at stopping Greader activity!

Morgred turned to the other cloaked figures beside him. 'Welcome, my dark brothers. You bring word from the Museum of Magical Miscellany?'

The two shorter figures stepped forward. The first pulled back his hood. Archie heard a sharp intake of breath beside him.

'It's Motley Brown,' hissed Bramble. 'He's the traitor.'

Brown was speaking. 'The Flame of Pharos is extinguished!' he said. 'We all serve the Dark Flame now.'

The second figure removed his hood. Peter Quiggley's round face looked out at them. Archie felt the bile rise in his stomach. Quiggley was in this up to his neck.

'The Word Smithy is cold,' he boasted. 'The Flame of Pharos is no more. I destroyed it with dragon's blood and the quenching spell. Long Live the Dark Flame!'

There was a murmur among the crowd, and then other voices joined in with the chant. 'Long Live the Dark Flame! Long Live the Dark Flame!'

People all around him were chanting now and Archie felt sick. And it was about to get worse.

The Dark Flame flared. A face appeared among the flames, its features ravaged by fire. Two cold grey eyes stared out. Archie would have recognised those eyes anywhere. Arthur Ripley stepped out of the fire.

Arabella gasped as she recognised her grandfather. 'He's the Dark Master,' she whispered.

Uther Morgred held up his hands for silence. He turned to the figure beside the Flame. 'We are your servants, master,' he said, bowing his head.

Arthur Ripley's cold eyes gazed around the room. 'So good of you all to come,' he said. 'I knew that you'd come around to my way of thinking eventually.

'I recognise some new faces among you.' He

looked at Rusp. 'Aurelius, so you finally realised the foolishness of following Hawke.'

'Some of you took longer than others, eh, Motley? If you had been a bit bolder, then we would have got here a lot quicker!'

Motley Brown stared at the ground. 'I had to be cautious,' he said. 'It would have done our cause no good if I'd been discovered.'

'You are a coward, Motley, and you always were. You kept your head down until you were sure of our success and only then did you act.'

'But I extinguished the Flame of Pharos!' cried Brown.

'No, I extinguished the Flame!' said Quiggley.

'So you used the boy to do your dirty work,' sneered Ripley.

'I taught the boy the quenching spell,' snarled Brown. 'And made the ungrateful wretch practise using rat's blood to snuff out candles until he could do it – and I got him dragon's blood when the salamander blood proved too weak. Without me he could not have put out the Flame.'

But Ripley ignored his protests. 'It is done and that is all that matters. The Flame of Pharos is extinguished. Only the Dark Flame remains. We stand at the threshold of a new era – a dark age of magic. We have waited a long time for this moment.

'And now it is within our grasp,' he said. 'And we have someone special joining us.' He turned towards the last two hooded figures. 'Show yourselves.'

The first figure pulled back her hood. Katerina Krone's dull eyes stared out.

Ripley's thin lips twitched into a smile.

'Welcome, Katerina. I trust my good friend Rumold treated you kindly at the asylum?'

Katerina bowed. 'Yes, master. He sends his apologies. He would have been here in person but he has things to attend to at the asylum.'

'Very well. He has served us well so I will permit his absence on this occasion. And now it is time to present our very special guest.'

He paused. 'My dark brothers and sisters, we have long sought the greatest prize in magic. I speak of *The Opus Magus* of course, the Great Work. Most of my life has been spent searching for it. All those years and it was closer than I realised. Finally, we can welcome the one person who knows its secret – Fabian Grey.'

The last hooded figure was pushed forward. In his hand he clutched the package from Folly & Catchpole. He looked to be in a daze as Uther Morgred pulled back his hood. Archie froze in horror at the face that was revealed. It was Gideon Hawke.

28

The Opus Magus

Archie's whole world collapsed. He stared in shock. How could Gideon Hawke be Fabian Grey?

And then suddenly it all made sense: Hawke's extraordinary magical ability, his mismatched eyes and his mysterious past, even his illness – his supposed madness! It all fitted. Why hadn't Archie seen it before? It had been staring him in the face all along.

Hawke had said that he felt like he was chasing his own tail – and he was. All this time he'd been desperately searching for Fabian Grey when in reality he was Fabian Grey!

Ripley snatched the package and tore it open. 'Thank you, Gideon,' he said, 'or should I call you Fabian?'

In his hand he held a slim white book. 'Finally, I have what I desire,' he cried. '*The Opus Magus* is mine and with it all the power of magic!'

He turned his greedy gaze on the book. 'For the first time in three hundred and fifty years new eyes will know its secrets, and when I commit it to the Black Flame then magic will enter a glorious new dark age.'

Ripley turned to *The Book of Night*. 'By the power of the Dark Flame, I command you my dark servants.'

Archie felt someone tug at his sleeve. It was Bramble. 'We've got to do something,' she hissed. 'We've got to stop him!'

The three Pale Writers rose from *The Book of Night* like a foul fog. Their faces flickered and their eyes burned with a hungry fire. Archie felt the same sudden terror grip him that he'd felt before. He recognised two of the three, but not the third. He felt the hairs on the back of his neck stand up.

Morgred stepped forward. 'Here is some azoth to write the spell with,' he said, producing a small phial of the magic ink and placing it on the plinth beside *The Book of Night*. 'I took it from the Royal Society. Let the new age of darkness commence,' he cried and his cry was picked up by others and rang around the room.

Ripley opened the white book in his hand,

and as he did the Pale Writers rose into the air. Their ghostly faces flickered with malice as they anticipated the ultimate act of darchemy. But in an instant their expressions turned to rage.

'What is this?' the first Pale Writer hissed.

'It is a trick!' spat the second.

'Someone must pay for this deception!' screeched the third.

Ripley was staring at the writing in the white book. He read out the words in disbelief. 'This is to remind me who I am and of the vision that I saw ...' he read. He riffled through the book.

'This is not *The Opus Magus*,' he cried. 'It is a changing spell. What good is that to me?'

He slammed the book shut. 'These are the ramblings of a madman!' he roared.

He turned his wrath on Hawke. 'Where is *The Opus Magus*?' he screamed.

Hawke shook his head. 'What you hold in your hand is my memoir,' he said. 'It is to remind me who I really am. No more and no less.'

'But you have a bibliographical memory,' raged Ripley. 'You remember every spell you ever saw. *The Opus Magus* must be in your head somewhere.'

'Perhaps it was once,' said Hawke. 'But I lost it along with all my other memories. And if it means you cannot corrupt it, then I am glad.'

Ripley stopped ranting. A knowing look passed

across his face. 'Wait. If you don't remember *The Opus Magus* spell then someone else has to – otherwise the magic would have been extinguished long ago. So if it's not you, then who is it?'

His eyes turned on the crowd of dark followers. 'It's Archie Greene!' he snarled. 'He's here somewhere. I can sense his presence.'

'He is Fabian Grey's heir. Somehow the memory of *The Opus Magus* must have passed to him. That's why he has a forked fate – Archie Greene is part of the prophecy!'

He turned to the Pale Writers. 'He's here, I know it. Find him!'

The three phantoms hung into the air. Archie felt their dark minds searching for him among the crowd. He could feel their evil presence as they used a dark delving spell to draw him out.

The person next to him pulled back his cloak. It was Rupert. 'I am Archie Greene,' he cried.

The Pale Writers hissed and turned towards him. 'That's not Archie Greene. The other boy is trying to shield him! Kill him!' screamed Ripley.

Archie threw back his own hood. 'Sorry, Rupert, but I won't let you do this,' he cried. 'I'm the real Archie Greene.'

'No!' cried Arabella. 'You don't have to do this, Archie!'

'But I do,' said Archie. 'I'm a Grey and only a Grey can stop the Dark Flame. My fate has always been intertwined with Fabian Grey's. This is my destiny.'

The crowd parted. A hush had fallen on the room. Archie walked towards the stage where Ripley stood.

'Finally, Archie Greene, I have you where I want you,' laughed Ripley.

There was a roar of outrage and a stooped figure charged towards the stage. 'You are a disgrace to the name of magic, Ripley!' cried Aurelius Rusp. 'You are nothing next to Fabian Grey!'

'Ah, Aurelius,' said Ripley. 'I should have known you were Hawke's man.'

'My loyalty was always to the museum,' snarled Rusp. 'I'm prepared to die for it!'

He hurled a banishing spell at Ripley, but Ripley blocked it. Before Rusp could use a guarding spell to defend himself, the Pale Writers descended on him, surrounding him and muttering dark spells. For a moment Rusp resisted and then Ripley pointed his hand at him.

'Power of darkness
Power of night
Take his soul
Put out his light.'

Rusp fell dead on the ground.

There was a shocked silence.

Archie had never liked Rusp but he'd died trying to protect the museum from the Dark Flame. Hawke had been right to trust him. Archie felt a surge of anger.

But before he could react there was a loud thumping sound – hundreds of ravens crashed against the leaded glass window. A huge flock of them had gathered outside the house. That was the black cloud Archie had seen in the sky earlier. Now he could hear their wings beating and the tapping of their beaks on the window. There was total chaos in the hall now as the birds blocked out the light from the moon, plunging the room into semi-darkness.

In the confusion Archie felt someone grab his arm. It was Hawke – or Fabian Grey as he now knew him to be.

'We don't have much time. Listen carefully. To extinguish the Dark Flame requires a sacrifice,' he gasped, 'an act of total selflessness. I have read the memoir now and I remember. The memoir contains the changing spell that will allow me to transform into a raven by choice, but once I use it I will need your help to save magic.'

'What is it I have to do?' asked Archie.

'When the time comes, you must rewrite *The Opus Magus*, Archie. It is the only way!'

'But where is it?' cried Archie desperately.

At that moment there was a blinding flash of lightning. When his vision returned, Grey had gone. He was alone. He saw the cold eyes of Arthur Ripley.

29

The Death Duel

'Where is Grey?' demanded Ripley. 'I saw him whispering to you. He told you where *The Opus Magus* is, didn't he?'

A knowing look had come over his distorted features. 'Or are you *The Opus Magus*? That's it!' he cried. 'Archie Greene is *The Opus Magus* – the primary spell is inside you. That's why Hawke was so protective of you.'

Ripley's mind was unravelling. It must be the Flame's malevolent power. He was so desperate now that he was clutching at straws. Archie could see a glint of madness in his eyes.

Ripley saw the look of confusion on Archie's face. 'Oh, but you did not know,' he cackled. 'That's because *The Opus Magus* is not in your head, it is in your heart! How touching! So if you are corrupted then magic will be corrupted, too. This is even better. Take him!' Ripley ordered. The Pale Writers flew at Archie.

The first of the three approached him. Its black eyes flared and its fiery voice hissed and crackled in Archie's head.

'You are full of doubts,' it said. 'I can feel them gnawing away at your mind like rats chewing on a corpse.' It swirled around Archie. 'What is it you doubt most?' it whispered. 'Is it the love of your family? Or is it your belief in yourself? But no, I sense it is something darker. You doubt yourself, Archie Greene. You do not believe you are worthy to be Fabian Grey's heir! That's it! That is your greatest doubt. And you are right! You will fail him. He has put his faith in you and you will surely let him down. You will let everyone down!'

Doubt moved towards him. Archie felt powerless to resist it. The vile creature was right. He doubted his worthiness to serve magic. For a brief second he was almost glad it was all over. Glad that he wouldn't have to keep up the pretence any more.

But in that same moment he heard another voice in his head. It was Hawke – or Grey, as he now knew him. 'I trust the boy completely,' he had said at the asylum. 'I have never doubted him and he has no reason to doubt himself.'

Archie felt his conviction come flooding back. He pushed the lingering doubts from his mind, driving them from his thoughts like a cat chasing rats.

Doubt recoiled. With a hissing sound like water being poured on a flame, it shrank back into the book.

'So you have overcome your doubt, Archie Greene, but that will not save you,' cried Ripley.

At his signal, the second Pale Writer, Dread, flew at Archie. Its touch was like ice on his skin and he felt the cold run up his spine.

'What is it that you fear most, Archie Greene?' whispered Dread, and the stench of its foul breath hung in the air.

Archie drew back. He tried to hide his fears but Dread was inside his head. He could feel its clammy cold fingers prying into the darkest recesses of his mind to find his most terrifying memories.

'Ah!' it cried, and its voice was a long frosty breath. 'What have we here?'

Archie felt the blood in his veins turn to ice. What had it found?

Dread opened out its withered hand and to Archie's horror he saw the Flare Wolf, the dark creature he and Bramble had encountered in the museum. Half dragon and half wolf, the beast fixed its staring red eyes on him. Then throwing back its head it gave a blood-curdling howl and began to stalk him. Archie felt his terror return. He tried to calm himself but his heart was skittering in his chest and his legs had turned to jelly.

His mind was spinning, but then he remembered something Hawke had said to him. 'The Pale Writers can only use real memories – not magical memories from a spell.'

As terrifying as it was, the Flare Wolf was a popper spell and Wolfus Bone had slain it. The creature was dead – and never real. As the realisation reached Archie's mind the Flare Wolf evaporated, vanishing with a loud pop.

Dread turned hateful eyes on him. Then it reached into his mind once more and plucked something else from his darkest memories. It opened its other hand. This time the sight that met Archie's eyes was so terrifying that he thought he might faint.

A claw-like hand reached out from *The Book of Night*. It had long black fingernails. In the middle of its palm was the Golden Circle firemark and beside it the Black Dragon. A tall figure emerged from the book's pages. He was almost seven feet tall, dressed in a long purple cloak with a red pendant round his neck. A hollow-cheeked face appeared, with a hooked nose like a bird of prey, and Archie found himself staring into the dull black eyes of Barzak.

Archie froze. This was his worst nightmare. He had no idea how he had managed to defeat the darchemist the first time.

Barzak's eyes bored into him. 'I bring darkness and death,' he thundered. 'This time there is no escape, book whisperer.'

Archie stood transfixed. But again Hawke's words came back to him.

'You used original magic to defeat Barzak and save Gloom. Those spells are your own. They are inside you.'

Archie closed his eyes and focused. The spell he'd used before came back to him.

Barzak raised his clawed hands and started to utter a dark spell. But before he could finish it, Archie cried out.

'I cast you back into the darkness
I command you return to where you
came from!'

And as he spoke, the words appeared in green fiery letters that hung in the air above his head. He smelled the scent of a star-filled night, the pure smell of amora, natural magic.

Barzak uttered a counter curse and black letters

formed above him. For a moment the black letters mingled with the green threatening to overcome them.

'We will see whose magic is the stronger,' roared Barzak. But the black letters began to fade.

'I cast you back into *The Book of Night*!' cried Archie.

Barzak's face twisted in anger as he fought to resist the spell. His mouth moved as he tried to utter a counter curse, but no words came out. And then with a terrible scream, the dark warlock was sucked back into *The Book of Night*, his clawed hands clutching at the air as he was swept away by the spell.

'So you have overcome your fears,' sneered Ripley. 'But the final Pale Writer is the most deadly of all.'

Archie felt the presence of the leader of the Pale Writers before he saw it. A dull, numbing sadness had entered him. He saw the phantom rise into the air, its spider-web strands loosely coiled to form the shape of a human. Its dead eyes gazed from its dismal white features. This was Despair.

Archie felt his hackles rise and a sense of impending doom. All the oxygen seemed to have been sucked out of the air. Far worse than either of the other two Pale Writers, this was a feeling of utter desolation and hopelessness.

When Despair reached out to him, he felt it drawing all the life from him. He felt a sense of bleakness and depression overwhelm him.

The phantom did not speak but he could feel its hunger like a vampire sucking his life force. He tried to resist it but his own thoughts turned on him viciously, twisting into a downward spiral of misery.

He thought about Bramble and Thistle and Loretta and Woodbine and Gran, and realised that he had failed them. He thought about his parents and that he would never see them again. He thought about the museum and how the Dark Flame would corrupt the magical books, and Fabian Grey had failed to save magic. The phantom's dull eyes mocked him. He felt utterly bereft and without hope. He had never experienced such misery or helplessness. There was no point going on.

For the first time in his life Archie felt the pointlessness of his own existence. His life was worthless. He was worthless. His hope had melted like snow in the rain. He felt himself sinking into a pit of wretchedness from which there was no escape.

Archie had never experienced anything so paralysing before. The white figure moved towards him like mist drifting in from the sea.

As it drew closer, Despair unsheathed a thin white blade like a shard of ice and pointed it at Archie's heart. For an unbearably long moment its mournful eyes looked into his. He felt as if his soul was turned to frost.

The Pale Writer held the ice shard over Archie's heart ready to stab him. He felt nothing. Just emptiness that seemed like it must go on forever. Inside, he felt himself falling, tumbling down into a bottomless pit.

He heard Bramble screaming and the beating of wings from the ravens outside the window. Rupert and Thistle tried to reach him but were restrained by Morgred and his henchmen. Arabella was screaming, too.

Despair moved closer to seal his fate. Archie could feel it leeching the life from him. The other two Pale Writers hovered beside it. As the last of Archie's hope ebbed away, the spaces were filled with Doubt and Dread. He felt them about to overcome him.

And then in his most desolate moment he remembered the raven's words.

'Look for me when all hope has gone.'

The words rang hollow. *The Opus Magus*, the only chance of defeating the Dark Flame, did not exist. The last hope had been that the primary spell was somehow in Fabian Grey's memory. But

Grey had vanished – abandoned him. All hope had truly gone. It was over.

Archie heard a roaring sound and the Dark Flame freed itself from *The Book of Night*. It engulfed Ripley whose laughing features could be seen inside the flame. It had claimed his soul for dark magic.

'Behold,' Ripley cried, clenching his fists so that the flame burned even more darkly. 'It is not Fabian Grey's destiny to save magic, it is mine! Let the reign of darkness begin. Let all of magic answer to its new master. I am reborn as the darchemist and ruler of the magical realm. Dark magic shall be restored to its rightful place. All shall kneel to me and do my bidding. And the first spirit I will enslave will be Archie Greene's – followed by his pathetic Alchemists' Club.'

The Dark Flame flared and Ripley reached out his hand. Archie could barely lift his head to watch.

'Where are you, Fabian Grey?' Ripley cried, and his voice was full of scorn. 'Or do you prefer Gideon Hawke? It makes no difference to me.'

Suddenly Archie heard Ripley laugh. 'A bird! You conjure a bird!' he mocked. 'Is that the best you can do? It would be laughable if it weren't so pathetic. The greatest alchemist the world has ever seen and this is your final flourish!'

Then Archie lifted his head and saw the raven. It stared defiantly back at Ripley. Ripley laughed again. But the raven took no notice. It flew into the air and landed on Archie's shoulder.

'The memoir, Archie,' it said. 'Pick up the memoir.'

With the last of his energy Archie dived for it. The Pale Writers tried to beat him to it but he got there first, snatching the book and holding it open.

'What foolishness is this!' cried Ripley. 'The book is worthless. It has no power.'

But Archie wasn't listening. He was staring at an empty page.

'I left it blank for you,' the raven whispered in his ear. 'I only remember *The Opus Magus* when I am in raven form, but as a raven I cannot write it down. You must do that for me.'

'So now you will never be able to change back into a man!' cried Archie, horrified.

'It was my choice,' the raven said. 'It was the sacrifice I had to make. We had forked fates, you and I. Our destinies were always linked. This is my destiny. And yours is to do what I cannot and write down the spell. Now listen well.'

Archie plucked Fabian Grey's ring from his finger and held it in the palm of his hand. The ring changed into Grey's golden quill.

The raven began to recite from memory *The Opus Magus*, the spell that had first created magic.

Using all his concentration and straining every magical sinew in his body, Archie gripped the golden quill. He dipped it in the phial of azoth on the plinth and wrote down the raven's words on the empty page in the memoir. As he did, green flaming letters appeared in the air above his head.

The Pale Writers reached out their grasping hands to corrupt him, but the power of *The Opus Magus* pushed them back.

The Dark Flame twisted and writhed as Ripley screamed at the three Pale Writers. 'The quill! The quill! Take it from the boy! Kill him before he writes the spell!'

The Dark Flame began to swirl around Ripley like a cyclone, its dark plumes of fire spinning faster and faster. As it span it made a whistling, crackling sound. The three Pale Writers were pulled into its fiery maelstrom.

Thick, dark smog was oozing from *The Book of Night*. The air around Archie was filling up with the poisonous darkness and he covered his mouth and nose with his hand to stop it seeping into his lungs. Still he carried on writing the primary spell of magic.

As he wrote each word of *The Opus Magus*, it blazed with a golden fire, but some vanished in black fire.

He heard the voices of the three darchemists whose spirits were trapped in the black flame. They were chanting their own dark spells, trying to break the primary spell. By now the darkness was all around him so he could no longer see the raven, only hear its voice in his ear. The stench of dark magic filled his nostrils. It smelled of putrefying flesh and something acrid like burning rubber.

Archie heard the raven whisper the concluding words of *The Opus Magus*. And still he did not flinch in his task. He gripped the golden quill in his hand and with the last of his remaining strength he formed the final letters of the spell. But the Dark Flame was nearly upon them. With a rising panic, Archie realised the fire was about to consume him. At the last moment, out of the corner of his eye, he saw the raven. In its claws it clutched the phial of dragon's blood.

'Farewell, Archie Greene. Do not forget me. When you speak of poor Fabian Grey, speak kindly and tell the world that he sacrificed himself to save magic.'

With that its dark shape arrowed past him and into the heart of the Dark Flame, and as it did, Archie heard Hawke's voice cry out.

'*Blood of Dracus*
Newly slain
Beast of darkness
Quench the Flame.'

The Dark Flame blazed brighter and then began to swirl in reverse. Faster and faster it span, shrinking back into itself until it collapsed into a single point. The dark fog burned off like mist in the morning sun, and *The Book of Night* burned with a golden flame. There was a flash of lightning and a crack of thunder, and all that remained of Ripley was a pile of ashes on the page of the open book.

A gust of wind riffled Archie's hair and blew the ashes away. Finally he understood. It was his and Grey's destiny to save magic *together*. Either one of them could have turned from the path but neither had. In the end Fabian Grey, or was it Gideon Hawke, had made the ultimate sacrifice. He had given up his human form to defeat the Dark Flame.

Archie was aware of a stabbing pain in his eyes. The hall was illuminated as if a light switch had been turned on. Dawn had broken and the sunlight streamed in through the tall leaded window. The flock of ravens had dispersed, letting the light in. The birds were perched on nearby buildings and in the garden.

Inside the hall, the hooded followers of the Dark Flame shielded their eyes from the bright glare of a new day.

'You are completely surrounded. Surrender or face the consequences,' declared a loud, clear voice.

Feodora Graves had appeared in the middle of the stage. Old Zeb stood beside her. They were flanked on either side by the bookend beasts, their golden griffin feathers resplendent in the sunshine streaming through the windows.

One of the beasts sniffed the air. 'I smell the thief who came to steal from our lair,' it thundered.

It turned its head towards Motley Brown. 'It was you!' it roared accusingly.

'No,' cried Brown, 'it wasn't me, it was the boy!'

He gave Quiggley a shove towards the giant griffin and tried to run. But the bookend beast would not be denied. It opened its beak and released a jet of icy breath that hit Brown squarely between the shoulder blades. The griffin's breath froze his blood so that he turned to ice and fell dead, shattering into a myriad of shards as he hit the ground.

There were terrified screams and the Greaders were thrown into confusion, colliding with each other as they tried to escape.

The doors at the back of the hall were thrown open and Woodbine and Loretta appeared in the doorway with Faustus Gaunt. Seeing their exit blocked, some of the Greaders tried to climb up into the minstrels' gallery, but Wolfus Bone and Gardenia Greene appeared above them, cutting off that escape route, too.

More of the Flame Keepers were arriving now, lining the hall so that the Greaders had nowhere to go. The Trevallens, the Drews and the Merryweathers were all there along with other members of the magical realm.

Archie spotted the Siren Sisters, Hemlock and Delphinium, and Geoffrey Screech. They stood shoulder to shoulder, lining the inside of Ripley Mansion.

Archie was aware of people moving around him. Bramble, Thistle, Arabella and Rupert were beside him. Rupert helped him to his feet.

'Are you all right?'

'I'm fine,' said Archie. 'Thanks to Fabian Grey. He fulfilled his destiny.'

At that moment there was a shout as one of the cloaked Greaders tried to flee across the stage towards the leaded window.

'Stop him!' cried Graves.

Pink stepped forward. 'My pleasure,' she said, sticking out a booted foot. The man went sprawling. Pink pulled back his cloak to reveal an angry face with bulging eyes.

'Amos Roach,' said Graves. 'I might have guessed.'

Roach's lip curled into a snarl. 'You may have destroyed the Dark Flame,' he growled. 'But the Flame of Pharos is no more. Magic is dead!'

'No,' cried Arabella. 'Archie has the Torchstone. The Flame of Pharos can be rekindled.'

Archie's heart sank. Peter Quiggley roared with laughter.

'Oh dear! There's something Greene hasn't told you. Shall I tell them, Archie, or will you?'

Archie felt his stomach twist. He shook his head. 'I'm sorry,' he said. 'I lost the Torchstone when the Pale Writer attacked me in the churchyard.'

Quiggley was taunting them now. 'Luckily, when he dropped it, I was there to pick it up. He couldn't see me of course because I was using the invisibility potion.'

'And what did you do with the Torchstone, Peter?' asked Graves, trying to remain calm.

Quiggley smiled. 'I extinguished it along with the Flame of Pharos!' he said. 'So you see, Archie, when you and Grey put out the Dark Flame you didn't save magic, you destroyed it once and for all!'

Graves gave a deep sigh. 'That's that then,' she said. '*The Opus Magus* has been saved. But without the magical flames there can be no more magic.'

Bramble coughed. 'Erm, actually, they're not

quite extinguished,' she said, reaching into her pocket to produce an egg-shaped object that gave off an amber light.

'The Torchstone!' gasped Archie, goggling at it. 'But how?'

'There were two, remember?' said Bramble.

'The spare!' cried Archie. 'So that was you?'

Bramble grinned. 'Just a precaution,' she said. 'I took it the same time you took the other one. I thought we might as well double up.'

'Why didn't you say anything?' cried Archie.

'I thought the fewer people who knew the better,' said Bramble.

Archie smiled. 'Yes, but you could have told us!'

'And spoil the surprise!' said Bramble, her lips curling into a grin. 'You know how we Greys like our secrets!'

'So we have saved magic after all!' cried Thistle.

'I think this calls for a celebration,' said Graves. 'Send out the ravens to every corner of the magical realm. Tell the magical world that the Flame of Pharos still burns and magic lives on!'

30

The Last Flame

It was the day after the showdown at Ripley Mansion. The torrential rainfall of the night before had been replaced by warm sunshine. The storm had passed and the air smelled clean and fresh.

There were celebrations going on all over the magical realm. At number 32 Houndstooth Road, Archie, Bramble and Thistle were getting ready to leave for a big party at Quill's.

Gardenia was standing in the kitchen in her best frock with Woodbine, who was in a crumpled suit that Archie recognised from the old newspaper cutting.

It had already been decided the night before that Archie and Bramble were to carry on living with the Foxes. Houndstooth Road was their home.

'I'll miss you all of course,' Gardenia said. 'But it won't be for long. As soon as I can sell my cottage I'm moving back to Oxford. There's no reason to stay away any more!'

'That's brilliant, news, Gran,' said Archie, giving her a big hug.

Gardenia glanced at the clock.

'What's taking Loretta so long?' she asked.

Thistle called up the stairs. 'The party's starting soon, Mum. Hurry up!'

At that moment there was a knock at the door. Woodbine went to answer it and Archie heard voices in the hall. Feodora Graves and Wolfus Bone walked through to the kitchen.

'We just dropped by to let you know that the Word Smithy has been relit,' said Graves. 'The Flame of Pharos burns brightly once more!'

'That's the best news ever,' said Archie.

'And the plotters have been rounded up,' said Bone. 'Rumold was arrested at the asylum and will be charged with crimes against magic, as will Morgred. Amos Roach will stand trial for killing Katerina's adopted parents and aunt.'

'And this is for you,' said Graves, handing Thistle an envelope. He tore it open.

'Wow! It's a letter from the museum,' he said excitedly. 'I'm to start in the mythical menagerie on Monday!' He beamed with pleasure.

'Congratulations,' said Gardenia. 'Rupert will be thrilled for you.'

'What will happen to Quiggley?' asked Bramble.

'He's too young to stand trial for putting out the Flame, so for now he'll go to the Home for Young Magical Offenders where he can't cause any more trouble. Katerina Krone will remain at the asylum. Orpheus Gloom is replacing Rumold in charge.'

Bone looked at Woodbine. 'We have Roach to thank for the drubbing we received. It was Motley Brown who tipped him and the other Greaders off that *The Book of Night* was being moved.'

'So Gloom wasn't part of the plot?' asked Bramble.

'No, he was telling the truth. He only found out about *The Book of Night* when he discovered the secret library. He reported it to the museum as soon as he realised what it was.'

'*The Book of Night* is now safely chained up with the other Terrible Tomes in the crypt,' added Bone. 'You'll be pleased to know, too, that the other books from the dark library have been locked away in the Darchive. Orpheus saw to that.'

'So all's well that ends well,' said Thistle.

Archie's expression changed as he felt a sudden sadness. 'I was just thinking about Fabian Grey,' he said. 'It's not surprising the vision almost drove him mad. Imagine finding out you had to turn into a raven to fulfil your destiny?'

'It's Gideon I feel for,' said Bone. 'He was my friend. He spent his life looking for clues about Fabian Grey without knowing that he was searching for himself. It's no wonder the pressure got to him in the end.'

'I'm not sure it did,' said Graves. 'The Greaders wanted him to think he was going mad. The medication Brown was mixing for him contained March hare's blood to dull his mind. Rumold admitted it under questioning. They wanted Hawke locked up in the asylum where they could keep him out of the way – they didn't want him somehow discovering how to extinguish the Dark Flame.

'The raven left the receipt from Folly & Catchpole in his room at the asylum for him to find. But Rumold saw it and thought it was for *The Opus Magus*, so they released Hawke and followed him to Folly & Catchpole's offices. When he came out with the package they grabbed him and took him to Ripley Mansion. By then they had guessed he was Fabian Grey and thought they'd got the primary spell.'

'But it was just Grey's account of what had happened to him!' said Archie.

'Yes,' said Graves. 'That was the clever plan

that Alex and Amelia Greene came up with. Alex persuaded Grey to write it all down so that he would remember who he was.'

'And *The Opus Magus* was in the raven's memory,' said Bramble.

'That's right,' said Graves. 'The *Grimoire*'s curse only affected Grey when he was a man. When he changed into the raven he still had his bibliographical memory so he could remember everything from before.'

Thistle looked thoughtful. 'Something I don't understand is why Hawke didn't have the streak of white in his hair?'

'Hawke had no memory of what he'd seen in *The Book of Prophecy*, so his mind was unburdened and his hair was untouched,' said Graves. 'The raven had the white streak because it remembered. As Hawke's memory started to come back, his hair started to turn white, too.'

'And I thought it was the stress he was under!' said Archie.

'I suppose it was really,' said Graves. 'It was the stress of being Fabian Grey.'

'That'd turn anyone's hair white!' agreed Archie.

'Grey gave his life to save magic. And we must never forget the sacrifice your parents made,' said Graves. 'But now is not the time for sadness. It is a time to honour them and celebrate their lives.

There will be statues of Gideon Hawke and your parents in the museum, and Rusp, too.'

'Fabian Grey will be remembered for what he was,' said Bone, 'the greatest alchemist of all.'

Archie looked thoughtful. 'I don't think any of that mattered to him,' he said. 'I think all he cared about was saving magic.'

Just then Loretta tottered into the room. She was wearing violet high heels and a large fuchsia-coloured hat.

'How do I look?' she asked.

'Very purple,' said Thistle.

'You look lovely . . . Mum,' said Bramble, giving Thistle a sharp dig in the ribs.

Loretta beamed at them. She took a mirror from her lavender-coloured handbag and puckered her lips.

'I've made a cake to take to the party. It's in the larder,' she said, applying some purple lipstick. 'Where are you going?'

'We'll see you there,' called Bramble over her shoulder. 'We're meeting Arabella and Rupert.'

'But what about the . . .'

The front door closed behind them.

'. . . cake?'

With the sun shining on their faces and the wind in their hair, Archie, Bramble and Thistle ran down the garden path and along Houndstooth

Road. They ran all the way to the Bodleian Library where Rupert and Arabella were waiting for them. Together the five of them walked to Quill's.

High up on the roof of the Bodleian, a raven with a white streak on its head sat watching. Its flinty eyes observed the five teenagers as they passed beneath it arm in arm. It listened to the magic of their laughter, and remembered what it was to be young. Then, with a cry of pure joy, it flew up into the air and arrowed across the rooftops of Oxford.

John Dee's Prophecy

When white burns black
And shadows prey
Then hope must lie
With all that's grey.

The raven knows
What was forgot
It holds the key
To magic's lock.

To stop the dark
There is a price
A selfless act
Of sacrifice.

Mudberry's
Magical Glossary

The following excerpts are reproduced from Mudberry's *A Beginner's Guide to Magic* (13th Edition), with grateful thanks to the Mudberry family.

Agatha's Emporium A magical shop in Oxford that sells astroscopes and other magical memorabilia. It is one of the best-known magical stores, along with the Flaming Tattoo Parlour, Mother Marek's Musical Muffins and Veruca's Secret.

Aisle of White The magical bookshop attached to the Museum of Magical Miscellany. The Aisle of White serves as a place to sort the magical books from other books that people come to sell, and is the only part of the museum open to the Unready. Its current proprietor is Geoffrey Screech.

The Alchemists' Club A group of seventeenth-century alchemists led by Fabian Grey, who tried to rewrite the magical books contained in the Museum of Magical Miscellany. Their magical experiments started the Great Fire of London and led to the introduction of the Lores of Magical Restraint. Their experiments also triggered the Alchemist's Curse.

Alchemists' Firemark The symbol of a golden dragon swallowing its own tail (also known as the Golden Circle firemark). The appearance of the firemark indicates that an apprentice is able to write magic. It is also the symbol of the Alchemists' Club.

Amora The smell of magic. Different types of magic give off different amoras. Natural magic smells of nature. Mortal magic smells of fusty rooms and fire smoke. And supernatural magic smells of cold tombs and dead flesh.

Apprenticeships The magical apprenticeships were developed as a way to pass on the magical knowledge to the next generation. The Flame of Pharos determines the order in which an apprentice learns the three book skills:

Finding (firemark symbol: eye)
Binding (firemark symbol: needle and thread)
Minding (firemark symbol: ladder)

Archive Located in the Department of Lost Books at the Museum of Magical Miscellany. The archive is where all the old texts relating to magical books are kept. The texts date back to the Great Library of Alexandria and the Golden Age of Magic that preceded it.

Azoth A magical substance highly prized by alchemists. It is one of the three requirements for writing magic. The other two are the Golden Circle firemark and an enchanted quill made from a feather given freely by a magical creature. The ancient magic writers wrote their master spells with azoth because of its long-lasting properties. It can also extend the life expectancy of mortals. The symbol for azoth is the caduceus.

Barzak The most feared darchemist of his time, Barzak wrote *The Book of Souls*, one of the seven Terrible Tomes, and was responsible for burning down the Great Library of Alexandria. He was subsequently imprisoned in *The Book of Souls* by Archie Greene.

Black Dragon The firemark of the Flame of Pandemonium – the Dark Flame.

Bookend Beasts Ancient stone griffins that guard magical books and artifacts. They can be identified by their amber eyes and can come to life if the secrets they protect are threatened. Bookend beasts are extremely loyal and able to perform remarkable feats of magic. The last known pair protected the magic books in the Great Library of Alexandria. Highly dangerous: do not approach.

Bookery The great vaulted space between Quill's

and the entrance to the Museum of Magical Miscellany, where magical books roost in huge bookcases like birds or fly around in flocks.

Books of Destiny The name given to *The Book of Prophecy* and *The Book of Reckoning*. *The Book of Yore* is also sometimes included.

Book of Night, The (proper title *The Book of Nightmares*) Was written by three darchemists to summon the Flame of Pandemonium from the underworld. Opening *The Book of Night* will release the Dark Flame and the Pale Writers, the spirits of the darchemists who wrote it. The Pale Writers seek *The Opus Magus* to control the primary spell and bring a dark age of magic.

Book Whisperer One who can talk to magical books, a very rare magical ability. Archie Greene is the first book whisperer in four hundred years.

Curiosity Compass A magical device for detecting the direction of magical energy. Curiosity compasses are useful for finding dragon hoards and other hidden magical artefacts.

Darchemist Writer of dark magic, including the authors of the Terrible Tomes.

Darchive A secret place in the Museum of Magical Miscellany that is kept in total darkness. The Darchive houses magical books and artifacts that must never see the light of day. A number of dark magical items are stored there. Over the years several famous and infamous members of the magical realm have gained access to the Darchive. In the seventeenth century, the alchemist Fabian Grey is known to have visited on at least one occasion. The last known visitor was Arthur Ripley.

Dark Flame The Flame of Pandemonium that was summoned from the underworld. It is the dark twin of the Flame of Pharos. The Dark Flame has its own firemark, the Black Dragon, and its own deadly servants called the Pale Writers – the corrupted spirits of the three darchemists who summoned it.

Door Ray The secret entrance to the back of house in Quill's Coffee & Chocolate House. The door ray provides access to the Museum of Magical Miscellany. It is disguised as a sunbeam to confuse the Unready.

Dragon's Claw One of the oldest seats of learning. The Dragon's Claw belonged to Fellwind the Destroyer, one of the great dragons of the North. Its claw was so large that it could hold two men, which is why the Dragon's Claw is one of a small number of double seats. The Dragon's Claw has a reputation for trickery and treachery.

Drawing Books Highly dangerous magical books that draw unwary readers into their pages. They include *The Book of Yore*, which contains the history of magic.

Emerald Eye The magical pendant that belonged to the magician John Dee and that Dee's ghost gave to Archie Greene as his keepsafe.

Enchanted Entrance A secret doorway underneath the Aisle of White that gives access to other magical buildings.

Firemark Magical symbol that appears on the palm of an apprentice's hand when he or she passes the Flame test. New firemarks appear when the Flame of Pharos determines an apprentice is ready for the next challenge.

Flame Keepers of Alexandria A secret community devoted to finding and preserving magical books. The Flame Keepers protect the Museum of Magical Miscellany in Oxford and are descended from the original guardians of the Great Library of Alexandria.

Flame of Pharos One of the two magical flames. The Flame of Pharos burned in the lighthouse in the harbour of Alexandria, guiding travellers from faraway lands to the books. When the Great Library of Alexandria burned down, the Flame was brought to Oxford. Legend has it that the Flame contains the spirits of the magisters, the ancient magic writers from the Golden Age of Magic, and is the conscience of the magical realm. The Flame now burns in the Word Smithy in the mending workshop beneath the Aisle of White and marks new apprentices with a firemark for the three apprentice skills: Finding, Minding or Binding.

Folly & Catchpole The oldest and most secretive law firm in England. Folly & Catchpole has been the legal firm of choice for the magical community of Britain for more than nine hundred years. Based in London it specialises in magical instructions and the storage of magical items and other secrets.

Forbidden Books Magical books that must not be opened. They include the Terrible Tomes and other books that are covered under prohibited practices.

Forked Fate Someone with a forked fate is said to have the forks on them. It means their destiny hangs in the balance and the outcome will be determined by a decision they have to make. A number of those with forked fates turned to dark magic, including the dark warlock Barzak and Hecate the witch.

Golden Age of Magic Most people have forgotten about magic or don't know it ever existed. But long ago there was a golden age when magic was practised openly. In those days, master magicians called magisters wrote the master spells that magicians have relied on ever since. As long as the master spell remains intact, someone else trained in magic can cast the spell by speaking it.

Greaders Sworn enemies of the Flame Keepers. In secret they still use magic for their own purposes and ignore the Lores of Magical Restraint. They are called Greaders because they are greedy for magical books and will go to any lengths to get their hands on them. The apprentices who work at the museum always have to be on their guard against them. Above all else the Greaders desire the Terrible Tomes.

Great Library of Alexandria The most famous library of all time, it housed the greatest collection of magical books ever assembled. The library was burned down in around 48 BC.

Happy Landing The place just outside the main doors to the Museum of Magical Miscellany, where the seats of learning deposit visitors.

Hecate Nightshade A darchemist, a writer of dark magic. Hecate was a witch who wrote *The Grim Grimoire*, a book of diabolical spells, which is one of the seven Terrible Tomes. A bolt of lightning killed Hecate as she was trying to complete the final spell, giving rise to its name, the Unfinished Spell.

John Dee (1527–1609) An English mathematician, astronomer, astrologer, alchemist and navigator. One of the most learned men of his age, Dee was Queen Elizabeth I's court magician and amassed one of the largest private libraries in Europe, including many rare and magical books. Dee's ghost gave his favourite scrying crystal pendant, the Emerald Eye, to Archie Greene as a keepsafe.

Keepsafe A magical gift usually given to someone to protect them from danger. Traditionally, a keepsafe is received from a friend or family member at the start of a magical apprenticeship.

Lost Books Department Located in the Museum of Magical Miscellany, the Department of Lost Books identifies magical books that have gone astray. When a new book arrives, it first goes to Lost Books to be classified according to its magical strength. Former heads of Lost Books include Gideon Hawke and the Greader Arthur Ripley.

Magic There are three branches of magic:

Natural Magic The purest kind of magic. It comes from magical creatures and plants and the elemental forces of nature, such as the sun, the stars, and the seas. (Symbol: tree with lightning bolt)

Mortal Magic Man-made magic. It includes the magical instruments and other devices created by magicians to channel magical power. (Symbol: crystal ball)

Supernatural Magic The third and darkest type of magic uses the power of spirits and other supernatural beings. (Symbol: smiling skull)

Magicians' Eye The condition of having eyes that are different colours. Magicians' eye is associated with rare magical abilities, including a talent for dark magic.

Magister Master magician and magic writer from the Golden Age of Magic.

Motion Potion An antigravity potion served at Quill's that is required to travel safely in the seats of learning. Motion potions come in a variety of flavours and names and can be mixed with hot chocolate (choc-tails) or fruit juices.

Museum of Magical Miscellany The secret building concealed under the Bodleian Library in Oxford that houses the world's most powerful magical books. All magical books must be returned to the museum for inspection and classification.

Oculus Large crystal orb used for communicating within the magical realm. The face of the person you are communicating with appears in the oculus.

Opus Magus 'The Great Work' is the founding spell of magic. The original *Opus Magus* was housed in the Great Library of Alexandria and disappeared when the Library was destroyed.

Only when the *Opus Magus* is rewritten will magic be restored to its former glory.

Pale Writers Servants of the Dark Flame of Pandemonium. The Pale Writers were once great magic writers who turned to writing dark magic. By writing *The Book of Night* they summoned the Dark Flame from the underworld of Pandemonium. They thought they could control it but its power was too great and they became its servants instead, each trapped within the book by his own weakness: the first by doubt, the second by dread and the third by despair.

Permission Wall An enchantment that disguises magical places so they can't be seen from the outside. Typically a secret mark or password is required as 'permission' to pass through a permission wall.

Poppers Magical books with spells that can escape if they are opened. There are two types: pop-ups are spells that can escape from a book but must remain with it; pop-outs are able to roam freely.

Popper Stopper A glass phial which, when uncorked, releases a white vapour that surrounds and captures wayward popper spells. Once used, a popper stopper must be returned to the museum so that the spell it contains can be put back into its book or disposed of in some other way. First- and second-hand apprentices are forbidden to use popper stoppers because they are deemed too dangerous.

Quill's Coffee & Chocolate House Founded in London in 1657 by Jacob Quill, Quill's became a favourite meeting place for the magical community. In 1667, Quill's moved to Oxford after the original shop was destroyed in the Great Fire of London. It has been in Oxford ever since. As well as its internationally famous choc-tails, it boasts one of the most impressive permission walls anywhere in the magical world, acting as the entrance to the Museum of Magical Miscellany.

Royal Society of Magic Founded in 1666 by King Charles II, the Royal Society was established to further the understanding of magic. Its mission is to recognise, promote and support excellence in magic and to encourage the development and use of magic for the benefit of humankind. A number of famous and infamous magical experiments were conducted there. It has a reputation for being elitist and several famous magicians and alchemists have been linked with it, including Sir Isaac Newton.

Seats of Learning A set of ancient enchanted flying chairs used for getting in and out of the Museum of Magical Miscellany to provide added security and secrecy. Those using the seats of learning must drink a motion potion. Each seat is unique and has its own colourful history.

Shadow Blade An enchanted blade made from the reflection of a shooting star captured in the black glass of obsidian. The Shadow Blade is a potent weapon against dark magical creatures because it can penetrate any darkness – and the darkest of hearts.

Snook It's one of the Museum of Magical Miscellany's traditions that new apprentices must bring a magical book – called a snook – on their first day.

Special Instruction A special instruction is a binding magical contract, usually an order to do something with a magical object on or by a given date. Special instructions may be placed many years in advance of the designated date. Once received, a special instruction may not be cancelled. Failure to comply with a special instruction is against the Lore and may have serious magical repercussions, triggering curses or other unpleasant spells.

Terrible Tomes The seven most dangerous dark magic books ever written. They are among the Forbidden Books that must not be opened. It is said that if the Greaders get their hands on just one of the Terrible Tomes, then they could destroy the world. The Tomes are kept inside the crypt at the Museum of Magical Miscellany in enchanted iron cages.

Torchstones Magical orbs made from amber and used by the flame carriers to transport the Flame of Pharos. The Torchstones were used to bring the Flame of Pharos from Alexandria to Oxford, and can be used to protect the Flame in times of danger. There are two Torchstones.

Unready People who don't know about magic.

Acknowledgements

I'd like to thank the people who made this book possible – many of whom have been on Archie's journey with me from the beginning.

To Lindsay – my plotting companion and friend for all those 'literary lunches' at the Crown in Horsted Keynes, Red Lion at Chelwood Gate, Swan in Forest Row, and the rest.

My own Alchemists' Club: the advance readers who reviewed the early chapters,

To Dan and Erin, whose enthusiasm for life is infectious and makes everything better.

To my nephew Harry, without whom Archie may never have seen the light of day.

To my agent Paul Moreton at Bell Lomax Moreton for his calm and always good humoured advice. To Jo Hayes who brought me to Faber & Faber and made it all possible. And to Eddie Bell who first saw potential in my writing.

To Leah Thaxton, my brilliant publisher and her fantastic team of editors at Faber: Alice Swan, who brought much-needed discipline and polish to my writing, to Natasha Brown for helping me juggle manuscripts and proofs and especially Naomi Colthurst who made writing Raven's Spell such a pleasure.

And to everyone else at Faber – especially Hannah Love, for getting me some great publicity and events, and Lizzie Bishop and her foreign rights team who did such a fabulous job with the Archie series.

To James de la Rue, whose illustrations add so much to the Archie Greene books, and who excelled himself with this one.

To Maurice Lyon, my helpful and insightful copy editor throughout Archie's adventures.

To Bryan – you know why. And to Ian for being there – always, and helping me make better decisions. And to Charlotte and Jane.

To Stuart and Ro for their support and (still) unwavering friendship.

To Sara for her editorial eye and unstinting encouragement.

Finally to my parents Peter Dearlove and Dorothy Dearlove (née Everest) for, well, everything.